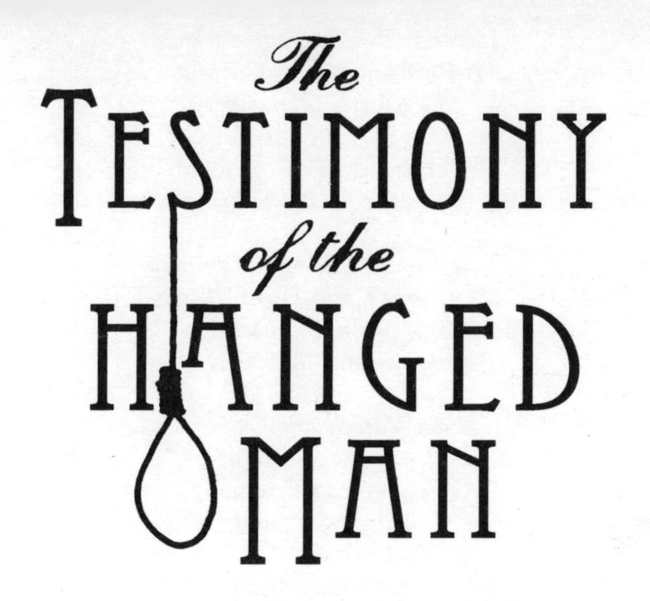
The
TESTIMONY
of the
HANGED
MAN

Inspector Ben Ross crime novels
A Rare Interest in Corpses
A Mortal Curiosity
A Better Quality of Murder
A Particular Eye for Villainy
The Testimony of the Hanged Man

Campbell and Carter crime novels
Mud, Muck and Dead Things
Rack, Ruin and Murder
Bricks and Mortality

Fran Varady crime novels
Asking for Trouble
Keeping Bad Company
Running Scared
Risking it All
Watching Out
Mixing with Murder
Rattling the Bones

Mitchell and Markby crime novels
Say it with Poison
A Season for Murder
Cold in the Earth
Murder Among Us
Where Old Bones Lie
A Fine Place for Death
Flowers for his Funeral
Candle for a Corpse
A Touch of Mortality
A Word After Dying
Call the Dead Again
Beneath these Stones
Shades of Murder
A Restless Evil
That Way Murder Lies

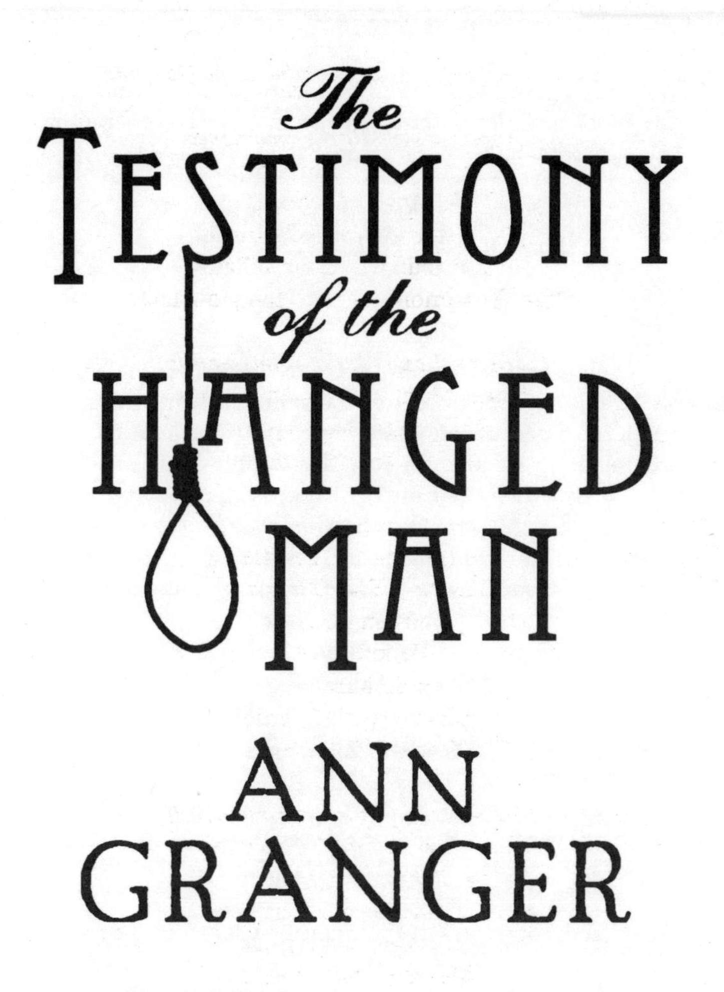

headline

First published in 2014 by
HEADLINE PUBLISHING GROUP

1

Cataloguing in Publication Data is available
from the British Library

Hardback ISBN 978 1 4722 0447 9
Trade Paperback ISBN 978 1 4722 0448 6

Typeset in Plantin by Avon DataSet Ltd,
Bidford-on-Avon, Warwickshire

Printed and bound in Great Britain by Clays Ltd, St Ives plc

Headline's policy is to use papers that are natural, renewable and recyclable products and made from wood grown in sustainable forests. The logging and manufacturing processes are expected to conform to the environmental regulations of the country of origin.

HEADLINE PUBLISHING GROUP
An Hachette UK Company
338 Euston Road
London NW1 3BH

www.headline.co.uk
www.hachette.co.uk

Author's Note

A guidebook of 1818, in my possession, says of Putney: 'a village in Surrey, four miles and three-quarters S.W. from London, is pleasantly situated on the southern bank of the Thames, over which there is a wooden bridge connecting it with Fulham.' This wooden bridge had been constructed in 1729 despite opposition from the ferrymen who saw their livelihood disappear.

Fifty years later, in 1868, when this story takes Ben Ross and his wife Lizzie to Putney, the old wooden bridge was still in use. There had been changes in Putney and it was a growing community, but was still at heart a large village. Despite some great poverty in certain areas, it had always been favoured by the well-to-do and boasted a number of substantial houses with gardens. But it had to wait almost until the end of the century to see a stone bridge replace the wooden structure, and a major increase in population with all the changes that brings.

The problem for the writer of any historical novel is to recreate a place in a way that will bring alive the spirit of it; while taking into consideration the needs of the plot. I may have created a few footpaths where perhaps there were none. But who is to say? At any rate, I hope I have evoked the 'feel' of Putney while respecting the facts wherever possible.

I cannot finish without expressing my sincere gratitude to the Reverend Ailsa Newby and Michael Bull of St Mary's Putney parish church. Both were kind enough to help me in my inquiries about Putney's Victorian burial grounds.

Chapter One

Inspector Benjamin Ross

'I FIRST set eyes on Francis Appleton while we were both up at Oxford, nearly forty years ago,' James Mills said. 'It was an uncommonly warm spring day, I recall, and I was walking by the Cherwell, not far from Magdalen Bridge. There were plenty of other people enjoying the sunshine, strolling on the college meadows as I was, and a varied collection of craft floated past me – rowing boats, punts and so on. Some were handled more dextrously than others!'

Mills paused, his gaze misting and focusing on some scene long gone by. Little light came through the tiny window and the candle, guttering on the table, sent both our shadows leaping fantastically about the walls. He'd lost weight in prison since I'd last seen him in the dock at the Old Bailey. He was still a sturdy man, though, robust for his sixty-something years.

I hoped the hangman did not bungle the job on the morrow. I did not like to think of Mills dangling, kicking and gurgling, as the life was slowly squeezed out of him.

The Newgate hangman, Calcraft, was notorious for the high number of executions he'd carried out and the prolonged death agonies of the condemned. If the job were to be given to him, I could not hold out much hope for Mills having a quick and painless end. I had heard reports of Calcraft pulling on the condemned person's legs to hurry things along. He probably justified that sort of behaviour as doing the prisoner a kindness. I had my own view.

It was not the only reason I had answered the call to Newgate Prison that evening with deep reluctance. The smell of the prison always takes a couple of days to wash away. It has a way of pervading everything. The sourness of unwashed humanity, the fatty stink of what passes for cooking in the great cauldrons, the staleness from lack of ventilation and, above all, the despair: for that has an odour all its own. All this seeps into your clothing, skin and hair. Even after it has been cleansed from these it lingers in the mind. The smell and atmosphere of the condemned cell, where I sat with Mills, was yet more sinister and unpleasant. It was as if Death himself sat with us in his rotting rags and smiled a ghastly grin at us as we talked.

Mills twitched and pulled his attention back to his present grim surroundings. 'Are you listening, Inspector?' he asked testily.

I assured him that I was and begged him to continue his story without unnecessary delays.

'Ah,' said Mills with a mirthless smile. 'You wish to be back home with your wife – I suppose you to have one – and family. Sitting at your own table, eh?'

I almost snapped that I would, indeed, be comfortable at home if I weren't sitting there in that wretched place at his behest. But I didn't say so, because Mills, with his calm manner, made me feel somehow embarrassed. I could walk out of there and he could not. He saw I grew restless and returned to his memories.

'Anyhow, Inspector Ross, I was telling you how I met Appleton. There I was, by the river, not a care in the world. Then a punt emerged from under the bridge, poled towards me by a young fellow I did not, at that time, know. He was about my own age, some twenty years, fair-haired and athletic in build. I admit I paid more attention to his passenger. A girl, and an uncommonly pretty girl, reclined in the punt, laughing up at him. She wore a white muslin gown, cut rather low, I recall. This was before the later ugly fashion for women to barricade themselves inside crinolines. Women then wore gowns with skirts billowing gracefully over layers of petticoats that rustled most delightfully as they walked. She had long white gloves, and wore a wide-brimmed hat of Italian straw, with blue ribbons, to shield her from the sun. Beneath it bunches of dark curls framed her face. She had a parasol, too. Oh, I dare say she was no better than she should have been; one of the town's many ladies of easy manners and easier morals. There were enough of them in Oxford then and, I dare say, still are. For all the white gown and gloves, she was laughing at him in such an uninhibited way, casting up such roguish glances and twirling that parasol – I can see her now! He was grinning at her like a sailor on shore leave. I envied him.'

The speaker paused again to chuckle. 'I never saw *her* again, more's the pity. I did see Appleton, only a couple of days later, scurrying along the Broad late for some lecture, and alone. The student walking with me knew him and called out. He introduced us and that's how I formally met Francis Appleton. It was an evil day.'

'And now,' I said, 'you have requested I come here this evening in order that, even at this late stage of proceedings, you can tell me you didn't murder him in a foul manner last Michaelmas – and I arrested the wrong man!'

'Oh, no, Inspector Ross.' Mills raised a protesting hand. 'By no means. You arrested the right man. I confess freely that I cut his throat with a carving knife, the same one we had used to carve the Michaelmas goose sent round earlier from the cook shop. The cold remains of our meal stood on the table. I first snatched up the knife in a fit of rage and stabbed him in the throat. That didn't kill him straight away so, needs must when the devil drives, I had to continue. I hacked at his windpipe a few times while he gurgled and flailed about, bloody bubbles of froth pouring from his lips. I severed the artery at last and that did it. Who would have thought it would be so difficult to kill a man? Oh, yes, I am a murderer; and in the morning I shall make the short walk from this condemned cell to the gallows here at Newgate. I understand the scaffold has been erected in the yard, inside the prison walls, not outside in the street. Is that so?'

'It is so. You are among the first to benefit from the

recent ruling by the government that hangings shall no longer take place in public.'

On my approach to the prison I had been struck by the absence of the black-painted barriers that would formerly have been set up the day before a hanging to control the mob come to view the show. Absent, too, were the eager visitors who had arrived early to secure the best places, and would pass the night drinking and gambling. But the crowd would gather, anyway, when dawn lightened the sky, I was sure of it. Even if they couldn't see the process, they would be drawn there by the knowledge of what was happening inside the walls. They would wait until someone came out and nailed the notice of the completed execution to the gate. Then they would probably raise a *huzzah*! I wondered whether hangman Calcraft would improve his technique now he would no longer have an audience. He was undeniably a showman and the crowd had always liked to see a victim dangle kicking at the end of the rope.

'Benefit?' Mills gave me an amused look.

To my annoyance, I knew my face betrayed my confusion. 'Forgive me,' I said stiffly, 'it was not a well-chosen word. I meant to say, you won't have to see the mob baying at you.'

'What a polite fellow you are, Ross.' Mills gave me a gracious nod. Then he frowned. 'There was a condemned man hanged outside in public view soon after I arrived here. That was in May. I heard the crowd roaring in delight. I even heard them singing.'

'That was Barrett, for his part in the Clerkenwell

bombings,' I told him. 'There was a crowd of some two thousand out there, so I'm not surprised you heard the noise.'

'Ah, yes, Barratt, the Fenian. He killed twelve people of whom he knew nothing and who had done him no personal wrong. I killed only one who had greatly wronged me . . .' Mills smiled at me but his eyes were cold. 'Of course I am relieved I won't have a drunken, stinking audience roaring their approval as they watch *me* dance.'

He leaned back against the wall. 'I was able to hear them building the scaffold earlier today, so much sawing and hammering. The racket penetrated the walls and I dare say all in here could hear it. The prison chaplain – a most tedious fellow – visited me earlier this evening. He droned on about repentance. I told him I had confessed; and did not see that I was obliged to repent as well! He insisted that I should. I told him the only thing of which I repented, most heartily, was that I had placed my confidence, trust and money in the keeping of a man I believed my closest and oldest friend. A man I had never imagined might swindle me, ruin my fortune and good name, bring shame on my wife and children, leave them destitute . . .'

He was becoming agitated. From my arrival until that moment he'd been unnaturally calm. I can tell you that his earlier outward serenity had rattled me far more than this. Others in his situation I'd seen gibbering and raving. He had been, to all appearances, relaxed. I felt some sympathy for the chaplain.

'So,' I said crossly. 'Why have you brought me across

London, depriving me of my supper? To hear for myself this confession? I didn't need the confirmation from your own lips. I am certain you are guilty and was so from the moment I arrested you.'

Mills relaxed once more and raised a hand, dismissing my protest. 'I am sorry you have missed your dinner. They asked me if I had any special choice for my last meal. I told them I had no appetite and only required good, strong coffee – which they brought. Perhaps I should have asked for a beefsteak pie and presented you with it. However, I told them that I did have a last request and it was that a message should be sent to you, asking that you be kind enough to attend me here, as I had something to tell you. I couldn't go to you, alas. I am obliged to you for coming.'

'Get on with it, then!' I snapped. I suspected he was taking some sort of revenge by wasting my time. A feeble revenge, perhaps, but in his situation, he could do little more.

I was wrong.

His manner changed again, becoming brisk and businesslike. 'What a man declares on his deathbed, knowing that his end is near, is held to be admissible in a court of law, is it not?'

'I have no experience of that in any case where I've been the arresting officer. Yet I have heard of it,' I replied cautiously. 'It would be in special circumstances, I expect. I am not a lawyer. I suppose it depends what is said, if it is before witnesses and whether the speaker, though dying, is of sound mind and not raving . . .'

'I am of sound mind. I am not raving. I wish to tell you I witnessed a murder.' Again he held up a hand to prevent my outburst. 'No, not the one *I* committed. I saw someone else commit a murder. It did not suit me at the time to speak of it. But it lies on my conscience.' He paused and frowned. 'Call it my conscience. I feel I should tell you about it in order to set the record straight. Yes, that's a better way of putting it.'

'Go on,' I invited without disguising my disbelief. He could still be playing at some form of revenge. He knew curiosity would make me ask more. It was possible he didn't so much want to unburden his mind as to trouble mine. 'Where and when?' I demanded. 'Who was the murderer? Who was the victim?'

'Patience, Ross, I beg you. Perhaps you don't believe me. But I have made great efforts to remain calm in my present distressing circumstances because I wish you to consider what I have to say as a declaration upon my deathbed. True, I am sitting at this table and not lying on that disgusting pallet over there. Also, I am in a good state of health, as we speak, for my age. None the less, please consider me a dying man. I go to the gallows in the morning so it comes to the same thing.'

The prisoner shrugged away the image. 'I wish that you, Ross, shall take what I say seriously. You will write it down and I shall sign it, in the proper manner of statements made to the police.'

I admit his earnestness impressed me. I was at a loss how to respond. 'Very well,' was all I could manage, although I wondered if I were rash to promise it.

It was all he wanted to hear.

'So, begin,' he ordered and pushed towards me a sheet of paper, a pot of ink and a pen lying in readiness – I now realised – for this purpose. 'I, James Mills, being of sound mind and aware I go to meet my Maker in the morning, declare—' He stopped suddenly and frowned. 'There must be a witness. Have the warder come in.'

The warder was duly summoned from where he waited outside the door. I think he had been listening at the grille because his face betrayed eager curiosity when he entered.

'On the late afternoon of the fifteenth of June, eighteen fifty-two, I was returning alone, on horseback, from a business visit at Putney,' Mills continued. 'It was a Tuesday. You see, the date is fixed in my memory! I was riding across the heath. It can be a lonely place. The criminal element that used to be a feature of it still hadn't entirely forsaken it sixteen years ago; so I had my eyes well open for thieves and vagabonds. Yet, in good weather, there are usually enough respectable people out there, taking exercise, or travelling across it as I was. Earlier, on my way to make my visit, I had even seen a drover herding cattle towards the metropolis for slaughter at Smithfield. But June is a fickle month. On that day it had been sultry and airless. Then, as I set out for home, and as bad luck would have it, a sudden summer storm blew up. The skies opened, sending down heavy rain, accompanied by a strong wind and great rolling claps of thunder. The heath was deserted. Any other travellers had been forced to seek shelter, and I knew I must do the same. It was all I could do to control my frightened horse. A clump of trees not too far away offered the nearest sanctuary and I turned towards it.

'It proved a small coppice. I dismounted at the edge and led my horse forward under the branches. They did little to shield the pair of us. I then realised that there was a house nearby, just ahead of me, beyond the trees. I tied my horse to a suitable branch and set out on foot towards the place, hoping it would prove to be an inn, as I calculated I wasn't far from the Portsmouth road. If so, I could retrieve my poor beast and the pair of us would find shelter. But it was a private house, of a style that suggested the earlier part of the last century. The eaves came down low and the windows were small. Smoke came from a chimney in fitful bursts when the rain didn't go straight down and must almost have quenched the fire below. The sky was dark – not because it was late but because of the weather – and all around gloomy. A lamp had been lit in a room on the ground floor. I approached and first thumped the knocker on the main entrance. But no one came and I supposed that, with the noise of the storm, no one within could hear me. So I made my way towards the lighted window and peered in.'

'You must wait a moment and allow me to catch up,' I requested. I had been scribbling as fast as I could but the candlelight was poor and the ink badly mixed. There was a risk I'd obscure half the narrative with blots.

Mills listened as I read back to him what I'd written down so far. He nodded to express his satisfaction.

The warder, called to witness the account, was breathing heavily and quite fascinated.

'I looked into a small sitting room, with a low ceiling and open beams across in the old style. It was comfortably furnished. I remember a grandfather clock stood against the wall to my right. There was a fire burning in the hearth.'

'A thunderstorm,' I interrupted, 'usually follows hot, sultry weather such as you mentioned prevailing before the rain poured down. Yet there was a fire?'

'I only report what I saw!' Mills replied testily. 'Yes, a fire. The rain was indeed finding its way down the chimney and the flames flickered, growing taller, then falling back almost to nothing. Remember, please, the fire was not the only source of light. There was an oil lamp, too, on a small table. The glow of that was what had attracted me from outside. Believe me, I could make out everything within quite clearly. That is important. I saw what I saw and did not imagine it.'

'Then what did you see?' I asked. 'If you don't cut it short, I'll run out of paper.' But despite my sharp words I had been drawn into his tale already. I felt myself on that windswept heath. I heard the hiss of the rain pattering on to the parched soil and pressed my face to the wet panes of the window. What could he have seen so dreadful that he could not face death without unburdening his mind of it?

Mills appeared unperturbed by my impatience. He knew he had hooked his fish – me – and was reeling him in.

'I could see an elderly gentleman slumbering in a chair. He had white hair and there was a cane leaning against the arm of the chair. The fire had no doubt been lit on his account. I tapped with little hope of awakening him. Then, as I debated what to do, the door of the room suddenly opened and a young woman came in. I had been hoping someone would arrive, perhaps a maidservant to tend the fire. But this was a young lady. She was no servant, I am sure of it. She was a handsome girl, perhaps twenty years old, in a gown of some dark colour, mauve or purplish. It had a lace collar and cuffs. Her hair was dressed in ringlets, much a fashion at that time, as you may yourself recall. She stood for a moment in the open doorway looking at the sleeping old gentleman. Then she went towards the hearth.

'Perhaps she had come to see how the fire did. But when she got there, she stood before the old fellow's chair for a minute or two, staring down at him. Believe me, Ross, there was no concern or affection on her face. Her expression was bitter. It both surprised and shocked me. Nevertheless, the rain was trickling down my neck in a most unpleasant manner, so I raised my hand again to knock at the windowpane. I hoped my sudden appearance, as a face peering in, wouldn't alarm her. If she screamed, then the old man would wake up with a start and there would be such a to-do. However, before I could knock, she moved in a sudden and determined manner as if her mind were made up. She went to another chair nearby and picked up a cushion. I thought she meant to make the old fellow more comfortable and stayed my hand to allow her time to do it. That was my unwitting mistake.'

Mills paused. The warder's hoarse breath seemed unnaturally loud. I wrote out the last few words and nodded at him to signal he should go on.

'She placed the cushion upon the old man's face,' Mills said bleakly, 'in a most deliberate and careful manner, and smothered him.'

'Strewth . . .' croaked the warder.

'You are certain of this?' I demanded.

'As certain as I am that the hangman is practising his knots, even as we speak. She held the cushion down with both hands, eventually picking it up again and bending over him to see if he still breathed. She even stretched out her bare palm and held it before his nose and mouth, to feel if there were yet breath.'

'He did not resist?'

'I doubt he knew what was happening. He started and put up his hands when she first pressed down the cushion. He made a feeble gesture or two, and then it was over.'

'And *you*? You did nothing to prevent this?' I asked.

He shrugged. 'I was quite frozen with the horror of it. Besides, how could I have done anything? I was outside in the storm.'

'You could have shouted, struck the window as forcefully as you could, broken it if necessary.'

Mills waved his hand irritably. 'Yes, yes, all this is very well and spoken after the event. Hindsight is a wonderful thing. But it was so unexpected, so sudden, and so quick . . . It was the very last thing in the world I might have anticipated. You don't walk up to a respectable house prepared to see murder done! I would have signalled my presence urgently, as you describe, had I the slightest inkling of her intention.'

I nodded to show I accepted the point he'd made. Mills took a deep breath. 'Satisfied the work was done, she walked quickly out of the room. She had left the door open on her entry, but now she closed it behind her. Her victim was alone, but for the spectator of it all, myself, still pressed against the wet windowpane as if frozen to it. The old fellow's head lolled sideways. One arm dropped down by the side of the chair, dislodging the cane propped there. He was lifeless, Ross, and I was in a pretty fix.'

'You could have gone back to your horse, remounted, and ridden to the next habitation to raise the alarm.'

'I intended that, I swear. I ran back to where I'd left my horse, dragged the wretched beast from what little shelter he'd enjoyed and scrambled into the saddle. But I had become disoriented in the storm, in seeking shelter, by the shock of what I'd witnessed . . . I must have ridden in circles and eventually, when I did make a straight line, I found myself almost at the river before I saw the tower of the St Mary's church, shops and houses.'

'Where you could still have raised the alarm or sought out the authorities.'

'You don't understand, Ross. As I rode, I had had time to reflect on what might happen if I raised a hue and cry. To begin with, a number of well-to-do folk have houses in the area and they don't want to be troubled with anything so unpleasant as murder! So it would not be an easy thing to knock on a door and tell someone. I was not sure where to turn.'

'To the Metropolitan Police!' I snapped. 'I accept you may not have found an officer to hand in Putney. But, for pity's sake, man, you had reached the bridge! You had but to ride across it and report what you'd witnessed to the first officer you saw.'

'You make it sound simple,' Mills said angrily. 'Let us say I found a constable – on either side of the bridge. There would still be questions, delays. I would be asked to return to the scene of the crime with the officers. I couldn't be certain of finding it again at once. They might think I was leading them on a fool's errand. If we found the house – and the old fellow lying dead – what then? More questions. More delay. Suppose they asked my business acquaintance at Putney to vouch for me? Eventually the whole wretched affair would find its way into the newspapers and what a time the reporters would have! They'd camp out on my doorstep demanding my eyewitness account. I couldn't allow that. The business matter I'd attended at Putney was of a very delicate nature. I – I could not admit to being there.'

The warder and I exchanged glances. We were of a mind, I fancy. It had not been a business visit that had taken Mills to Putney, but an amorous one. He seemed always to have had an eye for a pretty woman. The lady he'd visited in Putney had no doubt been married, quite possibly to someone of consequence. Mills's remark about wealthy people having homes in the area, and not wanting to hear of murder, had been made with one particular household in mind.

As if he could read my mind, Mills said defiantly: 'The old man was dead. I couldn't bring him back to life. I had to think of my own circumstances . . .'

'And you now wish me to investigate a murder that took place sixteen years ago? The gentleman's death was perhaps subject to inquiry at the time.'

He shook his head. 'I kept a close eye on the newspapers for some time afterward. Such a case, had it been investigated, would have been closely followed by the press, for obvious reasons. The old fellow's death must have been declared due to natural causes – of whatever kind – and this stated on the death certificate.'

'All the more difficult to investigate it now!' I pointed out. 'The news may not have reached the press and the absence of a report doesn't necessarily tell us anything. But let us say a professional man – a doctor or a coroner – ruled upon the death at the time. This is quite possible. Then he must, if he is still alive, be prepared to admit he made a mistake, or could have made a mistake. Why should he? What if he insists there was no error? It is far too late in the day to dig up the body, even if an order could be obtained. Most of all, after so long, who is there to care?'

Mills's smile this time was positively wolfish. 'I thought, my dear Ross, the police cared.'

I sighed. 'Have you the address of this house?'

'Of course I don't!' he fairly shouted at me. 'It was in the middle of Putney Heath. It was near a sizeable coppice. It was built, I'd guess, a hundred and twenty years ago. I have described it to you as best I can.'

'And you expect me to find it?'

'I have told you the date the death occurred,' Mills retorted. 'You know the approximate location. Good heavens, man! You are the detective. Must I direct you? The house was old, and indeed may once have been an inn, but it was certainly by then a gentleman's home. Perhaps that of a prosperous city businessman, now long retired? At any rate, the room was well furnished. The girl was a young lady . . .'

The warder burst out laughing. 'Some young lady, that! What, go smothering an old gent with a cushion?'

Mills gave him a withering look and turned back to me. 'I shall sign the document now. You sign it, too, Ross, and this fellow – as witnesses.' He indicated the warder.

We all signed.

'Now you can go.' Mills suddenly sounded tired. 'I have spoken my piece and cleared my conscience. Now it's up to you.'

I got up, folding the statement and tucking it securely into my breast pocket. 'Is there anything else you would like? A book, perhaps?'

'No, no.' Mills shook his head. 'Only, perhaps, more coffee if possible.' He looked up at me. 'I do not want to fall asleep,' he said, 'not now. I shall be doing that soon enough.' He paused. 'Besides, he watches me.'

'I have to watch you!' said the warder, affronted. 'It's my job. Fellows like you try and cheat the hangman.'

Turning to me, he explained, 'They go banging their heads on the walls or tear up their shirts to make a rope and hang 'emselves if they're not watched.'

'Not him,' said Mills to me, pointing at the warder. '*Him.*' He pointed at the opposite wall.

'Mind gone,' confided the warder to me in a whisper and tapping his own brow with a grimy forefinger. 'That happens, too, you know.'

But I knew whom Mills could see.

'Bring him some more coffee,' I said to the warder in a low voice and he nodded.

'Oh, Ross!' Mills's voice called, as I was about to step out of the cell. I paused and turned. 'There is one thing about that house. I've just remembered. It had a weather-vane attached to the chimney. It was whirling round and round in the storm. It was shaped like an animal, a running fox, I fancy, with his brush held straight out behind him.'

The warder pulled the door shut and locked it. He looked at me inquiringly.

'What about all that then, sir?'

'I must speak with the governor immediately,' I said.

'Bless you, Mr Ross, the governor's at home, most likely sitting down to his dinner or enjoying a glass of brandy after it.'

'Nevertheless, I must disturb him. He must be told of this at once, tonight. Tomorrow will be too late.'

'Aye,' agreed the warder, nodding sagely. 'It will be that.'

Chapter Two

THE GOVERNOR was indeed at home and, as if my disturbing him there at this late hour were not embarrassing enough, he was sitting with guests at dinner. They had reached the stage where the ladies had retired to gossip and the gentlemen were relaxing with the port and cigars. That's when I arrived, dishevelled and demanding to speak to him. Give the man his due; he agreed to see me in his study for ten minutes.

So there he sat before me, in his gleaming starched white shirtfront and cuffs and immaculate black tailcoat, his face red from good food and good wine, and from the luxury of a fire lit on a cool September evening. An aroma of cigar smoke wafted around him. I was put in mind of Charles Dickens's yarn, *A Christmas Carol*, a favourite read of my wife, Lizzie. It was not the time of year and there was no holly wreathing the man's brow, but in all other ways I could not but think of the ghost of Christmas Present.

And there was I, the ghosts of Christmas Past and Future rolled into one, speaking of old murder and soon-to-be-execution.

He heard me out, took Mills's statement, read it through. Then he put it down with a sigh. 'My dear chap,' he said, 'you appear to have had a most difficult evening. Will you take a glass of brandy?'

'You are too kind,' I told him ruefully, 'but I must decline. I shall arrive home late enough without doing it smelling of brandy.'

He chuckled. 'Now, see here, Inspector Ross. You were quite right to bring this to my attention. But I do urge you now to go home to your wife, your much-delayed dinner and your bed. Put this whole matter out of your mind. Frankly, there is nothing to be done.'

'Mills should be questioned again in the morning,' I protested. 'Taken under secure guard to Putney to help us locate the house . . .'

The governor waved a well-manicured hand. 'My dear fellow, there is no house. There was no murder witnessed through a window. What is it good Dr Johnson said? That when man knows he is to be hanged in a fortnight, it concentrates his mind wonderfully? It certainly seems to have inspired Mills's imagination.'

I uttered a yelp of protest.

He shook his head at me. 'See here, Ross, this prisoner, Mills, is to be hanged as soon as this coming morning. He may have been able to put on a good show till now, hiding any fears. But now the moment has almost come. Reality has concentrated his mind. He is prepared to do anything to delay the dreadful event. To gain a few hours, a few days . . . It may seem little enough, but not to a man in his circumstances.

'Let us suppose,' he continued, 'that, instead of making this declaration in the condemned cell, Mills had walked, as a free man with clean hands, into the nearest police station sixteen years ago and reported what he now claims to have seen at Putney. Even then, surely you will agree, that the first thing any police officer would do would be to establish what kind of man had made such a strange and serious accusation? In short, is the witness credible? Is he of good character? Respected and successful in his business? Has he a clear head? Is he likely to speak or act wildly? Only if they thought there was some reason to believe him – and not take him for drunk or mad or acting from malice – only then would police resources and public money be spent on an investigation. Am I not correct?'

'Yes,' I said reluctantly.

'Well, then, how – tonight – would you answer those questions with regard to Mills, the murderer? Is *he* credible?'

'I understand the argument you make, sir,' I told him. 'Perhaps I should be reluctant to take his word. But I cannot disregard any witness telling me of a murder.'

'And I cannot trouble the home secretary at this time of the evening with this!' He brandished the statement at me. 'It is the fantasy of a desperate man. Your wish to be thorough does you credit, Inspector Ross. But I have experience of dealing with men about to go to the gallows. Of course, they panic. They are like a drowning man. They flail about, grasping at any fragile scrap of flotsam to help them stay afloat and alive. Believe me, my dear

Ross, there is nothing to be done and no crime to investigate.'

Perhaps he saw I was still unconvinced. The governor leaned forward and went on earnestly, 'Mills is a clever fellow. I got to know him a little over the past weeks and he is an intriguing character; the very last man, you might have thought, to find himself in his present fix. You, also, Ross got to know him during your investigation into his crime and his trial. But here's the thing.' The governor raised a finger. 'So did *he* get to know *you*!'

This was true. I felt myself redden. The governor leaned back to expound on his theory, making a gesture in the air with his right hand as a conjuror might. '"Ross is a conscientious fellow," Mills says to himself as he sits in the condemned cell. "If I give him this cock-and-bull story, well dressed up to sound plausible, he will feel duty-bound to do something about it and seek to delay my execution." And he was right. You have done something about it. You have brought this work of fiction to me. I, in turn, have done my duty and read it. Is that not so?'

I had felt my face burn even more and hoped he'd put it down to the fire in his hearth. But he would know he was right, of course. Many a clever crook – or murderer – has sought to find a weakness in the investigating officer that can be exploited. My confidence was ebbing fast. I began to feel I'd been foolish. I should know better than to believe Mills. Of course he sought to delay the horror of what awaited him on the morrow. 'I am sorry to have troubled you with it, sir,' I said stiffly.

'Come, come, my dear Inspector, you did the right thing. Your conscience can be clear.'

Silence fell between us, only the fire crackled. I watched conflicting emotions play across the governor's ruddy features as he peered at the statement still in his hand.

His conscience might not trouble him but concern for his future career was disturbing him. After all, he had just made a splendid speech telling an officer of the law to disregard a report of murder. It was the sort of grand decision that might possibly come back to bite him.

In a more conciliatory tone, he continued. 'Well, well, on second thoughts, now that you have told me, I feel I am obliged to take some action. I'll tell you what I'll do. I will write to the home secretary in the morning, enclosing this document, and send it to him by hand, instructing my messenger that it must be delivered personally. Then you and I will both have done all in our power and can forget about it.'

And the home secretary will order it filed; or toss it into the fire, I thought, but did not say. Then, having much else on his mind, he will forget about the whole thing. Even if he does take it seriously, it will be too late, for Mills will already be dead.

I thanked the governor again for hearing me out; and rose to take my leave. At the door of the room I turned and asked him, 'The executioner will be Calcraft, I suppose?'

For a moment the governor looked embarrassed and avoided my eye as he replied, 'Yes, yes, Calcraft. He is the Newgate hangman.'

'He is a bungler, either through incompetence or by design,' I said. 'He ought to be sacked. This is my personal opinion.'

'He is nearing retirement, certainly,' replied the governor curtly, 'but he has served Newgate and other prisons well for many years, doing a task not everyone would wish to do. You, William Calcraft, and I, we all in our several ways serve justice in this country. Our individual personal opinions are of no account. Duty! That is what guides us! Goodnight, Inspector Ross.'

As the butler closed the street door behind me, I caught a snatch of male laughter from the direction of the dining room. The governor had rejoined his guests and probably forgotten Mills already.

I began to walk slowly homeward, still turning over what I should do. Should I let the matter go? I'd done as Mills had asked and reported it. I'd been promised action – even if that action would come too late. What else? Take it directly to a senior police officer? There is a hierarchy within the police force and I could not by-pass it. This meant I would have to disturb Superintendent Dunn, who would be at home now in Camden, and beg him, in turn, to by-pass anyone immediately his senior in order directly to disturb the commissioner of the Metropolitan Police.

It would take me time to get to Dunn's home, even if I took a cab. Dunn was a fair man and a good officer, but also impatient; and by nature respectful of those his senior. I would have to inform him the governor of

Newgate had promised to contact the home secretary in the morning. That would alarm Dunn enough. It would also count against his troubling Sir Richard Mayne, the commissioner. Sir Richard was a distinguished man. But it was well known that he did not enjoy a good relationship with the office of the home secretary. (This was due to some confusion during the police investigation into the Clerkenwell bombing carried out by Barrett: that same Barrett whose execution had been the last to be carried out before a cheering crowd; and had been overheard by Mills in his cell.) In short, I did not have to visit Dunn to know that the superintendent would no more take the matter to Sir Richard than he would run and knock on the home secretary's door in person.

I could do no more than I had done. Besides, it was quite possible all this was what is popularly termed a 'mare's nest'. Mills had spun me a fantasy of murder unsolved in order to delay his own merited execution. 'Yes,' I said aloud to myself, 'that is it!'

My voice echoed in the empty air. I had reached the embankment and been strolling alongside the river. I was just passing by the arches supporting the brick walls of Waterloo Station. The tide was high and the river lapped at the stone and concrete corset confining it only feet away. I could smell its acrid tang above the smoke from the great engines on the other side of the station's walls. There was no one around that I could see and I expected no response to my words. But my ear caught the faintest sound from beneath one of the arches. It was a woman's voice, I was sure of that. I couldn't catch the words. They were spoken too quietly and, I fancied, not addressed to me. Not a prostitute, then, patrolling the riverside and who thought she spotted in me a possible customer. This was someone else.

The arches were a known refuge for homeless souls. Had the voice been male, I would have put it down as belonging to one of them, and not inquired further. But this was a female voice, and now, to add to my curiosity – and some dismay – I heard a small child give a little cry, as a restless child will when sleep is fitful. I approached the arch and peered into the darkness.

Something moved, no doubt startled at my appearance. I heard the rustle of clothing. The child squeaked again.

'Who is there?' I asked.

There was no reply, other than the sound of rapid breathing. I took a box of lucifers from my pocket and struck one. In its flickering light I saw a woman's terrified face. She was huddled on the ground, wrapped in some kind of cloak or blanket. Before the lucifer's brief flame was extinguished, I saw the covering move and a small bare foot emerge.

'Don't be afraid,' I urged her. 'I am a police officer – not in uniform – but an officer of the law, none the less. I am Inspector Ross of Scotland Yard.'

'I am not begging, sir,' she whispered in reply.

'I know that. You are only sheltering here but that is still classed as vagrancy. There are places you can go if you have no other shelter. You should apply to a casual ward at a workhouse for a night's bed.'

'Have you seen those places?' she whispered in reply. 'You have not, sir, or you wouldn't suggest it.'

I had never had cause to enter a women's ward. But, as a younger officer, I had had occasion to search through a men's ward seeking a wanted man. I remembered it as a dreadful place, airless, stinking, crammed with drunken, diseased and desperate men, young and old. I had even had to throw open the door of the privy in the corner, to see if my fugitive was in there, and shall not forget the open pit, brimming with human excrement.

'But you have a child with you,' I argued, none the less. 'You cannot stay here.'

'We are safe here,' she replied obstinately.

'What has brought you to this state?' I asked next, as sympathetically as I could.

Almost inaudibly, as if shamed by the admission, she whispered, 'My husband left us. I do not know where he has gone. I had no money to pay the rent and buy food . . . We had to leave the place where we lodged.'

'Then apply to the parish!' I exclaimed.

'They will send us to the workhouse. They will take my child from me.' She wrapped her arms around the bundle beneath the shawl. 'Please, Inspector Ross, don't arrest me for vagrancy. I do no harm here.'

'But it is not suitable—' I broke off. Neither was a casual ward a suitable place for a child. 'I will leave you here tonight,' I said. 'But tomorrow, come to Scotland Yard and ask for me or for Sergeant Morris. We will see you are put in touch with a suitable charity.'

I could rely on Morris, whom I would forewarn, but I

hoped Superintendent Dunn never learned I was taking on the work of charities from my office at the Yard.

'What is your name?'

Reluctantly she answered, 'Jane Stephens, sir.'

'Have you no family?' I asked. 'Other than your absconded husband?'

'They're a long way from here, sir.'

'Well, well . . . come to the Yard in the morning. Remember, Inspector Ross or Sergeant Morris.' I delved into my pocket and extracted the few coins there. I held them out to her. 'Take it. It is not a trick. I shan't accuse you of begging. Buy something warm for breakfast for yourself and the child.'

She whispered her thanks and took the money. Her fingers, brushing my palm, were soft. This was not a working woman with roughened hands. 'See here,' I told her, 'for your husband to have abandoned you and fail to support his child is an offence and you can report it.'

Even as I spoke, I realised this was the reason she had not gone to the parish authorities and claimed relief under the Poor Law. She had a child and would be required to name the father so that he could be found and made to reimburse any money the parish spent on his family. But she did not want him found, that was it! I began to doubt the accuracy of her story, such as it was. Possibly even the name she'd given me was false. At any rate, the man had not left her. She had run away from him. She feared any authority would force her back to him. He must be a brute, that she chose this archway as a better and safer place for them both.

I went on my way. There were many who would have told me she would buy alcohol with the money, but I believed she would buy food for the child, if not for herself.

I completed my journey home, feeling unaccustomedly useless. I couldn't help the woman, other than leave her in the shelter she'd found and hope she'd come to the Yard the next day. (I doubted she would. She would be too frightened.) Nor could I do anything about Mills's testimony, with the result that a murderess remained free out there somewhere. London was full of wrongs and any police officer who thought he could right even half of them would be a fool.

But he could still try.

The house was quiet. The parlour clock told me it was nearly midnight. Lizzie was already abed and so was our maid-of-all-work, Bessie. I went into the kitchen and found a large plate of cold sliced beef, carefully covered over to protect from mice, and a jar of pickled onions. I didn't fancy either. But the kitchen was warm and comfortable and I sat for a while by the range and thought over what had happened. I would go to Dunn in the morning and report it. I had no hope of there being any action, but it must be officially recorded.

I heard a sound at the door into the kitchen from the hall, and there stood Lizzie in her nightgown and a shawl, with her long dark hair braided into a single plait, and holding up a guttering candle. The dancing flame chased shadows across her face. She was in her early thirties now but, to me, still looked a young girl. She had been a very young girl when I had first set eyes on her, back home in Derbyshire. We had been children, she the doctor's daughter and me the grimy lad who worked down in the mine. Her father's generosity had taken me from that life and seen to it I had an education. I doubted he meant I would reward him by marrying his daughter.

'You found the beef?' she asked. That meant, why hadn't I eaten any of it?

'I am not hungry,' I defended myself. 'I'm sorry if I wakened you.'

'I wasn't asleep, only dozing.' She sat down before the range in a chair facing mine. 'What happened at Newgate? Mills must be very distressed. One has to pity him.'

So I told her the whole thing from beginning to end. She listened without interruption. Then, when I fell silent, she said firmly: 'You could have done nothing else. You had to go to the governor.'

'Perhaps he was right and Mills was making a fool of me.'

'Of course, he *might* have been doing that!' she retorted. 'But you don't know.'

'I'll never know,' I said wryly.

After a moment, she stretched out her hand and placed it on my arm. 'You did the right thing,' she said. 'You have done all you could.'

I wished I believed her.

Chapter Three

Elizabeth Martin Ross

I HAD been awaiting Ben's return from Newgate all evening. I had gone upstairs to bed, but not to sleep.

We had been about to sit down to our supper earlier when the message came that he was required there. A condemned man had made it his last request that he speak to the arresting officer in his case. That had been Ben. He had stood up from the table, made a brief apology, and left at once. I had not attempted to delay him or suggest he dine first. But I had known he would not only be hungry when he returned, he would be in mental turmoil.

Any visit to Newgate has a depressing effect on Ben's spirits, as it would on any sane person's. I have never been inside the fortress-like walls of that dreadful place, although I have occasionally shopped in the market that thrives in the street just outside it. The market stall-holders and other shoppers seem never to give it a second look. For me, its castle-keep-like appearance, blind windows and the stone frieze of entwined manacles and chains above the main entrance send a shudder down my spine.

Now, on this occasion, Ben's visit had been made much more difficult by Mills's strange allegation. Could it be true? I wondered. Or was it just the invention of a desperate man about to climb the steps to the gallows? Even the thought of what must happen in the morning made me shiver.

Ben believed Mills's tale; that was the problem. Because he believed it, he would not be able to leave it alone. The idea of an uninvestigated murder would continue to prey on his mind; above all if he were unable to persuade anyone else to take it seriously.

There was nothing more I could have said to him that would have made things easier. I had offered the obvious words of comfort. I urged that he had done his best in going to the governor, that it was not his fault if the governor had dismissed the claim made. Mills should have spoken out earlier. After all, he had had sixteen years to do so, if his strange tale were true. In the end we had agreed to discuss it no more, as it was now in the early hours.

Ben slept badly and I hardly at all as he tossed and turned beside me. It began to prey on my mind, too. If Mills had given an honest account, then what had led to the awful scene he'd witnessed that fateful day on Putney Heath? What hatred had built up in the heart of an apparently respectable young woman and why? I knew already that I could no more leave the question unanswered than Ben could. That is to say, he could do little more than file a report in the morning at Scotland Yard. As for me, I could only lie awake here with images of the wretched Mills in his cell, dancing in the darkness before me.

Eventually I fell asleep to be awakened by a rattle of fire irons in the kitchen range beneath my feet. Bessie was up and about and encouraging the range to heat up and boil the kettle for hot water. I slipped out of bed, picked up the empty jug on the washstand, and went downstairs to help her.

It is not possible to keep much from our intrepid maid-of-all-work.

'The inspector came home very late from Newgate, missis,' she observed, hauling the kettle from the range and splashing most of the contents into the jug. As she was preparing to lug it upstairs, she added casually, 'Did he go and see that murderer?'

'Yes, he did.'

'It makes my blood run cold,' declared Bessie with so much relish I suspected the thought of the wretched Mills in the condemned cell had quite the opposite effect. She then added, with a glance at the clock ticking above the hearth, 'They're probably leading him out to the scaffold this very minute!'

'That's enough, Bessie!' I told her sharply. 'Take up the water or it will go cold again and the inspector not be able to shave.'

Bessie had previously worked in the household of my Aunt Parry. In those days she had called me 'Miss Martin'. Now, I am afraid, she called me 'missis' and there was nothing I could do to change this. Ben was always called by her 'the inspector' and I, when talking to her, had to do the same.

'Yes, missis,' she said obediently now.

'And don't ask him about Newgate!' I called after her.

'Of course I wouldn't, missis!' floated back down the stairs.

Inspector Benjamin Ross

Before I went up to bed, tired as I was, I had carefully written out Mills's story while it was still fresh in my mind. I took great care not to omit a single detail: the wild weather, the oil lamp in the parlour window, the old man dozing by the fire, the arrival of the young woman, her dreadful deed and her calm departure. I described how Mills, appalled and disorientated, had ridden aimlessly around the heath before finally coming to houses; by which time he'd decided to say nothing of what he'd seen, for reasons of his own. I read it through two or three times until satisfied and put it in my pocket. If I had a chance, I would hand it to Superintendent Dunn. It might never be investigated but it would be on record.

On my way to Scotland Yard I rehearsed mentally how I would approach the subject. When I arrived, however, and before I could get anywhere near the superintendent, I was intercepted by Sergeant Morris. He stationed his burly frame before me, obliging me to stop and pay attention.

'I have a message for you, sir,' he announced, looking, I fancied, slightly furtive.

'Is it from a young woman giving the name Jane Stephens?' I asked, remembering I had told the woman beneath the arches to come to the Yard in the morning.

'No,' replied Morris, his bushy eyebrows twitching in surprise. 'Who would she be, then, Mr Ross?'

'She – I told her to ask either for me or for you. It doesn't matter – but if she comes here, tell me and no one else. What is your message?'

Morris gave me an old-fashioned look but let the question about Jane Stephens drop. 'It's from Mr Dunn, sir. He came in early today and he wants to see you, straight away.' The sergeant leaned forward and added, sotto voce, 'I understand, sir, there has been communication.'

'Communication?'

'Between the commissioner of the Metropolitan Police – that is to say, his office – and this department, sir. There has been talks in *high places*. Only,' added Morris, 'I don't know what about, as is natural.'

'Natural?'

'High places,' said Morris, 'do not confide in me, Mr Ross. No more should they. Mr Dunn said to tell him – you, that is – to come direct, no delay.'

I sighed. The carefully memorised speech concocted on my way to work would not be delivered. There would be no need either of that or of my written report. Both the governor of Newgate and the Home Office had moved faster than I'd anticipated. I glanced at the clock on the wall. It was a little before half past eight. Mills had probably been dead this past two hours. His mischief – as I was beginning to view it – lingered on and was, in a sense, possibly only beginning to meddle in our lives.

Dunn appeared to have been pacing up and down the room as he waited for me. When I entered, he'd reached the far end and turned swiftly to face me. He was alarmingly red in the face and his sharp little eyes glittered beneath the shaggy brows.

'There you are, Ross,' he greeted me. 'I understand you think we have time on our hands here, at the Yard?'

'No, sir!' I replied, startled.

'It seems you do. As if we didn't have enough cases to investigate and enough criminals don't take to violence, you have dug up a murder, which, if it ever happened at all, took place sixteen years ago. It was committed in Putney, we are asked to believe. We know neither the name of the victim, nor exactly where he lived. There are no witnesses and no one reported it.'

He paused for breath and I took the opportunity to say quickly, 'There was one eyewitness and he told me last night what he'd seen.'

'Well, he won't tell anyone else,' said Dunn shortly. He marched to his desk and sat down, placing his stubby hands flat on the polished surface. He was a stocky man who looked more like a farmer than a police officer. His preference for suits of tweed material encouraged the country image. His wiry hair stood up, trimmed off level.

It made it look as if he had a scrubbing brush on his head.

'Mills has gone to the gallows, then,' I said dully.

'He has, at six o'clock this morning.'

'Did Calcraft make a decent job of it this time?'

'I haven't heard that he didn't. He's strung up enough of the condemned to know what he's about.'

I had my own thoughts on that, but I left them unsaid.

'Anyhow, that's quite by the by,' Dunn rumbled on. 'We no longer have to worry about James Mills. But you have stirred up the devil of a fuss and to-do by running to the governor. He sent a messenger to the Home Office last night, you know, not more than an hour or two after you left him. There were few staff on duty in the building and they did as might be expected – got rid of the thing. They dispatched a night clerk with the letter to the home secretary's London home. His private secretary not being on duty, a half-awake butler got the gentleman himself out of his bed at midnight.' Dunn eyed me quizzically. 'You are no respecter of persons, Ross.'

I had underestimated the governor. He had not waited until morning. I doubted it was efficiency or a desire to postpone the hanging that had made him send such a message in the middle of the night. It had been the equivalent of Pontius Pilate washing his hands. It had ceased to be the governor's responsibility. Perhaps, after I'd left him, he'd told his guests about it all and they had urged him to act without waiting for morning. The panicking clerk on the night desk at the Home Office had reacted in the same way and done the same thing. I need not have feared a delay in the news reaching the top man. The very fact that it had been sent after hours meant it had reached its final destination with fewer hands to impede it. If it had been scalding hot it couldn't have been passed on faster! But it had not prevented Mills reaching his final destination.

'They didn't halt the hanging.' I spoke more to myself than to Dunn but the superintendent answered, accompanying his words with a thump of a fist on the desk.

'Good heavens, Ross! Of course they didn't. It was not as if you had sent word of some new evidence in Mills's own case. Then there might have been some delay while it was investigated. But Mills was found guilty after a properly conducted trial and had later admitted his guilt. He said nothing to you last night to withdraw his confession. He had to hang.'

Dunn paused and went on in a persuasive sort of tone. 'Come now, Ross, you arrested him. You saw the scene of his dreadful crime?'

I nodded. 'Yes, I did; the room resembled a slaughterhouse, blood everywhere. I shall never forget it.'

'Then keep the image before you now. Remind yourself that Mills fell out with a business partner, attacked him, and all but sawed off his head with a carving knife. The newspapers' reports were full of the details of the dreadful business. Mills wrapped his greatcoat over his bloodstained coat and trousers, walked out and took a cab home. The next fare to climb into that same cab complained to the driver of fresh bloodstains on the upholstery. The cabman went to the police, the police to Mills's house . . . and from there to Appleton's lodgings to make the awful discovery. This is your man, your informant, Ross.'

'Yes, sir,' I said. I could see where this line of argument had taken us: into a dead end. Dunn, like the governor of Newgate the evening before, judged Mills unreliable as a witness, a condemned man living out his last hours in a nightmare.

Dunn nodded, as if confident I saw reason at long last. 'Now then, Ross, here we have a brand-new accusation concerning the death of an unidentified victim at the hand of an unidentified killer at an address no one knows and taking place sixteen years ago. And we are to take this report as gospel? We are to believe the word of a man like Mills! The *unsubstantiated word* of a self-confessed murderer? A man who apparently had sixteen years to speak out during which he was a respected citizen, not yet with blood on his hands.'

'Well, sir—'

'No!' thundered Dunn. 'We have a man who waited until he was almost at the steps of the gallows to unburden himself of a fantastic tale, giving no details but a date and a general area – Putney Heath – where this murder is supposed to have taken place! How could you, Ross, an officer of such experience and generally of such good judgement, be taken in by such an obvious ploy to gain time?'

'I had to make such a judgement, sir. I had no time to

think it over. It was, as you say, the eleventh hour. I couldn't ignore what Mills told me.' I took a deep breath. 'For what it is worth, I believed him.'

Dunn rolled bloodshot eyes at me. 'Did you, indeed? I recommend you, not only as your superior officer but also as a friend, to stop believing it, forthwith. Do not, Ross, go out of this room and start telling all and sundry that there was a murder on Putney Heath, at the home of some respectable citizen, sixteen years ago, and it was not only never reported, it was never investigated. Nor . . .' Dunn's voice rose. 'Nor will it be investigated now, Ross, do you understand?'

'Yes, sir.' It could not be investigated now. The only witness was dead and probably buried while his body was still warm.

Dunn's demeanour grew more controlled. He signalled towards a chair, meaning I should sit down. I sat.

He placed his hands together, fingers interlaced, and spoke in a low growl. 'What I shall say now is between us, Ross. It will not go outside this room.'

'No, sir, I understand.'

'There was some little difficulty earlier in the year between the Home Office and the Yard, concerning the investigation into the Clerkenwell bombings. That has all settled down. Nothing must disturb the – er – restored good working relationship. Now, I am not unsympathetic to your predicament when Mills spun you this wild story. In your shoes, sitting in the condemned cell last night with a man about to die, I should probably have done what you did. You were right, quite right, to follow it up.

But now it is settled, once and for all. The home secretary has decreed it. There shall be no further action in this matter.'

'I understand, sir.'

'Forget about it, Ross!'

'Yes, sir.' I paused. 'Thank you for your understanding.'

'I stand by my officers,' growled Dunn. 'I told the top brass you were one of the best and my regard for you is undiminished following this.'

'I am grateful, sir.'

'So don't make a fool of yourself or of me, nor of this service.'

'I shall endeavour not to, sir.'

'That's all. My regards to your wife.' The superintendent's expression was inscrutable.

I was startled. It wasn't the first time the superintendent had sent his good wishes to Lizzie. He had a soft spot for her, even though he disapproved of her talent for unofficial detection. But why he should choose to send his regards and mention her name at the end of this particular difficult interview, I couldn't imagine.

'I will pass them on, sir.'

'Everything all right, sir?' asked Morris in a worried tone, when I reappeared.

'Thank you, Sergeant, everything is . . . Everything has been settled.' I probably sounded both cross and mulish and Morris knows me well.

'Can't win 'em all, sir!' he observed.

'I have set the whole establishment of the Metropolitan

Police by its ears, Morris. I have invaded the privacy of the Newgate governor's home; and been responsible for the home secretary being awakened in his blameless bed at midnight, by a butler probably in his nightshirt. I have been fortunate not to be reduced in rank. I am, I fancy, on a warning.'

'Cor,' said Morris with some respect.

It was only fair to explain to him exactly what had been going on. I told him of Mills and his tale and what had followed.

'Ah!' said Morris sagely. 'That's a tricky one, Mr Ross. And this Jane Stephens, where does she come in?'

'She doesn't come into it at all. She was a female vagrant I came across under the arches at Waterloo.' I explained about Jane.

'Chances are,' said Morris, 'they will take her body out of the river.'

Well, that didn't make me feel any better. He was right, though. 'Send young Biddle over to the River Police at Wapping,' I told him. 'Have him ask if they have recovered from the water any female body or the body of a child, last night. And, if they should recover the corpse of a young woman or a child during the coming few days, perhaps they would be so good as to let me know. I would like to be kept informed.'

I was indeed informed but not in the way I'd requested. Towards the end of a trying day I received a visit from a member of the public. Initially I was glad enough of the distraction. All day constables had been whispering behind my back and casting me glances in which awe was mixed with glee. A new case would relegate the whole Mills episode to the category of five-minute wonder.

'A Mr Canning, sir,' announced Morris. 'He's very upset. He says someone has abducted his entire family.'

'If that's true, he has a right to be upset! How sure is he of this? Are there any witnesses?'

'No, but you'd better speak to him, Mr Ross. He's a—' A curiously bland expression crossed the sergeant's face. 'He is a taxpayer, sir.'

'Ah,' I said. 'I think I understand you. He believes he pays our wages and therefore we are here to do his bidding.'

'It's the impression he gave me, sir.'

'Then show this tax-paying gentleman in, Morris, without delay.' After all, I couldn't afford to offend anyone else today.

Mr Canning proved to be a gentleman of perhaps forty years, sporting a moustache and beard in the style commonly called Vandyke. He was not tall, perhaps a little over five feet high, and his tightly buttoned blue coat drew attention to a certain embonpoint. A round hat was crammed on his head almost to the level of his eyebrows.

'You are Inspector Ross?' he demanded as soon as he was fairly through the door. Morris had followed him and taken up a discreet position by the wall.

'I am, and you are Mr Canning, I understand.' I rose to my feet as I spoke, in order to greet him, but as I am just on six feet in height – in my stockinged feet – I found myself towering above him. This clearly did not please him and he glared up at me, pursing his small red mouth in the midst of the Vandyke whiskers.

Hurriedly I invited him to be seated and, when we had both sat down and so were now much of a height, he seemed mollified. He took off his round hat and set it on his knees. His hair was thinning and what remained was peppered with grey. I added a few years to my original estimation of his age, now putting him at fifty or even a year or two older.

'My name is Hubert Canning,' he said. 'I am a merchant in fine wines and of considerable reputation in the business. I supply the best households.'

'Indeed, sir? I know little of wine, I'm afraid.'

The look he cast me showed that he had expected nothing else. 'My business premises are adjacent to Charing Cross. My home is in St John's Wood.'

Mr Canning was a prosperous wine merchant, then. 'The sergeant tells me that you report your family has been abducted, Mr Canning.' I would have expected him to begin with this startling information. If unknown miscreants had snatched my family from me, I would have burst out with it. But he seemed anxious to establish his credentials first. There may have been method in that. It was intended to make me take him seriously. As both Dunn and the Newgate governor had been at pains to remind me, when someone reports a serious crime, the first thing the officer should find out is how reliable the informant is. I suspected, however,

Canning just wished to make me understand that he was an important man in the business community.

His face reddened. 'It's disgraceful. In St John's Wood! It is a highly respectable area. You must track down the villains at once and return my wife and child to me.'

'Ah, so by entire family, you mean your wife and one child. A boy or a girl? May I have your wife's name and that of the child?' I picked up my pen. 'Do you have other children?'

'What difference could it make how many children I have?' he shouted at me. Then he quietened with some visible effort and continued, 'My wife's name is Jane and my daughter's name is Charlotte. She is my – our – only child.'

The hairs on the back of my neck bristled but I managed to keep my voice level. 'When did this happen?'

'At some time the day before yesterday.'

'They have been missing *two nights*?' I exclaimed. 'Why have you only now come to the police? Do you have any suspicion who may have taken them?'

'Of course I don't! But there are those who are envious of me, Inspector. I am known to be a successful man of some substance.'

'You have received some communication?' I asked quickly. 'A demand for money?'

'No, no! I . . . See here, I do not know what to think. A dozen possibilities have occupied my brain. The only thing I know for certain is that they have gone.' He drew a deep breath. 'As to why I only today come to you, well, my reputation is important. I have told you I supply several very important households. I must avoid scandal. As soon as the police are called in to a matter, everyone knows and the tittle-tattle begins. I have spent the last day and a half searching for them. But they are nowhere to be found.'

I leaned back in my chair. 'Mr Canning,' I said, 'would you please tell me the whole story from the beginning. Let us start with the day before yesterday when you discovered they were missing. When and how did you do this?'

He puffed out his cheeks and hesitated. 'I returned from my place of business at around four in the afternoon, as I normally do. My wife was not at home. That was unusual. She is always there when I come home. She knows I like that to be the case. I inquired of the servants—'

'How many servants and what sort?' I asked quickly.

'A cook and two maids, together with a nursemaid for the child.'

'No menservants of any kind?'

'No. Does that matter?' He appeared genuinely affronted by the question.

I ignored it to ask, 'How long have the three women worked for you?'

'The cook-housekeeper has been employed by me for fifteen years. As for the maids, well, one of them for about a year and the other for about six months.' As if he thought I might think it odd that the housekeeper had been with him for so long and the maids so little time, he added, 'Mrs Bell, the housekeeper, has full charge of hiring and dismissing the maids. She sets high standards and does not tolerate slackness or insubordination. The nursemaid has been with us since the birth of my daughter. She came to us from an agency and my wife hired her.'

'I see, please go on.'

'I asked them where the mistress was and they professed not to know. I went up to the nursery where I found the nursemaid very distressed. She said she had not seen either her charge or my wife since mid-morning. My wife had declared her intention of going out with the child for a short walk. They had not returned. It is obvious they have been abducted. You must begin a thorough search at once! You must have informers among the criminal population. Ask among them.'

'Have you tried the hospitals, sir?' Morris's voice rumbled from his place by the door.

Without turning his head, Canning snapped, 'Yes! No accident victims have been brought in of my wife's – or my child's – description.'

'With regard to your wife,' I asked him, picking up my pen again. 'May I inquire how old the lady is, what is her general appearance, and any other details such as the names of family members or of friends to whom she might have gone.'

'Why on earth,' he stuttered, 'should she go and visit anyone and stay away two nights, leaving no word behind of her intention? Besides, she has no family other than a very elderly aunt of sorts who lives in Southampton. Nor has she any close friends.'

'You have the name of this aunt and her address?'

'Good Lord!' he cried. 'Are you to do nothing but inquire after irrelevant details? If you must know it, the aunt's name is Miss Alice Stephens. She must be nearly eighty now. She is, as I understand it, a great-aunt of my wife's and my wife lived with her before our marriage. I have her address somewhere at home.'

I confess my heart sank. It could be, of course, a coincidence that the name given to me by the female beneath the arches had been Jane Stephens. But . . .

'Perhaps you would be so kind as to look out the lady's address for me. And now, sir, you really must tell me your wife's age and description. Even better, have you a photograph? Also of the child?'

He seemed taken aback. 'My wife is twenty-six years of age. She is of medium height with fair hair. My daughter is three years old. I have photographs of them both at home. I should have brought some with me, of course. But whoever has kidnapped my family will have them well hidden.'

In the background, unseen by our visitor, Morris raised his eyebrows, looked at me, and then at Canning. The man was in a panic, that was true, and either did not know he was babbling what sounded like nonsense, or had persuaded himself that this was indeed the truth.

'Perhaps, Mr Canning, I could suggest you return home now. I will call on you there shortly, as soon as I have discussed this with my superintendent. If you could have ready any photographs and the address of your wife's aunt in Southampton, I'd be obliged. I would like to interview your servants. Be so good as to give Sergeant Morris your exact address.' I stood up.

He rose to his feet unwillingly. 'You are taking this seriously, I hope? I am a respectable taxpayer. I expect the police to make strenuous efforts.'

'Very seriously, sir. Now, go home and I'll be there as soon as I can.'

He still hesitated. 'Look here,' he burst out, 'my wife is utterly respectable!'

'Of course, sir.'

'Because I know how people gossip. They may suggest – they may suggest another man is involved. I assure you, that absolutely cannot be the case.'

'We will leave no stone unturned,' I assured him. 'And we make no assumptions.'

'I don't want you putting ideas into people's heads,' he said stubbornly. 'What do you intend to ask my servants?'

'That must wait until I see them. Now, Mr Canning, I am sure you don't want to waste any more time, so allow me to start the hunt straight away.'

'Oh, yes, quite,' he mumbled. 'But there must not be any gossip, you know. No scandal. I supply wines to important households. There must be absolutely no scandal.'

'See the gentleman out, Morris,' I said, adding, 'be sure to get the address in St John's Wood.' As Canning moved out of earshot I added quietly, 'Then take yourself, with a constable to help you, over to the river by Waterloo Bridge Station. See if you can locate anyone who was in the area of the arches last night, other rough sleepers, prostitutes, anyone who might have seen the person I encountered. Inquire of the workhouses, and anywhere else you can think of.'

Chapter Four

'WELL, WELL, this is a delicate business, indeed, Ross.' Dunn rubbed his chin.

I had gone at once to report the whole matter to him, and tell him of the woman giving the name Jane Stephens, whom I'd encountered the night before.

'You think,' Dunn continued, 'that the woman you met may well be the absconded wife of this fellow Canning?'

'I do think it, sir. I asked her name and she obviously did not want to give her married name, for fear we would connect her at once with her husband. She knew he'd have to go to the police sooner or later and declare them both missing, or it would appear very odd. She had to think up another name quickly and the only one to pop into her head was that of this elderly relative who lives in Southampton, Stephens. It may even be her own maiden name.'

'The woman under the arches claimed her husband had abandoned her and the child?'

'Yes, but I suspected at the time the truth was the reverse; that she had run away from him. I had the strong impression, sir, that she was a woman of good background and only recently fallen on such hard times.'

'How would you describe Canning's manner?'

'He is most anxious, above all, to avoid scandal. That would affect his personal reputation and he supplies wines, he was keen to tell me, to the very best households.' I made no effort to disguise my disapproval.

Dunn nodded. 'Not worried for their physical safety?'

'If so, he didn't mention it once, sir. He only talked of having enemies and being known to be successful. He insists he has received no communication from those he claims– or imagines – responsible. I had to ask him more than once to describe his wife and tell me her age. At best I put that down to his being in a state of confusion. Less charitably, I'd say because he is not anxious to draw attention to what I'd guess to be twenty-five years' difference in their ages. He did insist there could be no other man.'

'Hum,' murmured Dunn. He stopped rubbing his chin and scratched the crown of his bristly head of hair. 'So we are in a fix, eh? You have not mentioned the woman Stephens to Canning?'

'No, sir. After all, I don't know for certain that it was his wife I met. I suspect it, but unless I find her I can't establish it as a fact. As it is, if I tell him right away that his wife and child have been sleeping under arches by the river, I dread to think how he will react. He'll probably refuse to accept the very idea, and fly into a rage, as well. I couldn't blame him. It does seem preposterous, now that I say it aloud to you. A woman runs from a household with three servants to sleep under the arches? If I were Canning, and someone told me that, I wouldn't believe it.'

Dunn interrupted me. 'But there is a strong possibility that you came across the missing woman and child last night and, if we don't find the wife anywhere else, then the husband must be told.'

He gave an irritated sigh and scrubbed once more at his hair. 'You chased all over London last night following Mills's allegations, yet you left this well-spoken woman and her child under the arches. I understand you took pity on her, Ross, when you did not arrest her for vagrancy. But you should have done so, or found the constable on that beat and directed him to do so. If you *had* done so, this matter could have been sorted out already today. Jane Stephens, whether she is the missing wife or not, would have appeared before the magistrates this morning. If her story was false, they'd have realised it and got to the bottom of it.

'As it is, we have to start seeking her all over London with little or no idea where she might be. The woman, if she left of her own accord, cannot be forced to return to her husband, but the child is another matter. At the moment, the little girl is under the age of seven. Were the parents to divorce, the mother might have some hope that the court would allow her to have custody until the child reaches seven. But, even so, at age seven the law will return the child to its father. His rights in that matter are clear.

'I must say,' Dunn added, 'that as she left the

matrimonial home in such an irregular way, and as it's possible she took the child with her to sleep in the streets as a vagrant, I doubt very much that any judge would consider her a fit person to have custody! At any rate, in the absence of any application to a court, Jane Canning does not have custody of her daughter. The rights are therefore assumed to lie with the father. Thus the mother has abducted the child. What led up to this sad situation is not our affair, Ross. Our job is to find the infant Charlotte Canning.'

'Yes, sir, from what I've seen of Canning,' I told him, 'I can't believe he'd ever agree to a divorce. He's terrified of scandal.'

Had I taken pity on Jane Stephens last night, when I left her and her daughter under the arches? I wondered. Or had my mind been so busy with Mills's tale and the consequences that I simply had not bothered to do anything about Jane? At any rate, my failure to apply the strict letter of the law with regard to vagrancy would do nothing to restore my standing with the high commissioner.

'The puzzling thing is . . .' Dunn peered at the clock on the wall as if it might supply not only the time of day but also the answer to our problem. 'Why did she leave him, eh? He's a well-to-do, respected man. She lives in a good part of town in a house with three servants plus a nurserymaid. Canning insists no lover is involved, you say. But he would not be the only man to discover his wife's interest has strayed; and the first he knows of it is when she decamps. In this case, however, Mrs Canning has taken the child with her.' Dunn shook his head. 'That suggests she has not run to a lover.'

Dunn turned his gaze from the clock to me. 'Well, Ross, bearing all that in mind, what *does* it suggest to you?'

'That there is something amiss in that household,' I said promptly. 'I am anxious to interview the servants. Morris is down by the river with a constable, trying to find anyone who saw Jane there and may have spoken to her.'

'River Police?' Dunn asked in a flat tone.

'I had already sent young Biddle over there to ask about bodies, sir.'

'It's late.' Dunn glanced again at the clock. 'You had better hurry over to St John's Wood and speak to those servants before their employer has too long to coach them.' The superintendent pulled a face. 'Though he has had two days to do that! You might be lucky enough to find a neighbour who saw her leave the house.'

The superintendent leaned back in his chair. 'If it does indeed turn out that you met his wife last night by the river, then Canning may have good reason to bless the fact. If he'd simply come in with the tale of an unexplained disappearance without witnesses, we might have suspected him of being responsible. Husbands have murdered inconvenient wives before now.' Dunn scowled. 'I will make inquiries about his business affairs, Ross. No doubt he has his family insured. If his business has got into difficulties, he may have concocted some plot . . . but you can leave that to me. See what you can turn up at St John's Wood.'

Canning's house proved to be a solid, detached building standing behind a high wall. The house was rendered in white stucco and boasted an elegant porch supported on classical columns. There was evidence of a basement beneath and two more floors above the ground floor. The windows of the topmost one were small and probably indicated rooms given over to the domestic staff. All this confirmed Mr Canning was a wealthy man. Moreover, seeing this imposing dwelling, I had to wonder what on earth had led his wife to take their child and run away from it. I also wondered that he only employed a staff of three (nursemaid excluded), and no butler or footman.

Canning was awaiting me with some impatience and opened the front door to me himself.

'The staff are in the back parlour. It seemed to me a suitable place for you to conduct the interview. This way . . .' He stepped out briskly but I called him back.

'There is no need to take me yourself, sir. Just tell me which door it is.'

I wanted the staff to speak freely and the sight of their employer would only serve to reinforce any instructions he'd given them.

Canning turned, clearly nonplussed. 'If you insist,' he agreed with clear reluctance.

The women were all waiting for me, standing in line. They must have heard my voice in the hallway. The oldest of them was a stern-faced matron of some fifty to sixty summers garbed in black and with a white lace widow's cap pinned atop her steel grey hair. She stepped forward as I entered.

'I am Mrs Bell, the cook-housekeeper,' she said.

'And I am Inspector Ross, Mrs Bell. I need to speak to you all, but I wish to do it separately.' The maids would not speak freely in front of this dragon.

Mrs Bell opened her mouth as if she would object. Before she could speak, I added, 'That is the normal procedure.'

She could not argue with that, no matter what Canning may have instructed. 'Very well, sir.' She turned to the two maids and a very small, pale-faced girl no more than nineteen who must be the nursemaid. 'The three of you wait in the kitchen.'

They filed out obediently. I noticed, as she passed by me, that the nursemaid had very swollen and red-rimmed eyes. She must have done a lot of weeping since the disappearance of her charge. The younger of the two maids cast me a curious glance but the other kept her eyes fixed firmly ahead of her.

'Well, now, Mrs Bell,' I said when we were alone. 'Let us sit down.'

She sat, with back ramrod-straight and hands folded in her lap. Her eyes were fixed on me without any sign of nervousness and her mouth formed a straight line. I would have my work cut out to learn anything from her.

'When did you last see your mistress?' I asked.

'The day before yesterday, sir.'

'At what time of the day and in what circumstances?'

'It was half-past eleven in the morning, sir. The parlour clock had just chimed the half-hour. I came into the hall by chance and saw Mrs Canning tying the ribbons of her cape. She was wearing a small hat. The little girl was with her, also dressed for the street.'

'You spoke to her?'

'Yes, sir. I asked, "Are you going out, madam? Will you not take Ellen with you?"' At my raised eyebrow, she added, 'Ellen is the nursemaid.'

'And Mrs Canning replied, what?'

'That she had no need of Ellen and would not be more than an hour at the most. She fancied the child needed exercise and fresh air. She then left and did not come back.'

'What did you do, when you realised she had not returned? How did you learn it?'

'I am also the cook, Inspector. I had expected to serve her some luncheon. But Purvis – the parlourmaid – came to tell me that the mistress had not returned and luncheon would have to be delayed.'

'Were you surprised?'

'Yes, of course, sir. Mrs Canning had told me herself she would not be away above an hour.'

'Did you make any effort to find out the reason for her continued absence?'

'I sent out Ellen to look for them – for Mrs Canning and Miss Charlotte. Ellen scoured the streets around and asked passers-by but could get no news of them. Then Mr Canning came home.' The housekeeper's mouth snapped shut. I could imagine the scene when Canning got there. The staff would all have been blamed, as if it could be in any way their fault.

'Have you any idea what could have happened to Mrs Canning?'

'None whatsoever, sir,' Mrs Bell said firmly. 'Unless, as Mr Canning believes, they have been snatched away by some dreadful criminals.'

'Why do you think that?'

'Mr Canning thinks it,' she said simply.

'Do *you* think it?' I asked her gently.

'It is not my place to speculate,' she said, meeting my eye.

'Had Mrs Canning ever done anything like this before? Gone out – with or without her daughter – and returned late?'

'No, sir.'

'Would you say Mrs Canning was a happy woman?'

'Of course, sir.'

I tried another approach. 'You are the cook here. Do Mr and Mrs Canning entertain much? It would be a good deal of work for you with only the two maids to help.'

'Mr and Mrs Canning do not entertain.' But my question had riled her. She did not mean to let me go away thinking she couldn't manage a simple dinner party. 'It would be well within my competence but I believe Mr Canning entertains his business acquaintances in town. I am the cook-housekeeper, Inspector. I take my orders and I supervise the other staff. I do not ask any questions. That is not my place.'

I would make no further progress in this conversation today. I thanked her and asked her to send in Purvis. I did not get on any better either with the parlourmaid or the housemaid, whose name was Higgins. The three women would have given the celebrated wise monkeys a run for their reputation in seeing, hearing and speaking no evil. That left me with my last hope, the nursemaid, Ellen Brady.

The nursemaid was probably a pretty girl in normal circumstances, soberly dressed in grey with a snowy white apron like a little Quakeress, with a starched white cap covering her brown hair. But her face and manner were ravaged by her distress. She sat down at my invitation and promptly burst into tears. I urged her to take heart and still her sobs. Privately, I was not displeased. After the rigid self-discipline of the previous three witnesses, at last someone who might let something interesting escape her lips.

After much lamentation, Ellen had regained enough control – hiccups apart – to stop snuffling into a handkerchief. She raised a tear-streaked countenance to look at me. 'It's not my fault, sir.' The words came out in a soft Irish brogue.

'No one is suggesting that it is, Ellen.'

'They all say I should have gone out with her, with the mistress and Miss Charlotte, sir. I did offer, so I did. I asked her particularly if she would not take me with her because the master—'

Here Ellen broke off and looked fearfully at me. Good, she had been about to say something other than the carefully rehearsed script she'd been given.

'What had Mr Canning ordered?' I asked casually.

'Nothing, only that if they went out, I was to go along with them.'

'Why so?'

Ellen dropped her eyelids. 'To help with the little girl, sir. She's three. She can be mischievous. Run away and not come back when called, that sort of thing.' Ellen's face turned scarlet.

'Run away?' I asked as gently as I could. It was the first time the significant words had been spoken. 'Do you think that is what Mrs Canning has done, Ellen?'

'Oh, no, sir!' Ellen looked as if she would faint. She swayed on the chair.

'Don't be afraid,' I urged her. 'What you tell me does not get back to Mr Canning nor to Mrs Bell or the maids. You can speak to me in complete confidence.'

But Ellen had realised the pit yawning at her feet. 'I only meant, sir, that the little girl was playful.'

'Would you describe your mistress as a happy woman, Ellen?'

There was a silence. Ellen was afraid of her employer and of Mrs Bell, but she was at heart a truthful girl. 'Sometimes I fancied she was a little sad, sir. But she loved Miss Charlotte dearly.' Ellen leaned forward. 'She would never have left Miss Charlotte or let any harm come to her, sir.'

'She took Miss Charlotte with her,' I pointed out.

It was as if I'd unlocked a barrier. Her hands clasped and pleading eyes fixed on my face, words poured from the nurserymaid as in a torrent previously held back by a dam.

'As God is my witness, I tried to find them, sir. I looked for them everywhere, up and down the streets about here, and in the park, asking all the people.' The tears began to roll again. 'When I came back, there was Mrs Bell blaming me all the more, because I'd told other folk the mistress was lost somewhere; and Mr Canning doesn't like other people knowing his business.

'Mrs Bell says that if she had had the hiring of me, I would never have come to work in this house. But it was Mrs Canning who chose me from all the girls sent by the agency. She is a kind, good lady and I have always considered that I work for her – for the mistress, although it is the master as pays my wages, of course. Mrs Canning it was, who told me I was not needed to go out that awful day when they vanished off the face of the earth, snatched away by some devils and perhaps murdered.

'Mrs Canning said to stay home. Mrs Bell said to go out and look for them.

'Then I'm in trouble because I didn't find them and asked people . . . So what was I to do, sir? Whatever I did, it would be wrong and they'd be blaming me. They blame me still! I don't think I've slept a wink since. I only stay here in this place because I hope to see Miss Charlotte come running in, quite all right and no harm come to her. She's a blessed angel, so she is, that child. Now, for all I know, she is with the angels.'

With that, poor Ellen threw her apron over her head and sobbed into it.

I took pity on her and let her go. She had, in any case, confirmed what I had suspected. Jane Canning had run away, taking her daughter. They all knew it, Canning included.

When I returned to him he was pacing up and down the drawing room. 'Well?' he demanded.

'Thank you, sir, I think I have a fair picture of what happened leading up to Mrs Canning's departure from the house.'

Canning looked at me sharply and, I thought, with some alarm.

'Now, sir, it is a painful business but it is my duty to ask a few personal and distressing questions. Was Mrs Canning in good health?'

'Excellent health!' he snapped.

'She could not, for example, have suffered some nervous crisis? She could perhaps be wandering in London, with the child, a victim of loss of memory, perhaps?'

'Don't talk drivel!' he roared at me. 'Are you the best man Scotland Yard can produce?'

Sooner or later I had to let him know there was a possibility I had already encountered his missing wife. 'There are many in London sleeping beneath arches, in doorways, any little corner where they can hide away. Even respectable people might come to such a pass if—'

'This has nothing to do with the matter,' he cut short my speech. 'I shall go to the Yard tomorrow and demand they put another man on the case. My wife has been abducted and instead of looking for the malefactors who have done this heinous thing, you stand here and babble of the wretches who sleep in doorways. Not that anyone should be sleeping in a doorway! Are there no laws on vagrancy? What are the casual wards of the workhouses for? I pay my taxes, Ross, and I expect value for them. Find my wife.'

'I am trying to tell you, sir, that last night, quite late on my way home, I encountered a woman, with a child, who was sleeping rough near the river. She gave me the name Jane Stephens.'

His ruddy complexion drained of all colour so quickly I took a step forward, fearing he might be about to collapse. But he was of stronger stuff.

'If you are going to suggest that my wife has taken leave of her senses and, in her madness, has taken my daughter and is sleeping with her on the streets, then – then I fear you may have lost *your* senses, Inspector. The woman may have given you the name Stephens. It is coincidence.' His eyes glittered in rage and his little Vandyke beard was thrust forward belligerently.

I said nothing. He turned away and walked over to the window where he stood for a couple of minutes staring out into the street, his hands clasped behind his back. Eventually he swung round to face me, his composure regained.

'In any event, whether you came upon my wife last night or not, my daughter has been abducted and you are required to find her. I pay my taxes and expect the guardians of the law to carry out their duty.' He marched over to the circular table in the centre of the room, decorously draped in a lace cloth, and picked up an envelope. 'These are photographs of my wife and daughter. Let me know as soon as you have located them. The address of my wife's great-aunt in Southampton is also there, since you asked for it. But you will not find Jane on the coast.'

'You are sure of that, sir?'

'Of course I am sure! Do you try and vex me, Ross?'

'No, Mr Canning, but I hope you understand the importance of being entirely frank with us? We cannot investigate any matter if we are not given the full facts.'

'You have been told all that you need to know,' he returned icily.

I left the house, knowing he watched me go. However, due to the high wall around his property, I doubted he could see what I did next. I inquired at the houses on either side. I went to the back doors and asked the domestic staff there. No one had seen Mrs Canning on the day in question. But a couple of interesting facts did emerge. Mrs Canning never went out alone. In fact, Mrs Canning was hardly ever seen at all.

Back at the Yard I studied the photographs contained in the envelope. One was a studio portrait of a very young woman with pleasant, regular features. Not conventionally pretty, perhaps, but suggesting an open, generous nature. The sitter fixed the camera with a trusting look. She had a great deal of fair hair parted centrally and swept back to a just-discernible bundle of hair at the nape of her neck. The whole thing was artfully arranged. She was posed on a sofa that had the delicate, gilded style of a century earlier, and held a book in her lap, closed but with her forefinger marking the place, as if she had been reading when the photographer came in. The rococo sofa and the book probably belonged to the studio. I could not say whether this was the young woman I'd encountered by the river because I had not been able to see much of her face. But nothing suggested she could not have been the unknown vagrant.

There were two other photographs. One was of a little girl posed by a pedestal with an urn of flowers atop. I suspected these were also supplied by a studio. She was a round-faced child, with fair curls, wearing an elaborate dress with a flounced skirt and button boots. A slight frown seemed to pucker her forehead as if she studied the photographer while he studied her. I fancied she had the look of her mama, but more determined.

The third photograph was a family group and had been taken earlier, only a month or two after the child's birth. Mrs Canning sat with the baby Charlotte on her lap. The child was so wrapped up in petticoats, ribbons, and a large bonnet it was difficult to see much but a pouting baby face and a pair of chubby fists poking out. The mother looked older than in the photograph taken seated on the sofa alone. I picked up the first photograph again and compared the two. Yes, the studio portrait had been taken probably very soon after the marriage. There was a bloom on the young woman that had been lost by the time of the family group study. Childbirth might account for that . . . or marriage itself. Canning stood at his wife's shoulder in the family group. His hand rested proprietarily on the back of her chair. His Vandyke beard bristled as he tilted his chin and he glared fiercely at the camera. It was not, I decided, a happy picture.

It was time to enlist the help of the Hampshire Constabulary. I took a sheet of paper and carefully composed a message to be sent by electric telegraph that very evening.

I saw from Lizzie's face when I arrived home that night that she had been waiting for me with concern. So, as we ate, I described my long and frustrating day to her. When I told her of Canning and of my fear I had already encountered his missing wife and child beneath the arches of Waterloo, Lizzie looked even more worried.

'You say the servants could tell you nothing? Perhaps if you tried again?' she said, when I described my visit to St John's Wood. 'In my experience the staff of a large – or even modest – household generally know what is going on in the family.'

'They are under the control of the eagle-eyed Mrs Bell,' I replied with a sigh. 'Even the nursemaid who could, I'm sure, tell me a great deal more, did not give away much. She lamented and was genuinely distressed, but as much for her own situation as for the loss of her mistress and charge, I fancy. It was enough, though, to confirm my suspicions. Canning appears to be a very possessive man with regard to his wife. He expected her to be home every day when he returned from Charing Cross. He didn't like her to go out unaccompanied. She appears seldom to have gone out at all, and they didn't entertain at home.'

'He's jealous, perhaps?' Lizzie suggested. 'If she is much younger, and he is how you describe . . .'

'His possessive behaviour wouldn't be grounds for her to obtain a legal separation,' I mused. 'At least, not unless there were something else. If he were violent, perhaps?'

Lizzie said quietly, 'Whatever the law may say, it is almost impossible for a woman to divorce her husband. If Jane has no money of her own, protected legally in some way from her husband's grasp, then she is penniless now. If her only family is that one very elderly lady in Southampton, she has nowhere to go. The aunt would be horrified if she turned up on the doorstep. Whatever the truth of the matter, from now on she will be marked out by the scandal and her reputation ruined. You know as well as I do that whatever a divorce court may decide, in the public mind the blame always rests with the wife. Besides, there is the little girl. Superintendent Dunn is right. In the circumstances, a judge would not even allow her to keep the child until she is seven years old. It is very hard for women like poor Jane.'

'Be careful whom you marry!' I said with a smile in an attempt to lighten the gloomy conversation.

'I was fortunate to meet you again, Ben, after so many years. Jane Stephens, if that is her maiden name, met Mr Hubert Canning. No doubt he appeared an excellent prospect and the elderly great-aunt would have been anxious to see Jane comfortably established. I do wonder where she is now, and the little girl. It's terrible to think what a state they may be in.' Lizzie glanced at the clock. It was getting very late.

I, too, hauled myself wearily from my comfortable chair. 'I wish I could even hazard a guess. The best I can say is that, so far, her body has not been hauled from the Thames. I have telegraphed a request to my opposite number in Southampton tonight, asking him to send someone to call on Jane's elderly relative. It may help to find out the background to her marriage. I will do my utmost to find them, Lizzie,' I added.

My wife smiled 'Yes, Ben, I know you will. If anyone can find them, you will do it.'

'What I cannot do is investigate Mills's murder at Putney.' I picked up the poker and rattled it in the grate.

'Was Dunn very angry about that?'

'He wasn't so bad, quite sympathetic. But he was firm I should leave the matter alone. So nothing can be done.'

'Mm,' was all the reply. My wife had a thoughtful look on her face that I recognised only too well.

'No!' I said firmly.

'No, what?'

'This is not something for you to take an interest in!'

'It seems those like the governor or the home secretary, who could do something, will not. If they won't, you can't. So, if I don't, who will?' Lizzie asked serenely.

This was true. It still didn't make it a feasible proposition – or a desirable one. I did my best to explain this, all the time sensing my arguments were bouncing off a brick wall. 'What can you possibly hope to find out?' I pleaded at last. 'The whole thing happened, *if* it did, in the middle of Putney Heath – and sixteen years ago. I have no address. I wonder now if Mills himself could have found the house again. He says it wasn't far from the Portsmouth road but that's a vague location, for the main route down to the south runs right across the heath. Above the roof was a weathervane fashioned like a running fox with his brush held straight out behind him. That could have blown down in a gale since then. Or there might be two or three houses with such a weathervane.

'Perhaps if I could find some additional evidence to support Mills's statement, I might get those in authority to take an interest. But the likelihood of finding any such evidence is – well – it's impossible now.'

She had listened patiently to my argument and, as always, had an answer. 'I could find Wally Slater and get him to drive me out to Putney in his cab. With Wally, when I get there, I will have freedom of movement. The house, Mills told you, stands apart from others.'

'It was sixteen years ago,' I reminded her. 'There will almost certainly have been changes. It is not only hereabouts that London has seen such a mania for building. Putney will have seen many more houses built in the last twenty years. Who knows if that particular house is still the lonely dwelling it was when Mills came on it. Besides . . .' I reached for the last brick in my argument. 'It's too far for you to go, anyway. Setting aside the cost, that old nag of Slater's will never make it there and back without dropping in the shafts.'

'He doesn't have Nelson any more. He has a new,

younger horse. It's called Victor.'

I allowed myself to be distracted. 'Victor?'

'It would have been called Victory, to keep the memory of Nelson going, you understand. But Victor is easier to say.'

'You still can't drive all over the heath hoping to find a house that might not exist.' Here, I thought, I had put up an insurmountable obstacle.

My wife smiled at me. 'Oh, I can find out if it exists. When did this suspicious death occur? The fifteenth of June, eighteen fifty-two, I think you said.'

'I did. Mills informed me it was a Tuesday. It is one of the details that makes me think he did see something. He might, of course, have been mistaken in what he thought he saw.' As I spoke, I resigned myself to the inevitable.

'Then my first visit must be to Somerset House. They have records of all deaths, don't they?'

'Well, don't let Dunn find out, at least!' I begged.

'Oh, Superintendent Dunn,' said Lizzie. 'He's such a nice man but he does fuss so.'

Fuss? The image of Dunn, scarlet with rage, was hardly conveyed by such a mild term. But there was a more urgent consideration than Dunn's fury should he learn that Lizzie had once again involved herself in police business.

'Listen to me,' I begged her, 'for once, at least! Let us suppose you would not be going on a wild goose chase. Let's accept there was a murder done and witnessed by Mills. He says the killer was a young – very young – woman. That means she is today probably no more than forty years of age. Let us say she is still living in the house with the running fox weathervane and you manage to find it. Then you also find *her*, my dearest Lizzie, and she is a murderess.'

'Ben, do have a little confidence in me! I am not likely to forget that,' she said, clearly put out.

'Do, please, be tactful, Lizzie,' I begged. 'And don't let Bessie out of your sight. Or Slater, come to that. The three of you can't just run round talking of murder.'

'As if we would,' retorted my wife, affronted.

'In Bessie's case, as if she wouldn't!'

Chapter Five

Elizabeth Martin Ross

I UNDERSTOOD Ben's dilemma. He had once told me that any police officer should try and keep a personal distance from the case he was investigating. That he must concentrate on the facts. That he must not let his emotions take over. But Ben cared about other people's suffering. He had seen too much of it as a child. If he could help, he would. Only if convinced he could not, would he reluctantly accept that he must set the matter aside.

Now, in addition to the case of Mills, he had that of a missing woman and child to think about. He felt he had failed to help the woman when he found her sleeping beneath the arches. So that, too, preyed on his mind.

It was time for me to take a hand. I could do nothing about the case of Jane Canning. But I might be able to find out something about the background to the story Mills, the murderer, had spun. If I could discover anything, even if it indicated Mills had invented the whole tale, it would help set Ben's mind at rest. Frankly, to find Mills had lied would be the most helpful result of my inquiries. Ben would gain peace of mind. To learn that Mills might have spoken the truth could be unbearable. But I would do my best. 'And you have not yet begun, Lizzie!' I told myself optimistically.

When Ben departed for Scotland Yard the following morning, I sought out Bessie in the kitchen where she was washing up with the usual vigour. I wondered we had an unchipped plate left.

'I am about to tell you something in confidence, Bessie,' I informed her.

Bessie abandoned the dishes, wiped her hands on her apron and positioned herself before me with shining eyes. 'Yes, missis?'

I told her what I had omitted to tell her before: Mills's account of what he claimed had happened sixteen years earlier at Putney.

'Cor,' said Bessie with a deep sigh.

'You don't tell anyone else about this,' I reminded her.

'You know I won't, missis.' She sounded affronted.

I did know I could trust her. 'There are difficulties in the way of the inspector looking into this story.'

'We can do it!' said Bessie promptly.

'It may not be necessary,' I warned. 'The police may yet take it up and then we must not interfere.'

'Wouldn't do us no harm to go out to Putney and take a look round,' said Bessie.

'That's true, but it will be unofficial and we must be very, very careful.' I explained that I wanted her to seek out Wally Slater, the cabman, and commandeer his four-wheeled growler for the next day, explaining it was to go to Putney (and to enquire the cost). I fully intended to pay Wally a fair price for the journey there and back. However, when Ben found out I really was going to make the trip, the first – or almost the first – thing he would ask would be how much it would cost, so I had to have the answer ready. To travel there by train or omnibus, and walk around the area when we got there, would slow inquiries considerably.

'I'll find him,' promised Bessie. 'He's usually waiting up at the station in the cab rank there. I'll wait there and if he don't turn up, I'll tell the other cabbies I want to talk to him. The message will get round quick enough. Of course, I won't tell the other cabbies what I want him for.'

'Today,' I said, 'I will go to Somerset House, and see if I can at least find out the identity of the old gentleman who died on that date in eighteen fifty-two at the house with the running fox weathervane.'

Unfortunately, my own investigations did not begin very well. I soon arrived at the imposing pillars of Somerset House where records of births, deaths and marriages were kept. When I stepped inside, I stood bewildered. Here some of the greatest in the land had once lived, but now the whole great palace resembled nothing so much as a busy beehive, filled with scribbling clerks serving a dozen government departments.

As I stood staring, a friendly uniformed porter approached me. 'Morning, ma'am! What would you be looking for?'

Grateful for his help, I explained I hoped to track down a death certificate. He appeared to find this the most natural thing in the world. He then directed me down a corridor and up a stone staircase, where I found myself in another corridor, eventually entering a room where I found a desk presided over by a clerk.

This official was a pallid, podgy young man in a tightly buttoned blue coat. His hair was artfully curled, I guessed with the aid of tongs, and held in glistening immobility by a lavish application of Macassar oil. His whole demeanour was that of one who feels he should be engaged on better things than answering the public's questions. I began to fear things would not go on as well as they'd started. I was right.

I explained politely I was inquiring about a death at Putney in 1852, on the fifteenth of June, to be exact. Decedent was male.

'So is half the population,' he returned, heaving a deep sigh. 'Name?'

'I don't know his name.'

He stood and leaned across the desk to bring his plump cheeks and shining curls unpleasantly close to me. 'Then how, madam, is anyone to look him up?' His breath smelled of violet cachous.

'In the volume containing records or references for that year.'

He let out a squawk and then a shout of laughter that caused other people in the room – busy looking things up – to look at us instead. Ripples of disapproval flowed over us.

'The total of deaths in this nation during a whole year fill more than a single volume! There is a row of them. You must know the name. Then I will show you the appropriate volume – names beginning with that letter – and you may search through it.'

'But it's his name I want to find out!' I protested.

'Why?' he asked suddenly.

'It is of interest to me.'

He pursed his lips, which made him look like a mature cherub. 'You can't be a relation or you'd know his name.' He looked even more pleased with himself at having made this deduction.

'I am not, to my knowledge, related to the gentleman.'

His scornful look turned to one of suspicion. 'Not a relation, thought as much! Then what's his death to you, eh?'

'That,' I said sternly, 'is my business.'

'Is it, now? Well, keeping and protection of the records is my business. We have to be sure they won't be misused. I am not convinced you are doing anything but waste my time – that is, if you don't have some nefarious purpose in mind?' His features creased into the pantomime sneer of one who has just uncovered a dastardly plot.

'*Nefarious* . . . What kind of nefarious purpose could I possibly have?' I gasped.

He leaned forward again. 'Impersonation!' he hissed.

'How,' I snapped, 'am I to impersonate an elderly gentleman, let alone one who died sixteen years ago?'

'You could be acting for someone else. Or it might

have to do with a will. I can't help you – not unless you bring me the deceased person's name and his address at Putney. Now, madam, you are causing a disturbance and I must ask you to leave.'

Watched by everyone in the room, I made a dignified exit.

'Hullo!' said my kindly porter. 'That didn't take you long! Get what you wanted?'

'No,' I said shortly. Then, not wishing to be rude to someone who had been nothing but polite to me, I added, 'The clerk wasn't very helpful.'

He eyed me thoughtfully. 'What was the problem, then?'

'I don't know the deceased man's name,' I explained. 'I know when he died and where: at Putney. But I don't know the exact address.'

'Putney, eh?' said the porter with a frown. 'You say you know *when* the gentleman passed on?' He pointed a finger heavenwards.

I felt a glimmer of hope and told him, even though the doorman was probably no more than bored and curious. 'In eighteen fifty-two, on the fifteenth of June.' For good measure, I added, 'I believe there was a summer storm at Putney on that day.'

He nodded slowly. 'Your best bet,' he informed me, 'is parish records. Putney . . . that'll be St Mary's church.'

Seeing my surprise at his omniscience, he added, 'I know Putney. My wife was in service at Putney when she was a girl. Lots of toffs have houses in Putney, you know. There's people of quality has died in Putney. Some of

’em died in duels on Putney Heath in my old father’s day. They don’t allow that now. Of course, them – the gentlemen what blew one another’s heads off with a set of duelling pistols – they would have driven out to Putney for the occasion; and their dead bodies would have been put in their carriages to be driven back again and buried in town.

‘But if they live and die in Putney, folk are buried in Putney. St Mary’s church’s register of burials, that’s where the gentleman will be found. Not the date he died, but the date they buried him and that won’t be more than a week later, not if he died in June. In June it’s starting to warm up and you say there had been thunderstorms? You can’t have a corpse lying about the house in thundery weather. It’d go off in no time. Yes, parish records, that’s where you’ll find it all written up. Then, when you know he’s there, why, you will be able to see his grave and his headstone, especially if he only died back in eighteen fifty-two. That will give you the exact date he passed, more than likely. Headstones, that’s what I tell people like yourself who come here seeking their forebears. If you want to know about the late lamented, then go and find his headstone. It’ll tell you all about him, and the names of his wife and his children into the bargain, more often than not. Marvellous thing is a headstone.’

His powers of deduction left me speechless for a moment. Even Ben would have been impressed. They should employ the porter upstairs at the inquiry desk, and the plump clerk with the curls down here minding the door.

'Your wife wouldn't know a house at Putney, on the heath, an old house . . . with a running fox weathervane?' I asked in a burst of optimism. 'Possibly it's located not far from the road the coaches take going down to Portsmouth.'

'I'll ask her,' he said. 'You come and see me tomorrow.'

I had sent Bessie to arrange with Wally to take me to Putney on the morrow but time there might be saved if I paid a brief visit to the porter beforehand. Wally would get me there and back quickly. I thanked my new friend and went home not entirely displeased.

Inspector Ben Ross

I should have been worrying what Lizzie might be getting up to in her visit to Somerset House, but I had plenty of other things to occupy my mind and my time and, whatever Lizzie had learned, I'd find out that evening.

I'd sent out information on the missing Jane Canning to all the London police stations. Nothing relevant had come back to me. I had also written to my colleague in Southampton by the previous evening's post and he should receive my letter today, probably by his local afternoon post. With luck I would hear from him within a day or two. All of the London workhouses were contacted and none reported any female applicant by the name of either Canning or Stephens. Canning had told us he had inquired of the hospitals. We, nevertheless, inquired anew. No adult victim of any accident had been brought in of that name, and no unidentified child except for a boy, a crossing sweeper, crushed beneath the wheels of a cart. It was more than possible that Jane would not have given either of the two surnames we knew for her, if she had been admitted. But showing her photograph at the hospitals also took us no further forward. They had not seen her.

A little before twelve we received a message from Wapping that a woman's body had been recovered from the Thames. I hurried over there, fearing the worst.

I was conducted by a constable of the River Police into the mortuary set up for reception of bodies taken from the water. An attendant drew back the sheet to reveal a woman, no longer in her first youth, with a bruised face and other contusions on the torso. Her skin was coarse, her hair appeared coloured by henna, and when I picked up one of her hands and turned it over, the palm was callused. This was not Jane.

My first reaction was to be thankful it was not the woman I'd encountered beneath the bridge that evening. It is important, when investigating any case, not to take too personal an interest. But I did feel a personal responsibility for poor Jane Canning. Dunn was right. I should have seen that she was arrested for vagrancy. Then the whole matter would have been investigated at once and Jane returned to her husband, with her child. But would that have been for the best? I really didn't know. All I did know was that, if my mind had not been so full of Mills and his story, I'd have paid more attention to a well-spoken woman who was inexplicably sleeping rough with a young child in her arms.

My initial sense of relief was replaced by a curiosity about the bruising on the body before me. I asked the constable who had conducted me there if a police surgeon was available and, after some delay, a short, dishevelled individual in a grimy frock coat appeared.

'What do you want?' he demanded. 'I am a busy man with a waiting room full of patients.'

'I apologise for inconveniencing you, Doctor,' I said, 'and appreciate that you've come. Would you look at this woman's body and tell me what you consider the cause of her injuries.'

He hissed in annoyance, bent over the body and announced, 'Caused by the impact when she hit the water. Did she jump off a bridge?'

'No one saw her go in, sir,' said the constable. 'A ferryman reported seeing female clothing caught against some railings on steps going down into the water. He thought there was a body in the clothing and so there was, that one.'

'Not been in the water long,' said the surgeon. 'Rigor may have been delayed by the temperature of the water, but I would hazard a guess, without further examination, that she went in some time during last night, before the tide went out. Some time before midnight, say? If her clothing caught against the railings, as described, that would have prevented her sinking to the bottom. As to whether she was alive or dead, that I cannot say without opening her up and examining the lungs. If she was alive, there will be river water in them and in the airways.'

'I understand the face being bruised from hitting the

water,' I said. 'But the bruises on the chest and abdomen, beneath the clothing?'

The surgeon looked up at me, a surprisingly keen expression on his face. 'Ah, you think you have a murder victim, do you? The body bruises look older to me than the ones on the face. She has been the victim of some violent assault, certainly, within the last week. I can tell you no more, Inspector, without further examination. All I can say is that those bruises didn't kill her.' He moved to the top of the trestle on which the poor wretch lay, and carefully parted her hair and turned her head, raising it to look at the back of the skull. 'No visible head injury,' he said. 'You must be patient, Inspector, and await the result of the internal examination. Then I – or whoever conducts it – can tell you whether she was alive or dead when she went into the water.'

I returned to Scotland Yard and told Morris I was satisfied that I had not seen Jane lying dead. As to what postmortem examination of the unknown corpse might reveal, that might not land on my desk. I would wait until it did, if it did.

I also found a visitor awaiting me when I returned, Mr Canning. He jumped up from the chair Morris had provided for him and advanced on me, red in the face and little Vandyke beard aimed like a dagger at my chest.

'I have been here almost an hour, Inspector Ross!'

'I had to go and view a female body recovered from the river,' I said brusquely. I had had more than enough of Hubert Canning, the respectable taxpayer.

He paled at my words. 'My wife?' he gasped.

'No, Mr Canning, not your wife. But I had to view the corpse to make sure.'

The visitor sat down suddenly on the vacated chair, pulled out his handkerchief, took off his round hat and mopped his sweating brow. While I had him at a disadvantage, I listed all the steps we'd taken to find his wife. He nodded but appeared speechless.

'Mr Canning, are you quite sure you have no idea what caused Mrs Canning to leave home in such a way? It does appear to have been quite voluntary on her part. We have found nothing to indicate a criminal gang such as you claimed had kidnapped her and Charlotte.'

That rallied him. He stiffened, tucked away the handkerchief and said firmly, 'She had no reason at all to behave in such a disgraceful way. She must have taken leave of her senses. Have you tried the asylums for the insane?' He paused but I didn't oblige him with an answer. In an obstinate voice, he went on, 'I must have my daughter returned to me. As for my wife . . . See here, you must find the child.'

With that he got up and stalked out. I was more than ever convinced that he knew why his wife had fled. Nor was he particularly concerned to have her returned. But his daughter, he did want her – and to find little Charlotte, I had to find her mother. I wondered whether Canning had gone back to his place of business or to his house. I decided it more likely to be his wine emporium, somewhere he felt in control. Being in control, I had decided, meant a great deal to Hubert Canning.

'I am going to St John's Wood to interview that nursemaid again,' I told Morris.

The door of Canning's house was opened to me by the maid named, I recalled, Purvis.

'The master is not here, sir,' she said, as soon as she saw who stood on the step.

'I have not come to see Mr Canning. I have come to see Ellen Brady, the nursemaid. Is she here?'

Purvis blinked and a look of panic crossed her face. 'If you would wait here, sir, in the hall . . .' She fled towards the rear of the house.

As I anticipated, Mrs Bell appeared, advancing towards me like an avenging Fury. Without any greeting, she asked immediately, 'Why do you want Ellen?'

'Is she here?' I asked again.

'Yes,' Mrs Bell drew a deep breath. 'I must ask you again, Inspector Ross, why you wish to see her?'

'Why must you ask me that?' I asked as mildly as I could.

'Why?' Her complexion, that had been very pale, flooded with colour. 'I am responsible for the servants here, Inspector Ross, in the absence of Mr Canning.'

I smiled at her. 'But not, Mrs Bell, responsible for the investigation into the disappearance of Mrs Canning and Miss Charlotte Canning. Now, will you call down Ellen Brady? Oh, and tell her to bring her bonnet and shawl.'

She was obliged to give way, but not without marking her displeasure.

'Very well, Inspector Ross, if you insist. However, if

you have reason to call again in the absence of the master, I would be grateful if you apply to the back door of the house.'

She turned on her heel and marched away; and I heard her instructing Purvis to go up to the nursery and fetch down Ellen, complete with outdoor clothing.

In due course Ellen appeared from the direction of the back stairs, wearing a grey cloak and a minute bonnet perched on the front of her hair, secured with a large pearl-headed pin and tied with ribbons under her chin.

'Yes, sir?' she asked apprehensively, eyeing me as if I'd come to accuse her of some crime and haul her away in handcuffs.

'Don't worry, Miss Brady,' I told her. A faint rustle at the rear of the hall told me that either Mrs Bell or Purvis lurked there, listening. 'On the day she went missing, Mrs Canning took Miss Charlotte out for a walk. Now then, I think it likely that she followed the route she normally took on these occasions. You usually accompanied her, did you not?' Ellen nodded. 'So you can show me exactly the way.'

We left the house and Ellen indicated we should go to the right. We set off sedately. When we were out of sight of the house, I said, 'Don't be alarmed, Ellen, but I am anxious to talk to you without anyone else eavesdropping.'

'Yes, sir,' said Ellen, still apprehensive. 'I thought as that was your idea. Are we still to walk the way Mrs Canning normally wanted to go?'

'Yes, if you would.'

'Well, then,' said Ellen, 'we'd walk to Regent's Park. Miss Charlotte liked to visit the boating lake. Not that we ever went on it, of course. We'd walk right round it. That was in good weather. In bad weather, we'd cut the walk short, but we always went out, unless it was fairly pouring it down.'

'It was good weather the day they left the house and disappeared?'

'Yes, sir, it was a very fine day. I wasn't surprised Mrs Canning wanted to walk out with the child. Only surprised she didn't want me with her.'

So, I thought, that was a change to the normal routine. Something had happened to bring that about.

Aloud, I said, 'Then let us go to the boating lake. Now, Ellen, you must believe that anything you tell me I will use only as necessary for finding Mrs Canning. I will not report to Mr Canning, or Mrs Bell, or anyone else other than another police officer, what you tell me. You can speak absolutely freely.'

She didn't answer, so I added, 'It won't cost you your place!'

At that Ellen burst out, 'I won't have a place if Mrs Canning and Charlotte don't come back, will I? I dare say that I won't have a place in that house any more, even if – when they do. Mrs Bell is so angry with me – and the master – that for two pins they'd turn me away today, so they would! It is only because they want to keep an eye on me that they keep me in the house at all.'

'Oh, why so?'

'So that they know what I do and whom I speak to, such as to you, now, today.'

'Ellen,' I said gently, 'what is it they are afraid you will tell me?'

I received no answer to this for some minutes. Then Ellen said stonily, 'I'm sure I don't know, sir.'

'I'm sure – or reasonably so – that you do know, or can hazard a guess,' I said.

'I don't gossip, sir.'

It was time to be as obdurate as she was being. 'See here,' I said to her, 'Mrs Canning may be, almost certainly is, in danger, to say nothing of even greater danger to the little girl. Don't you want them to be found and brought back home safely?'

'Yes,' said Ellen simply. After a moment she added, 'I've scarcely slept a wink for thinking of them and worrying, and that's the truth.'

We walked on in silence until we reached the park. Another short walk inside the park itself brought us to the boating lake, where I indicated a wooden seat. Ellen sat down and I beside her.

'We should have brought some bread for the ducks,' I said.

'We used to do that,' said Ellen. 'Miss Charlotte liked . . .' She fell silent and I waited patiently. I sensed she had decided to tell me something but was not sure how to begin. A nursemaid pushing a baby carriage walked past us. A small boy carrying a hoop trotted alongside her.

'Mr Canning is a strange sort of feller, so he is,' said

Ellen suddenly, her Irish brogue more pronounced. 'He won't let anyone into the house, you know. There's never a visitor. They never go out together except to church of a Sunday morning. Then it's straight there and home again. No family comes. I don't know that Mr Canning has any. I know that Mrs Canning has an elderly relative, an old auntie, down in Southampton. She lived there with her before she was married. She told me so. She told me, she missed the sight of the sea and the air being different in a big city. She would like to take Miss Charlotte to the seaside somewhere, for a little holiday. But Mr Canning always said he couldn't leave his business. Sometimes Mrs Canning said she felt she couldn't breathe at all, here in London. I understood what she meant for I feel the same way myself. I grew up in the countryside.'

'When I was a boy back in my home in Derbyshire,' I told her, 'I was sent down the pit to work at ten years old. There was precious little fresh air there.'

'In the dark?' asked Ellen, looking anxiously at me.

'Very dark.'

'Were there rats, sir?'

'Big as a small dog.'

'Weren't you scared?'

'Terrified. It made no difference, I had to go down. There were younger boys than me down there.'

'You won't mind being in the city, then,' said Ellen, 'for all the smoke and the stink of it. It must be better than being buried down there with the coal.' She folded her hands in her lap. 'Mrs Canning was a very unhappy person, sir. Mr Canning – I'm not saying he's the only man in the world to be like it – but everything must be done how he wants it. Mrs Bell runs the household, down to the smallest detail, without any consultation with Mrs Canning, because he will have it so. Mr Canning goes to his business selling the wine to the gentry. Poor Mrs Canning has no say in anything and is allowed to go nowhere, not to meet with other married ladies or anything like that, no tea parties or charity circles, such as a lot of ladies give their time to. That's why she and I and little Miss Charlotte walked out every day.'

'Yet it was Mrs Canning who chose you to be the nursemaid, I believe.'

'So she did, sir. Mrs Bell hires and dismisses the maids – and they do come and go at a fair old clip, you can believe me. They don't like working there. Purvis doesn't mind so much. She's a walking streak of misery like old Mother Bell herself. Only Mrs Bell was never a mother and when it came to engaging a nursemaid, Mrs Canning – for the only time ever, I do believe – put her foot down and said she must choose whom it would be. The agency sent several girls and she chose me. Mrs Bell didn't like it. She doesn't like me. But, perhaps because Mr Canning was proud to be a new father and all, he let Mrs Canning have her way in that. Mrs Canning and I always got on famously.'

'So what do you think caused Mrs Canning to take the child and run away?'

I wondered whether Ellen would deny that was the

case. Instead, said, 'The master and mistress had a terrible argument, sir.'

'When was this?'

'Well, they'd had a few of them this last month or two. But this particular one was the evening before – before Mrs Canning left. She told him how unhappy she was, and lonely, and wanted it all to change, to be allowed to make friends. There were ladies at the church who had called and left cards. But she was not allowed to call and leave cards back. She wanted to do that. Mr Canning would have it was all nonsense and he wouldn't have her "running about the town" in his absence. He said all manner of things, besides, unkind things. Mrs Canning was in tears and he only shouted at her.'

'How did you come to hear all this, Ellen?'

'Miss Charlotte had been restless. She woke often at night and called out. I think she was aware her mama was unhappy and that made her unhappy and frightened, too, not understanding it, you see. So I would get up to go to Miss Charlotte and I could hear, the house being so quiet at night, how Mr and Mrs Canning argued. I sleep in the nursery, sir, and it's on the same floor as Mr and Mrs Canning's room. Mrs Bell and the maids are on the floor above and probably don't hear. That night, my, oh my, they made so much racket perhaps the staff sleeping above did hear. But you won't get any of them to admit that to you, sir.'

'So, this has been going on for a few months?'

'Yes, sir. It began, I do believe, after Mrs Canning had the misfortune to lose the baby.'

'What baby is this? I asked, startled.

'She was expecting another child, sir. But with three or four months she miscarried and was quite ill for some weeks. This happened last year, towards Christmas.'

'So Mrs Canning had been down in spirits for almost a year, since losing the baby,' I mused.

'Yes, sir. Women do get that way after a healthy birth, even. Any midwife will tell you so. With losing a child, well, what would you expect? But Mr Canning couldn't see it. He just lost his temper and shouted at her, as usual. Then she'd be sobbing and he'd storm out. I'd go in and try and comfort her. That fool of a doctor he called to examine her made it worse. He told Mr Canning that Mrs Canning was suffering from hysteria. He said it was a sickness of the womb, and very common among women. Mr Canning told her she must "pull herself together" – that's his phrase. If she didn't, he said, he would send her to a clinic recommended by that doctor, and they would treat her there.'

'What sort of clinic?' I exclaimed.

'The master and the doctor both called it "a special place for treatment of female hysteria". I've heard of such places, sir. They do all manner of indecent things to women there; and take such liberties . . . It's what no kind, gentle lady like Mrs Canning should have to put up with. Don't ask me to speak more of that, sir, because I won't. It's not fitting. I'm a respectable girl, and the dirty words won't leave my lips. But the poor lady isn't ill, sir! She's only unhappy.'

So, having driven the poor woman into a nervous

decline, he intended to send her off to be locked up in what amounted to a private asylum, though it might call itself a 'spa' in the fashionable Continental way. There she would be subjected to goodness knows what by way of treatment. Jane had panicked and fled, taking the child. Canning knew the reason for it. He'd never admit it. Her actions probably, in his view, confirmed the doctor's diagnosis of hysteria. Well, I am not a doctor, but if a man acts more like a gaoler than a husband, he ought not to expect his wife to like it. Canning was a bully, and that was the only word for it.

'We should go back now, sir,' said Ellen firmly, getting to her feet. 'It will be bad enough as it is, when I go back, for they – Mrs Bell first and Mr Canning when he gets home – will want to know every mortal word we exchanged. But you needn't worry, sir, that I will tell them what I told you. I am not afraid of them. They can send me away; but they can't do it with a bad reference because of what I might go telling people.' Ellen cast me quite a mischievous look. 'I do believe, sir, that Mr Canning is a bit frightened of me!'

No, I needn't worry about Ellen. She was more than able to look after herself.

When I arrived home that evening, I found Lizzie ready to tell me what had happened at Somerset House and her hope that the porter might have information for her on the morrow.

'Well, there is no harm in going back there and finding out if his wife has any memories of her time in Putney of help in this case,' I said cautiously, 'but do please be very careful, Lizzie. Asking questions can be a dangerous business.'

Chapter Six

Elizabeth Martin Ross

'THAT ANIMAL,' declared Wally Slater, the cabman, with pride, 'that is your genuine hackney vanner. That animal is bred for the purpose and is, as working horses go, a regular diamond. He'll keep going all day without going lame or starting to wheeze or otherwise breaking down. He's a young horse, too, you know, only a six year old. I had to pay handsome for him,' added Wally confidentially, 'but he'll repay me with years of hard work, reliable as Big Ben is at telling the time.'

A smile of pride creased his battered ex-prizefighter's features and rendered them, if possible, even more alarming.

The three of us, Wally, Bessie and myself, gazed at Victor as he waited, one hind hoof tipped, in the shafts of the four-wheeled growler, just outside our modest house. Victor in turn rolled a large brown eye at us, as if assessing what Bessie and I might weigh, without baggage. What he saw must have reassured him, for he sighed and settled down as if to doze off.

'He looks quiet enough,' observed Bessie. 'He's half asleep.'

'He's an excellent temperament. You've got to have a cab horse with a good temperament. There are those cab-men,' continued Wally, 'who look to buy a horse cheap. You know, some old carriage horse no longer fit to be part of a smart gent's carriage pair. An animal like that might be more showy, but it's not used to the work, can be difficult to handle, takes a chill easy, and don't last more than a couple of years. I've seen horses like that drop dead in the shafts. No, Victor and me, God willing, will be together as long as old Nelson and me were.'

'Speaking of youngsters, Mr Slater,' I said. 'Is young Joey still in your employ?'

'That street urchin you foisted on me?' Wally chuckled. 'He's come along very well. Of course, we had a few problems. F'instance, my wife won't stand for bad language, as no more she should. So I had to tell him a few times to mind his. Trouble was explaining to him what was bad language, as he seemed to think all language was fit for anyone's ears, females included. But we got that straight. He took to my old horse, Nelson, straight away and Nelson took to him. Why, when Nelson's time was finally up, and he had to go to the knacker's, young Joey was in tears, as was my wife. I had a tear in my eye, for that matter,' added Wally. 'Of course, you'd hardly recognise the lad if you saw him now. My wife has been feeding him up and he's grown and filled out, though he'll never make a prizefighter.'

Wally became business-like. 'You want to go to Somerset House first and then out to Putney. We'd better get started.'

Victor recognised from the tone of his owner that we would shortly be off. He threw up his head and looked alert. Bessie picked up the small basket containing apples to sustain us, and we climbed into the growler.

I had been worried that the friendly porter might not be on duty. But there he was at his station and greeted me like an old acquaintance.

'Pleased to see you again, ma'am. I knew you'd be back and I haven't let you down! I told my wife all about it last night. She was very happy during her time in service in Putney when she was a young girl, and it got her reminiscing right off. I told her about the house with the weathervane as you described it, a running fox.'

'And she knew the house?' I asked eagerly.

'Well, she remembers a house with a weathervane like that,' the porter replied cautiously. 'Not to say it's the same one, of course! But it was near the Portsmouth road, as you said. It belonged to a gentleman name of Spelton or Shelton, she cannot be sure which, and she knows no more about it than that. It was not a household that was on friendly terms with the people my wife worked for. By that I mean they didn't go visiting back and forth, so she never saw any of the people who lived there. The only thing she has in her mind is that Mr Spelton (or Shelton) was an elderly gent and something of an invalid. The reason she knows that is because the doctor used to call regular on a member of the family in her house. Quite often when he arrived he would say, as he was taking off his hat and coat, that he was coming from Mr Spelton (or Shelton). Or, when he was leaving, he would say, "I must be off to see Mr Spelton," (or Shelton).'

'I am extremely obliged to you, Mr – I am afraid I don't know your name,' I told him.

'Hogget, madam.'

'Then I am very obliged both to you and to Mrs Hogget. I wonder if I might trouble you to ask her one more thing. Can she remember the name of the doctor?'

'I'll ask her,' he promised. 'Let me know how you get on.'

I returned and conveyed what I'd learned to Bessie, who became thoughtful. 'You know what, missis, you may have started a hare, that's what. Hogget will go home and tell his wife that you're really interested and now you want the name of the doctor! If Mrs Hogget is still friendly with anyone from her days in service out at Putney, she'll be sure to mention it. You've set a rumour going, that's what.'

Mindful that this was exactly what Ben had feared, I said firmly, 'I am only making a general inquiry.'

'People going to all the trouble you're going to,' retorted Bessie, 'aren't making general inquiries. They've got a very particular interest, that's what. Begging your pardon for speaking out, missis,' she added belatedly.

Well, she was probably right but what was done was done. I settled back and let Victor take us all to Putney.

* * *

I need have had no fears about locating St Mary's church for it was just across Putney Bridge, standing by the river, and we saw its ancient square tower from the far side. We clattered over the wooden bridge, which echoed hollowly beneath us, and found ourselves in the High Street. Bessie and I descended from the growler and Wally clambered down from his perch.

'Seeing as,' Wally pointed up at the clock on the solid stone tower, 'it is past twelve, Victor will be wanting his oats, to stay nothing of a rest. I suggest to you, Mrs Ross, that I take Victor somewhere suitable, that has a stable yard with a water trough, and I can see to him and to myself there.'

'You mean to a public house,' said Bessie.

'Yus, Miss Sharp-as-a-razor, I do.' Wally turned back to me. 'Public houses is also very good places to get into conversations. You can find out a deal from a bit of chat over a pint of ale.'

'You will be careful, Mr Slater,' I begged.

'Don't you fret,' he assured me. 'People looking at me can see what I am; and there will be Victor outside busy chomping in his nosebag, to prove it. I ain't the law, like your husband. I'm just a cabbie. I'll come back here to collect you and her – ' Wally nodded towards Bessie – 'about half past one, how's that?'

We watched the cab roll away.

'Well, now, missis,' said Bessie as we turned back towards the church. 'What do we do now?'

'We visit the church,' I said, 'as anyone new in Putney

might do. That will occasion no gossip. Then, we look for a likely burial.'

The tide was out and the river low. A group of bare-legged urchins scavenged on the mudflats below the church. The exposed riverbed glistened grey or brown and, here and there, patched with a fetid green, and was strewn with all kind of debris. The swollen body of a drowned dog had been left by the retreating water as if the river gave it back to the land. Gulls wheeled overhead and the familiar odour of human refuse assailed our nostrils as we walked up the path to the doorway. Even with Mr Bazalgette's new sewer system now in place, Father Thames was still more than full of all kinds of filth.

We hurried to the church and stopped to survey the graveyard with some dismay. At first sight it was a jumble of tightly packed, sunken graves and mossy headstones and tombs, none of which looked recent. There were no new flowers or urns. The church noticeboard told us the building itself was in use, but its burial ground appeared to have been abandoned.

'It don't look like they buried the old fellow here,' said Bessie glumly, gesturing at the scene, 'whatever that porter told you.'

'They must have buried him somewhere,' I insisted, quelling my own doubts. 'We'll just have to search. Let's see if there is anyone in the church who can help us.'

We were about to enter the building when an elderly man appeared suddenly from within. We almost collided and he began to apologise profusely.

'I do beg your pardon, ladies! I was hurrying home to my luncheon and didn't expect anyone to be coming inside now. I trust you are not harmed? I am parish clerk of this church, ma'am,' he added to me. 'Did you want to go inside? There's no service due, not until this evening, six o'clock, when there will be a service without any music, as it isn't Sunday. Our organist doesn't play except on a Sunday or at weddings and funerals.'

'We only wanted to look at the building,' I told him. 'Is it very old?'

Closer to hand, parts of the church did not look so ancient, though the tower appeared to have age to it.

He was anxious to confirm my suspicions. 'Some parts of it are indeed very old, ma'am, as is this tower above us. It was in this church, you know, that in sixteen forty-seven after Cromwell had defeated King Charles, a great debate was held to decide what should follow. But if you will go inside now you will see there was a deal of repair and alteration some thirty years ago. There was a fire then, ma'am, and much of the building destroyed.'

'I couldn't help but notice your churchyard,' I went on, as he seemed disposed to chat. 'I see it is very full and the graves appear very old. I suppose some of them must be of historical interest.'

'It is indeed full, ma'am, and no one has been buried there in my lifetime, and I am sixty-four! They ran out of space at the end of the last century.' Then, with an astuteness I had not expected he asked, 'Was there a particular burial you had in mind, ma'am?'

It was time to confess. 'There is, but it would have

taken place some sixteen years ago, in eighteen fifty-two, and, from what you tell us, it cannot be here.'

'Ah,' said the clerk, 'then it will be in the ground given to the church for burials by a very generous and pious gentleman by the name of the Reverend Dr Pettiwand. But after a hundred years of burials since he gifted it, that is also full, alas, and we must bury our departed loved ones elsewhere. If however the person of interest to you died in eighteen fifty-two, there is a good chance he was given one of the last plots in Pettiwand's ground.' He shook his head. 'Putney has grown apace since I was a boy. Who would have thought it? What we require now is a large public cemetery such as has been set out elsewhere. What would be the name of the deceased, ma'am?'

'It may have been Spelton or Shelton,' I told him.

I should not have been surprised that this amiable parish clerk was as particular as the clerk in the blue coat at Somerset House. I felt I had to explain.

'I am asking on behalf of someone who knew the area many years ago, a Mr Mills. He did not live here but used to visit often. Unfortunately he is no longer able to come himself.' So far, so true . . . stretching a point.

The parish clerk shook his head. 'Spelton, eh? I know of no one of that name, and I am a local man as I told you, and have been parish clerk here for a good few years. We can look in the register of burials, ma'am. But I do not have on me the keys to the cupboard where it is kept.'

Was I to face defeat? I urged, 'Mr Mills did not remember the name of the gentleman's house, only that it had a weathervane designed like a running fox.'

To my delight, this struck a chord with the clerk. 'Indeed, yes, ma'am! The gentleman, Mr Mills, is quite right. Fox House, it's called, and was formerly an inn. It must be nigh as old as this church here. But it had long ceased to be a hostelry when I was a boy. I never knew it but as a private house and belonging to Mr Sheldon most of that time. Mr Mills, if you will forgive me, has not got the name quite right and that misled me!' He shook a triumphant forefinger at me. 'It is not Shelton, ma'am, but *Sheldon.*'

'That'll be him!' exclaimed Bessie impetuously. Then she blushed brick red, cast me an apologetic look and stared down hard at the ground.

But the parish clerk was anxious to tell me more. 'Oh, yes, I remember old Mr Sheldon. He was a fine old gentleman and very generous. I fancy he had made a good deal of money in the coffee trade. Mr and Mrs Lamont still live there. Mrs Lamont was Miss Sheldon before she married, and old Mr Sheldon's relative. She lived there with him.'

'That is indeed probably the one,' I told him.

'Then I can tell you that you will find him in the burial ground I spoke of. I can give you directions but it will be a good twenty minutes' walk for you ladies, and uphill.'

I assured him we were good walkers. He gave us the directions and added that if we failed to find Mr Sheldon, we should return to tell him that afternoon, but not before four. He bid us a cheery good afternoon and set off for his luncheon.

He was a reliable informant and although it was a warm walk, and uphill, we eventually found the burial ground he'd told us of. We divided it between us, Bessie beginning on the far side and I on the nearer side and working methodically towards the central pathway. The parish clerk had been correct in telling us this graveyard, too, was full. I wondered how long our search would take us. Wally would be wondering what had become of us. But then I heard a cry of triumph from Bessie and looked in that direction to see her waving energetically with one hand and indicating downward with the other. I hurried towards her and found she pointed at a headstone fashioned in gothic style.

'Found him!' she crowed. 'Here's Mr Sheldon, just like that old clerk fellow said.'

I read the inscription eagerly.

ISAIAH MATTHEW SHELDON
Born 17 April 1769 at Fulham
Departed this life 15 June 1852 at Putney
A pious and charitable gentleman remembered
with gratitude by many

Behind me, Bessie was still uttering little exclamations of triumph. I almost exclaimed aloud myself, for this was surely the old gentleman of whom Mills had spoken.

'Would you believe it?' asked Bessie, her glee mixed

with awe. 'We found 'im. We found the old gent as was murdered.'

'Hush, Bessie!' I said quickly. 'Don't speak of that here. You don't know who might overhear us.'

My warning came in the nick of time. Other people were approaching. I heard women's voices and turned.

Coming down the path towards us were two women, one still a fairly young woman, probably about my age, and dressed very fashionably. The other was slightly older and dressed very plainly, a lady's maid, perhaps. I had only a fleeting impression of a pale face. She walked behind the fashionable one. Both were looking towards us in a manner I could only describe as unfriendly.

'Good day,' I said cheerfully.

This did not cause them to soften their expressions. The elegant lady asked, in an icy tone, 'You are visiting my uncle's grave?'

I sent up a quick silent prayer of thanks that the parish clerk had not accompanied us and couldn't speak of my interest. He might do so later, of course, if he encountered the former Miss Sheldon, as this must surely be, now Mrs Lamont. She was what is called a handsome woman, with strong regular features and fine dark eyes. A few years earlier, with the bloom of youth on her, she might even have been called beautiful. Ben had told me that he believed Mills had had an eye for a good-looking woman. Was that, I wondered, what had kept Mills watching at the window, that dismal night in the rain, when this woman, if it were the one, had entered the room where the old man dozed by the fire? He had not raised a hand to rap on the windowpane – and perhaps save a life – because he had been transfixed by the sight of a lovely girl?

I spoke up with as much confidence as I could muster. 'We are only walking round and viewing all the headstones out of interest. I am a visitor to Putney and one can learn so much about a place from the headstones in a graveyard.' Again, all true. 'I see,' I went on, 'that your late uncle was a very charitable gentleman. He must be much missed in the community.'

'Yes,' agreed Mrs Lamont with no thawing of her voice. 'I trust you will find other things in Putney to take your interest.'

That was a clear dismissal. There was nothing more to do but smile and bow and make my departure, Bessie following behind.

'My!' said Bessie, when we were outside the burial ground and in the street. 'That was a close one.'

'It was, indeed, Bessie,' I agreed with feeling. 'Thank goodness the clerk had to hurry off to his meal, and didn't come with us.'

'I suppose that was her, then, the one who . . .' Bessie remembered she must not mention the word 'murder'. 'The one Mr Mills saw.'

'It might well be. Come along, we ought not to linger. I am sure Mrs Lamont is watching us. Let us take an interest in some of the other buildings in Putney.'

We made our way back to the High Street, where we strolled along, pausing occasionally to look in a shop window or gaze up at the frontage.

'That other one,' Bessie said suddenly, 'the woman who was walking with her. I didn't much like the look of her.'

I had to admit I'd paid very little attention to the woman I had assumed a lady's maid.

'Mrs Lamont,' went on Bessie, 'wanted to know what interest you had in her uncle's grave, and that might be a natural question. But that other one, my! If looks could kill, why the pair of us, you and I, missis, would be laid out flat on the grass alongside the dead!'

Our stroll had brought us to an old inn with an arched carriage entrance leading into a cobbled courtyard.

'There's Victor!' I exclaimed. 'Mr Slater must be inside. Come along, Bessie.'

We ventured into a narrow wood-panelled entry. A stout female descended on us and asked if she might be of assistance.

I explained to the landlady, as I supposed this to be, that I was seeking somewhere a lady might obtain some luncheon. Bessie and I were shown, with some ceremony, into a very small room, called by the landlady 'the Sun'. It was otherwise uninhabited and appeared to have been disused for some time, if the amount of dust was anything to go by. We squeezed ourselves on to narrow benches in a window bay, where there was a round table. The landlady informed us that the establishment's veal pie was famous all over Putney and beyond, diners travelling across the bridge from Fulham to sample it. Would we not have the veal pie with some boiled potatoes and a dish of tea? I said we would.

'Now, Bessie,' I said when the landlady had gone to see to our order. 'Just slip out and take a glance into the taproom and see if you can see Mr Slater. You don't have to hail him or do anything obvious, just let him catch sight of you and he will know we are here.'

Bessie did as bid and returned to tell me that Wally was settled comfortably with several companions, ale tankard in hand, and talking nineteen to the dozen. 'And they say women gossip!' said Bessie scornfully. She was sure he had seen her in the doorway, as his face had crinkled up fit to frighten the cat.

Bessie had encountered the landlady again and, to explain why she was not waiting in the Sun, requested if there was some place to which a lady might retire 'for necessary purposes'. The landlady had told her there was a privy in the yard but hardly fit for a lady's use. If two respectable persons like us were in need, let her know and we could go upstairs to the landlady's private living area where there was an earth closet, of which the landlady was extremely proud.

Either the veal pie was as excellent as promised or our efforts that morning had made us very hungry, but we made short work of the food and the tea. Having paid we ventured upstairs to the earth closet. The landlady sent up a servant girl with us to guide us to the very spot. She took us to what appeared a large clothes cupboard, but when she had flung open the doors we beheld the contraption itself. The girl insisted on demonstrating exactly how we must crank the handle on the side of the hopper above the wooden seat to release the ashes within down into the bucket below it. She eventually left us but not after informing us, in a hushed voice, that 'the Queen, God bless her, has got one just like it.'

'Really!' exploded Bessie when the girl had gone. 'As if neither of us had ever seen one before!'

After our adventures with the earth closet we made our way back down to the stable yard where we found Wally Slater waiting beside Victor in the shafts of the growler.

'If you want to take a look at Fox House,' said Wally, 'I've found out where it is. It's all right, Mrs Ross, no need to worry. No one has suspected anything. I just got talking to the locals and I found out a deal of interesting facts, as you might like to know. But I can't tell you here.'

'We could drive slowly past, Mr Slater, but we must not stop or appear interested!' I warned him. 'Bessie and I have already encountered the lady who lives there.'

'And she was very suspicious, if you ask me,' added Bessie.

'I suppose,' Wally told her, 'that whether we was to ask you or not, we gets your opinion, free and gratis!'

Bessie and I clambered into the cab and Wally on to his perch. We heard him whistle to Victor and we set off.

Bessie was by now so excited by the whole adventure that she fairly fizzed alongside me and could hardly keep still, despite my twice begging her to stop fidgeting. We had left the main area of habitation and began passing by scattered houses. Wally turned on to another road, leading across some open heath scattered with clumps of bushes and occasional trees. We then lurched and bumped across some rough terrain before arriving on another stretch of modest highway. Wally had slowed Victor to an amble and we proceeded at this gentle pace until the little trapdoor above our heads flew open and Wally shouted down, 'Up ahead, on your left, Mrs Ross!'

'Remember, don't stop!' I shouted back in warning, but the trap had already snapped shut.

The house came into view to our left. It was much as Ben had described it – following Mills's description. It was long, low and very old. It would be easy to believe it had once been an inn. I longed to put my head out of the window so that I could see the very top of the roof, to establish whether the running fox weathervane was still in place. But I dared not show so much interest in case we had been observed from within.

'Lonely old spot, ain't it, missis?' observed Bessie. 'You could get up to any amount of mischief out here and no one see you.'

'We must be following some medieval track leading to London from the south, a drovers' way,' I told her. A quick glance to my right took in a small clump of trees facing the house across the road. That was where Mills had tethered his horse on the night of the storm, sixteen years earlier. I felt a tingling as if I, too, were in the midst of an electric storm. It was just as Mills had told Ben, quite unchanged in every detail. The condemned man's testimony was to be trusted. I certainly did not doubt he'd witnessed a murder that dreadful day.

Just then I heard another loud whistle above my head, and a rap on the trapdoor, although it didn't open. Victor broke into a trot. Something was happening and Wally was sending us a warning.

At that moment we overtook a pedestrian, walking towards the house. We saw him briefly as we bowled past, a tall, dark-haired, moustachioed man in a country suit of tweed and a soft hat. He was striding out, walking stick in hand. We were aware of his sharp gaze fixed on us, and the look of suspicion and surprise on his face, before Victor carried us past and onward. Had we, I wondered, encountered Mr Lamont, on his way back home? If so, he might mention our cab to his wife – and she, in turn, mention the strangers who were so very interested in her uncle's gravestone.

'It can't be helped, Bessie,' I said to her. 'But I think we have stirred things up.'

'If you don't stir up the soup-pot, you don't find out what's at the bottom of it!' said Bessie in a surprisingly wise observation. 'Mrs Simms used to say that. Her what is cook-housekeeper to Mrs Parry.'

'Oh, I remember Mrs Simms!' I said. I remembered everything about my time as companion to my Aunt Parry. It had been full of surprises, not least in bringing me together with Ben again for the first time since childhood.

'I won't ever forget her,' said Bessie with feeling. 'She had me working from dawn till night in that kitchen. I never got a chance to sit down.'

The growler had slowed. We reached an area of open heath and stopped. The growler rocked as Wally's substantial frame clambered from his perch. He appeared at the door.

'It's dry underfoot, ladies. I got a rug I can set down so you can make yourselves comfortable. Then,' said Wally cheerfully, 'we can have what they call a council of war.'

He handed me down ceremoniously from the cab, Bessie scrambling down unaided behind me and pausing to reach in and retrieve the basket of apples. Wally fetched an old but spotlessly clean travelling rug from the box and spread it out for us. We settled ourselves and Bessie handed out apples. Victor was tearing at the rough grass a few feet away. Bessie put one apple back in the basket.

'That's for the horse,' she said, and Wally beamed his terrifying smile.

Anyone passing by would have taken the three of us for a slightly unusual but perfectly innocuous picnic party. But no one did pass by. I was pleased about that because in Putney people seemed to have a disconcerting way of popping up when least expected.

'Well, that's the house, then,' said Bessie. 'I couldn't see if there was a weathervane on the roof.'

'It's up there, right enough,' said Wally. 'Running fox, brush held out straight behind him, like you said, Mrs Ross.'

Bessie gave a little cry of triumph and clapped her hands. It was all I could do not to follow her example. We had indeed found Fox House, down to the last detail. 'So what did you learn in the taproom, Mr Slater?' I asked him.

Wally gave a comfortable sigh and settled in for a long

narrative. 'They all know one another's business around here,' he began. 'That suits our purpose very well, you might say.'

'What did *they* say?' interrupted Bessie, who also suspected we were in for a long address.

Wally turned a reproachful eye upon her. 'I took my time and a lot of trouble to learn all this,' he told her. 'So you just pipe down and listen.'

Bessie bridled and opened her mouth but I signalled her to silence.

'As I was saying,' began the cabman again. 'If you want to know anything about any of the big houses around here, you've only got to ask in that taproom – casual-like, of course. Fox House is well known because it's one of the oldest houses. Everyone complains how many new houses have been built over the last few years but I told them, if you lived across the river, in London proper, you'd be pleased to get out of the crowds and the dirt and the smells. It's like being in the country here. Fox House belonged to Mr Sheldon and he had made a mint of money in the coffee trade. Locals called him the "coffee king". In later years, of course, he'd retired from the active side of his business and being very comfortably placed – from the money point of view – he was seeing out his days very nicely, with an orphaned niece to look after him. Miss Amelia Sheldon, she was, and now she's Mrs Lamont.'

'We've met her,' burst out Bessie, then reddened and pressed her lips together, casting me a guilty look.

'Old Mr Sheldon,' continued Wally, 'was a . . .' Wally

scowled and creased his brow in effort. 'He was a *phil - threpist.*'

'Philanthropist?' I suggested.

'That's it!' Wally nodded. 'He gave away money to good causes; and he had plenty of money so good causes knew where to go and ask. He was over eighty and a bit chesty, but he took good care of himself and people were surprised to hear he'd died. He did that very sudden, although, as they all said in the taproom, at his age and with the weather being so changeable that year, it ought not to have been a surprise.'

Wally paused to crunch his apple, more for dramatic effect, I suspected, than because he felt peckish.

'Well, now,' he began, after a mighty swallow, 'after the old gent died, it was all change at Fox House. The charitable causes soon learned to stop calling at that door for help. Miss Amelia, she inherited the lot, house, fortune, everything. But she didn't inherit his generous ways! First off, she dismissed all the servants including the old fellow as had been Mr Sheldon's valet. He was as old as his master, so that wasn't so unexpected, and a young woman don't need a valet. But Mr Sheldon, in his will, had left his valet an annuity, since they had been together, master and man, for over forty years. Mrs Sheldon, she tried to get the lawyers to say that clause of the will had not to stand. But the lawyers said, yes, it did, because Mr Sheldon had been of sound mind when he caused that bequest to be written in. So the old valet got his annuity and lived on very nicely on it for another ten years. But it wasn't a very nice thing to do, so they reckon in the taproom, to try and stop him getting it. She'd have let him go to the workhouse, if she'd had her way. As it was, she didn't get her way that time, and he lived to spend his bit of a pension in that very taproom where we were sitting talking about it all.'

'Why, I wonder,' I mused aloud, 'did she dismiss all the servants?'

'All but one!' Wally held up a forefinger. 'There was a maidservant, Rachel Sawyer, and Miss Sheldon kept her on. She needed someone to look after her, I suppose. Made her her housekeeper and companion. Miss Sawyer took on engaging all new staff, cook, maids, gardener, stableman, the lot.'

'Amelia Sheldon meant to make it her own household,' I mused, still aloud. 'Perhaps she felt it easier that way. But it was a pity for a loyal staff, all to be dismissed without reason.'

I was married to a police detective and in my head I was thinking: Ben would say a reason existed. We just don't yet know what it was. Leaning forward, and lowering his voice although there was no one around, Wally added, 'They say, in the taproom, as Miss Sawyer is paid sixty pounds a year!'

That was too much for Bessie to bear in silence. 'What? Pay a servant sixty pounds!'

'Of course,' warned Wally, 'that might be a rumour, a bit of 'zaggeration. Then,' went on Wally with something of the air of a magician producing the white rabbit from a hat, 'to top it all, scarce a year later and hardly out of mourning, but Miss Sheldon ups and marries. She married a man called Lamont – and nobody likes him. They reckon him to be a regular fortune hunter. He's not a local man but comes, some of them say, from one of those islands out in the English Channel that are nearly in France.'

'The Channel Islands,' I said. 'Did anyone say which one? Jersey or Guernsey? Alderney or Sark?'

'They didn't say, ma'am.' Wally shook his head. 'But they do agree that he's worse than his wife for being tight with money. It was her money, of course, when they wed. But it got to be his money afterwards because the old man hadn't left it to his niece in any kind of a trust, but just outright.'

'There is talk of the law being changed and a new act passed to protect married women and allow them control of their own property and fortune,' I told him. 'It cannot happen soon enough, in my opinion.'

'Mrs Slater not having had any property when we got married, and me not having any now, other than the cab and Victor over there, it won't make any difference to us,' Wally said. 'I mean to train up young Joey to be a cabman, like me, so that if I departs this mortal coil, Mrs Slater will inherit the cab and the horse, and she can engage Joey to drive it. That's my plan.'

'And a very good plan, Mr Slater. But unless there is a new act of parliament to protect women's rights in this matter, then Mrs Slater will have to take care not to remarry. Not, of course, that she would!' I added hastily.

'I ain't thinking of going yet,' Wally retorted, a little testily. 'But I'll pass on your advice, as it was meant well.'

Bessie had no interest in Mrs Slater's future, either as wife or widow. 'Miss Sheldon, as she was when her uncle died, she would have got married to someone, sooner or later. I mean, she couldn't go on living there all on her own, being young and nice-looking and rich. They'd be queuing up at the door, hat in hand, to propose to her. If she hadn't accepted one of them, it'd have looked very odd.'

And up to that door at Fox House had walked Mr Lamont, with his moustaches and walking stick, and presented his case so well he'd become its master.

Bessie had, in fact, hit the nail on the head. The former Miss Sheldon's situation, as a rich young woman with no family to protect her, must have left her very vulnerable and in a strange social position. There would soon have been gossip, if she had not married. Invitations to other houses to dine or to balls would have been few, or difficult to accept, since she could hardly arrive all on her own without even an elderly aunt as duenna. Even Jane Stephens, later to become Mrs Canning, had had her Aunt Alice. Although much good Aunt Alice's chaperonage had done to protect the poor girl.

But we had done very well that day in our investigations. I could hardly wait to tell Ben all about our discoveries that evening.

Chapter Seven

Inspector Ben Ross

LIZZIE WAS back at home already when I returned that evening. Bessie opened the door, her face scarlet with the effort of suppressing all the news. Lizzie, too, had a look of triumph on her face. I didn't know if that was for the good or meant trouble.

Over supper, I learned all they'd been doing. At last, Lizzie fell silent and waited expectantly for my comments. Bessie, who had come in ostensibly to clear the dishes, lingered by the table with a vegetable bowl in her hands, face now so red she was almost purple.

I began my response with care. Treading on hot coals might have been less fraught with danger. 'Well, you – and Bessie and Wally Slater – have certainly been busy. I didn't anticipate you'd meet Mrs Lamont herself.'

'The murderess!' exclaimed Bessie dramatically, unable to keep silence any longer. 'And she looked so normal, too.'

'Generally, Bessie,' I told her, 'murderers look just like anyone else. That's what makes my job so difficult. The wretched Mills, whose information started this hare, looked just like any middle-aged man of business, tough in his dealings with competitors and suppliers, perhaps – but capable of dreadful physical violence?' I shook my head. 'No. Nor, Bessie, should you refer to Mrs Lamont as a murderess. If you let that slip in front of the wrong person and it gets about, we are all of us in a lot of trouble!'

'Yes, sir, sorry, sir,' said Bessie, downcast.

I turned to Lizzie. 'Nor do we know, for sure, that she is responsible for the late Mr Sheldon's death. But one thing I am sure of, Lizzie dear, and that is you must not return to Putney.'

As expected, this earned me gasps of dismay and indignation on my wife's part. Bessie uttered a series of suppressed yelps. When I'd calmed them both down, I explained. 'They will be suspicious of you there now, whether or not they have anything to hide. You were lingering in the burial ground and taking a keen interest in that headstone. You'd earlier spoken to the parish clerk who will almost certainly tell Mrs Lamont about you. There is little doubt she will attend that church. Lamont himself – if it was Lamont you spotted walking back to Fox House – will remember the cab driving past. It's a lonely, mostly disused road, so why should any hackney carriage be driving along it? Going to or coming from which address? Inquiry on their part will reveal that the mystery cab had no business in the area. The word will get round. Someone who was in the taproom of that public house may remember a cabman who stopped by to refresh himself, leaving horse and cab in the yard. They will recall with what interest Wally listened to gossip about Fox House, and tell Lamont all this. Innocent or guilty, the Lamonts will be suspicious and with good reason. Possibly they'll fear the house is to be burgled.'

'What?' burst out Lizzie, 'by *us*?'

'So it is very important,' I went on, ignoring her indignation and the fact that Bessie looked about to combust, 'that you do not go back there – at least not immediately.'

'I may, I suppose,' said Lizzie with a glint in her eyes, 'go back to Somerset House and see if the porter's wife has remembered the name of the doctor?'

'Well, yes, since you have already asked him. But don't ask him to do anything else. I mean, don't ask him to quiz his wife any further.'

'So,' declared Lizzie, 'what are *you* going to do?' Battle lines were clearly drawn up here. Bessie, still with the vegetable dish in her hands, had moved round to stand at my wife's shoulder. 'I have discovered several facts that point to Mills's story being true,' continued Lizzie. 'Are you going to ignore it all?'

I wanted to tell Lizzie that she looked remarkably attractive. A strand of hair had escaped and dangled very fetchingly by her pink cheek. Her eyes still sparkled . . .

I became aware of Bessie's gimlet gaze.

'No, I shall go back to Superintendent Dunn in the morning, tell him what you've learned and suggest I send Morris to Somerset House for the certificate of death,' I told them both.

'He may have more luck at that than I had!' said Lizzie grimly.

'He will know the name of the deceased and the date. He should have no trouble. My concern is what Dunn is going to say when he learns you've been investigating.' Although, I thought, he won't be surprised.

'Why, sir, do you think Miss Sheldon, as she was, dismissed all the servants?' asked Bessie. 'Once she come into her inheritance, that is. She just kept on the one. If she was the woman we saw with her, sir, you can take it from me, she didn't like seeing us there in that churchyard!'

'Yes, Rachel Sawyer. That is a strange business.'

'That must have involved so much disruption and taken so much time,' mused Lizzie. 'Interviewing new staff . . . getting them settled in . . . It does make it odd that she did it all at once, only keeping Rachel Sawyer to run the household.'

'It's certainly very curious,' I agreed. 'But since we don't know her reason, well, we can't speculate. Or at least,' I added, 'not aloud – not to anyone outside of this house.'

That gained me stony looks from both of them.

'Oh, bother,' said Lizzie at last, with a sigh of frustration. She put up a hand to tuck the loose strand of hair back into place. It immediately fell down loose again and was joined by another chestnut curl.

'Bessie!' I said firmly to our one and only maidservant. 'Haven't you got some washing-up to do?'

When I returned to work the following morning, I found a message on my desk from my opposite number at Wapping. The woman, whose body had been taken from the river and about whom I'd inquired, had now been named as Maria Tompkins. She was a known prostitute, aged forty. Water in the lungs and airways indicated she had entered the river alive. Bruising to the face had probably been caused on forceful contact with the river surface. The marks on the torso were about a week older. The man with whom she lived, who controlled her and took her wretched earnings, was a known bully-boy. Currently, however, he was in prison charged with procuring for prostitution a girl under the age of twelve (the age of consent). Coroner's verdict, therefore, was suicide. In the absence of a close relative or legal husband to claim the body, it had been sent to a school of anatomy.

It was a sad but not unfamiliar story. Maria had no longer been in her first youth and her looks had gone. Her man had been seeking younger flesh to peddle on the streets of London. Once he found it, he'd turn her out. She had no future but further and rapid decline into complete destitution. She had apparently leaped from the bridge at Southwark, an area she was known to frequent. A witness had now come forward to say Maria had been seen there the night before discovery of her body. The witness, who was a fellow lady of the night, stated that Maria had complained of business being slow. She had spoken of being 'very tired'.

There had been no such luck in finding any witness who'd seen Jane Canning or her daughter. Of them there was no news. Canning appeared in my office a little after nine, Vandyke beard bristling with aggression as usual.

'What, still no news? I am not surprised because you

appear to have a very odd way of looking for my wife, Inspector Ross. I believe you have been at my house yesterday, where my wife clearly is not. I am at a loss to understand what took you there. You cannot have achieved anything by troubling my household and taking the nursemaid out walking! For what purpose, may I ask, must you promenade with Ellen?'

'To establish the route she normally took with your wife and child,' I said as mildly as I could.

I often have to deal with awkward customers, even outwardly respectable persons such as Canning, but I'd never yet come across one I would so dearly have liked to punch on the nose. Alas, I could not do that. I also had the ignoble and undignified urge to reach across and tug that ridiculous beard.

'If this continues and you can bring me no evidence of progress,' Canning declared, drawing himself up to his full height, and thereby only succeeding in drawing attention to how modest his stature was, 'I shall be forced to engage a private detective.'

'Do as you wish, sir,' I told him curtly. 'We shall continue to do our best to trace the lady and the little girl.'

He stormed out.

'What are we to do, sir?' asked Morris, casting a worried look after our visitor. 'About the missing lady, I mean. He's going to make our lives a misery, that's my view. Not that anyone can blame the gentleman, since his wife and his daughter have vanished into thin air. But he's what you might call a prickly customer, isn't he?'

'I share your view, Morris. What can we do, but what we're doing already? Tell Wapping to keep us informed about any more female bodies recovered from the river. Send Biddle round the workhouses and hospitals again. She may have applied to one of them for help in the last twenty-four hours. In any case, whatever Mr Canning may think, he is not the only problem we have to tackle. I have to go and see Superintendent Dunn about the late Mr Mills's story. I think we may have cause to look into it, after all.'

'That'll be tricky,' said Morris.

Dunn listened with remarkable, not to say unusual, patience as I recounted Lizzie's adventures in Putney. Towards the end of my tale, however, he began to look worried.

'Mrs Ross isn't going back there, is she?' he asked. 'I trust not?'

'I have made it absolutely clear to her that it would be inadvisable,' I told him.

'Think she'll listen to you?'

'I am confident, sir, that she will. Lizzie is very sensible. She won't go back to Putney.' I did not mention that she meant to speak to the porter at Somerset House.

Dunn got up and walked about the room for a minute or two, rubbing his close-cropped head of hair and scowling. Eventually, at the far end of the room, he stopped, swung round to face me and announced, 'I shall take responsibility, should the necessity arise, for Mrs Ross's actions.'

This was such an astounding statement, that I couldn't answer for a moment. I stood there, probably with my mouth open, and gazed at him. At last I rallied and asked, 'Why, sir?'

'Oh, come, Ross. Let's not be naïve. When you came to me before about this and I told you we could not investigate, I more or less dropped a hint I wouldn't object to Mrs Ross deploying her undoubted skills.'

At the time he had, indeed, suddenly inquired after Lizzie. 'Mr Dunn,' I said firmly, 'if anyone is to take responsibility, it lies with me. She is my wife, after all, and I knew all about her trip to Putney before she went. The thing is, now we know what she found out, is it not possible for us to carry out some quiet investigation of the points raised? Lizzie can't go back to the scene of the crime, if there was a crime. We are agreed. Lizzie understands that. But someone – that is to say, we, as the police – should follow up in some way. For example, may I not send Sergeant Morris to Somerset House to obtain a death certificate for the late Isaiah Sheldon? It would be helpful to know the cause of death stated on it.'

'Yes, there is no reason why we shouldn't take a look at it,' Dunn agreed. 'But the whole thing must be kept very quiet.'

'Yes, sir, I understand.'

I sought out Morris immediately and dispatched him to Somerset House. He had not been gone very long when Constable Biddle appeared, his youthful features wearing a strangely secretive expression.

'I have a note for you, sir,' he said in a hoarse whisper that somehow carried more clearly on the air than his normal voice.

'From whom?' I asked.

'From Mrs Ross, sir.'

Biddle is a well-meaning youth and promising as a constable, but being young he is apt to dramatise events. His favoured reading in his leisure moments are the so-called 'penny dreadfuls', those tales of highwaymen, pirates, vampires, explorers stumbling upon lost civilisations, that sort of stuff. I know this because he lends some of the less lurid ones to Bessie, with whom he has a sort of unofficial arrangement. That is to say, they are not walking out, as both Lizzie and Mrs Biddle *mère* agree they are too young. But on a Sunday afternoon, it is not unusual to find Biddle sitting in our kitchen, drinking our tea and eating our cake. Delivering this week's reading matter is often given as an excuse for his presence. I did ask Lizzie if she approved of Bessie reading yarns of that kind. Lizzie replied that she preferred Bessie to have a taste for swashbuckling men of action in her literature, rather than for tales featuring swooning females with adoring swains.

'She might,' I objected, 'identify Biddle with a swashbuckling gallant, and from there it could be only a step to adoring swain.'

'Oh, really, Ben,' retorted Lizzie. 'Bessie has her head screwed on the right way. Besides, Biddle is nothing like a pirate or a highwayman. As to his being a gallant . . .'

This was true. Bessie was of a practical turn of mind.

In any case, Biddle hardly looked the part of romantic hero. He was also clumsy and apt to fall over his own stout boots.

'Is Mrs Ross waiting downstairs?' I exclaimed, rising to my feet.

'No, sir, she's left. She said she would not disturb you, but asked me to give this to you as soon as possible, *direct into your hand*.'

He stood there, looking hopeful. Awaiting part two, no doubt.

'Thank you, Constable!' I told him. 'Off you go.'

Biddle withdrew, still looking furtive and a little disappointed.

'*The Shadow strikes again . . .*' I murmured as I unfolded the piece of notepaper he'd given me.

The note was brief and to the point.

The doctor's name was Croft.

No signature but I knew my wife's handwriting. It seemed the constable was not the only one with the taste for drama. So, Dr Croft had attended Isaiah Sheldon. The porter's wife has a good memory, I thought to myself, refolding the note and tucking it into my waistcoat pocket. But is Dr Croft still to be found and will Dunn agree to my seeking him out?

The next thing to happen was that the post arrived and was brought to me. Amongst it was a large envelope with the Southampton postmark. 'Aha!' I exclaimed to myself. 'This will be in reply to my request for someone to call on Miss Alice Stephens. It seems they discovered too much for a telegraphed reply.' I tore it open eagerly.

The report of Inspector Reuben Hughes

I have now called, as per your request, on Miss Alice Stephens at her home in Southampton. She expressed great alarm on learning that her great-niece, Jane Canning, was missing, together with her young child. She declared she had neither seen nor heard from Mrs Canning. Miss Stephens struck me as an upright, religious lady of strong principles. She is the sort who would tell the truth, however painful. I fancy we can therefore believe her when she says she has no knowledge of Mrs Canning's whereabouts.

I also inquired about the husband, Hubert Canning, and whether she had heard from him. To date, she has not. This struck me as odd. I asked about the circumstances leading to the marriage. Miss Stephens told me that Jane Stephens (as she was before her marriage) met Hubert Canning in Southampton. He was there on a matter of business, visiting a wine shipper. During this visit, he mentioned to the wine shipper that he (Canning) would like to find himself a wife. The wine shipper, by the name of Graham, told his wife. Mrs Graham was acquainted with Miss Stephens, and Jane, through their common attendance at St Michael's church. The older ladies were engaged in charitable work and sat on several committees. Miss Stephens is in her late seventies and had begun to worry what would become of Jane, should she herself become infirm or pass away. A dinner party was arranged at the Grahams' house, attended by the Stephens ladies. Jane found favour with Mr Canning. Mr Canning found favour with Miss Alice. It was true that he was somewhat older than would have been ideal, but he was comfortably situated and her niece would have a large house and servants.

It is not clear whether Mr Canning found equal favour with Miss Jane. But the great aunt told her she could not hope for a better offer. I gather that Miss Jane had no money of her own and depended absolutely on her elderly relative for a roof over her head and all necessities. Miss Alice indicated to me that her resources were not limitless and she admitted that it would be a great help to her personally to have 'Jane off my hands'. I quote her words, although, after she had spoken them, she coloured and hastened to assure me that having Jane with her had always been a pleasure. Miss Alice then became anxious and asked me whether Mr Canning had misrepresented his financial situation to her. I replied that, as far as I knew, he had not. Miss Alice expressed astonishment that Jane should have left such a comfortable home and taken the little girl with her.

It is my private impression that Miss Alice Stephens revealed a trace of guilt when expressing her dismay. She had, after all, urged the match on the young woman. Miss Stephens is not, I believe, a woman generally given to Doubt. But I may have left her with a trace of it in her mind. She will contact me at once if she receives any kind of news, or if Canning contacts her. I will, however, call on her again if I do not hear from her. This is in case Canning gets in touch with her and dissuades her from contacting the police.

Inspector Ben Ross

I now understood the background to the Cannings' marriage. Lizzie had been right in her interpretation of the reasons for the match. Jane had not been in a position to refuse Hubert Canning when he came a-courting.

My colleague, Inspector Hughes, had done an excellent job and I was much obliged to him. He must have visited Miss Stephens as soon as my message arrived and he had been at pains to elicit as much background information as he could. Hughes thought it odd that Canning had not contacted Miss Stephens to find out if she had heard from Jane. I had met Canning and, to me, it was consistent with his desire to keep the scandal from becoming known. If he'd told Miss Stephens, she might well have told her friends, the Grahams, since it was at their suggestion, and in their home, that Canning had met his future wife. Graham was a wine shipper and would have mentioned it to others in that line of business. Soon everyone would know – everyone in Canning's limited world, that is. Canning would be very displeased to find the news had reached Southampton. Good, let him sweat.

Now all I could do was wait. I took the letter to Superintendent Dunn who read it through and snorted.

'Keep an eye on that fellow, Canning,' he said. 'I'm still not sure he's not done away with them both.'

'She and the child were alive when they left the house,' I pointed out. 'The housekeeper and nurserymaid are witnesses. I saw mother and child – at least the child's foot and heard her whimper – two evenings later beneath the arches.'

'But no one has seen them since!' snapped Dunn. 'If you found her beneath the arches, so might he have done. You told him where to look.'

It seemed I could do nothing right.

A little later that morning, Morris arrived back from his visit to Somerset House.

'Got it, sir!' he exclaimed, waving a piece of paper in the air.

So here it was, the death certificate of Isaiah Matthew Sheldon, retired coffee importer. He had died at his home, Fox House, at the age of eighty-three. Cause of death was given as cardiac failure and certified by W. Croft MB. The death had been reported to the registrar by – at this point I could not prevent myself uttering an exclamation of surprise.

'Charles Lamont!' I cried. 'So he was already acquainted with the family!'

'Hanging around the young lady,' said Morris in dire tones. 'Scented a fortune when the old fellow died.'

'Yes, I wonder what Mr Sheldon's opinion of Lamont was? He had been many years in business and he probably – as you suggest, Morris – recognised a fortune hunter. So I fancy we're safe in assuming that Mr Sheldon was an obstacle to his niece's marriage.'

Morris felt he should remind me. 'It wasn't Lamont that was seen pressing a cushion down on the old man's face. It was the young lady.'

'Men and women have done all manner of strange things for love, Morris.'

'So I've heard,' said Morris disapprovingly.

I returned to the cause of death and the doctor's name attached to it. 'Dr Croft was called and gives the cause of death as cardiac failure. He does not appear to have had any suspicions.'

'The old gentleman was eighty-three, Mr Ross.'

'I wonder,' I mused, 'if Dr Croft is still alive and to be found.'

'I took the liberty,' said Morris, 'of calling by a library and consulting the medical registers. Dr Croft was still living in Putney and practising medicine in eighteen sixty-four. Later than that, I can't find him. He may have died, sir, or retired.'

People sometimes make the mistake of underestimating Morris. He is a shrewd officer and utterly reliable. What's more, he is capable of acting on his own initiative, an invaluable trait.

'If we are in luck, then he has only retired. He may still be at the same address where he resided only four years ago.' I contemplated the death certificate again. 'I must try and speak with this medical gentleman.'

'Doctors don't like talking about their patients,' Morris reminded me.

'This patient died sixteen years ago. Besides, I am a police officer.'

'Mr Dunn might not go for it, sir.'

'I don't like it, Ross,' said Dunn, confirming the sergeant's forecast. 'Even if this medical man is still alive and you can find him, he apparently had no doubts at the time about the cause of death and was happy to have his name on this certificate. He won't like having you arrive on his doorstep to suggest he was mistaken. At any rate, he will want to know the reason for your interest in something that happened sixteen years ago – and has not occasioned any comment since then until now.'

Dunn stopped to draw breath and peer at me with a gimlet eye.

'I will be very tactful, sir,' I assured him.

'You will have to show the diplomacy of an ambassador and enjoy a fair measure of good luck. He will be entitled to throw you out, police officer or not. What are you going to say when he asks the reason for your investigation?'

'I shall say –' I searched my brains – 'I shall say that a rumour has been reported to us and we are anxious to settle the matter quickly and close the file.'

There was a silence. 'You have got your teeth into this, Ross, haven't you?' said Dunn. 'You have considered, I suppose, the possibility that Croft will report your visit to Mr and Mrs Lamont?'

'I shall ask him to keep the matter private, sir. Besides, he won't want to start a rumour of his own that he might have made a mistake on a death certificate.'

When Dunn still looked unhappy, I added, 'I will go this evening, sir, in my own time.'

Dunn sighed. 'This matter has already been discussed at the highest level, Ross, and a decision taken then that there was no case to investigate.'

'That was when we had nothing but the unsubstantiated word of Mills. Now we know that the place and date of the death tally, and the description of Fox House and its location are also just as Mills told it; and that the deceased was an elderly man. Everything we've learned has confirmed Mills's tale.' I hesitated. 'From Lizzie's visit, and what she and the cabman learned, there was some gossip at the time about Miss Sheldon, as she was, and Mr Lamont – how soon she married . . . and that he was considered locally to be a fortune hunter.'

'I cannot give you the authority,' said Dunn suddenly. 'I must take it further up. I will consult the assistant commissioner and his decision, Ross, will be final! Is that understood?'

'Yes, sir,' I said, with sinking heart.

I returned to my office and told Morris that his efforts that morning had probably been in vain. But here I was unexpectedly proved wrong. Dunn appeared an hour later in my office, a place he rarely set foot in.

'Ah, Ross,' he said. He looked somewhat confused, and even redder in complexion than normal.

'Yes, sir? Have you spoken to the assistant commissioner, sir?'

'I have. He was good enough to listen but showed little sign of any real interest in what I had to tell him. Until, that is, I chanced to mention the name of Charles Lamont. The assistant commissioner has come across

Mr Lamont, it seems. Mr Lamont is a gambling man. The assistant commissioner, I should stress, is not! However, not long ago he attended a private party at a gentleman's residence in the country. There among other guests he met Charles Lamont. We know it is the same man because Lamont mentioned that he was originally from Guernsey. Late in the evening, after dinner, the tables were set out for cards. The assistant commissioner did not play. But he did observe play and was startled at the amounts of money being wagered, won and lost. Mr Lamont, apparently, lost heavily, having played, in the assistant commissioner's opinion, recklessly. Lamont was also rather drunk and reacted initially to his considerable losses with anger. He declared the cards had run against him all evening, but that he would "make it up next time". In view of this, the assistant commissioner has, you might say, developed a personal interest in the matter. He declared to me that he would not want a fellow like Lamont in his family. He agrees that you should seek out the doctor. But you are to say as little as possible and make your visit brief.'

I told Morris this, hardly able to disguise my elation. Even Morris displayed moderate enthusiasm. I next sought out Biddle and asked him if he would be so good, on his way home, as to call by my house and tell my wife I would be late and not home in time for supper. Biddle replied that he would be delighted to oblige. Thus we all ended the working day on a note of optimism.

Chapter Eight

WHEN I had finished my day at the Yard, I hired a fly to take me out to Putney. I trusted that, as my visit was now official, I might be able to reclaim the cost as expenses. Accordingly I made good time and arrived before the house given as the doctor's address in the 1864 medical register. It was still light, a windless, mellow September evening. The house was a square, redbrick building standing on a large plot of ground. I thought it had probably been built at the beginning of the century.

I asked my driver to wait and set off to knock at the door. It was opened by a neatly dressed maidservant with the look of a country girl about her. She appeared to be about eighteen or nineteen, and had a suggestion of a squint. On my inquiring whether Dr Croft still lived there, she replied at once:

'The master don't see patients no more. He's given up all the doctoring.'

At least that meant he still lived there. 'I don't want to see him about my health. It's another matter.'

The maid looked doubtful. 'Who shall I say wants him?'

'Inspector Ross from Scotland Yard.' I handed her my card.

She peered at it in some dismay. 'We didn't send for no policeman.'

I was beginning to wonder if the doctor had engaged this maid as an act of charity.

'I know you didn't. I'd like to see your master, if you'd be so good to take in my card? Please tell him, I will not disturb him for long.'

The maid retrieved a small silver tray from a side table, placed my card carefully in the centre of it, and bore it away, leaving me on the doorstep and the door wide open. She was gone for almost ten minutes. Eventually she reappeared to announce: 'The master will see you in the garden. He always goes out into the garden after dinner. You can come through or go round the side, as you wish.'

'I will go round the side,' I said. 'I just go straight down the garden, do I?'

'I'll show you,' the maid offered in a burst of efficiency.

I followed her round the outside of the house and we set off down a narrow garden path until we reached a small forest of rose bushes. Above the scent of roses, I smelled tobacco.

My guide pointed to a curl of smoke rising into the air. 'That's him,' she said cheerfully. She then abandoned me and set off rapidly back to the house.

I made my way round the bushes and came upon an elderly man sitting on a wooden bench, peacefully smoking his after-dinner pipe.

'Dr Croft?' I asked, hat in hand.

He rose to greet me. This revealed him to be tall, lean in build and sinewy. He had a fine head of silver-grey hair and wore a shabby velvet jacket that had a look of an old friend.

'To give me that title would be a courtesy. I am but a bachelor of medicine and I no longer practise. Please join me . . .' He gestured at the place alongside him on the bench.

I sat down and observed, 'You have a fine garden here, sir.'

'Yes, yes, the roses have done very well this year. Last year they were plagued with greenfly. Soapy water is the best remedy for that, you know.' He had retaken the place beside me.

'Indeed, sir?'

'Yes. Now, this year, we had a great many ladybirds and that's an insect that devours greenfly. So we had far less trouble. Nature's balance, eh?' Seamlessly, he went on, 'Did you have any difficulty with Mary?'

'The maid?' I guessed. 'She appeared a little alarmed to learn I was a police officer.'

'She's very good girl, excellent worker, utterly reliable, but not very bright. I attended her birth. It was difficult. I fancy the infant was starved of sufficient oxygen.'

Mary had, then, been engaged by the doctor as an act of charity, or because he felt some responsibility for her slow wits.

'What can I do for you, Inspector Ross? I am sure you have more purpose to your visit than to discuss my roses.'

The doctor's tone was comfortable, but there was a touch of steel behind it. I had thought carefully how to begin this conversation; but I had now a shrewd suspicion that I might not be the one in charge of it.

'Well, sir, it is a somewhat delicate matter. It concerns a former patient of yours who died some sixteen years ago, a Mr Isaiah Sheldon, of Fox House.'

'Sixteen years ago, eh?' said Croft, puffing at his pipe and watching the smoke rise into the air.

'You do recall Mr Sheldon, sir?'

'Indeed, I do. I am surprised you have come all the way out here to ask about him now.' He took the pipe from his mouth and studied it. 'A doctor is, you know, somewhat loath to discuss a patient with anyone who is not a family member. There is a duty of confidentiality, rather like that of a priest or a lawyer. Even, I might venture to suggest, like an inspector of Scotland Yard?'

'That would depend, sir, whether it proves relevant to inquiries. What I want to ask you about is, in any case, a matter of public record. It concerns the death certificate.'

Croft turned his head to look at me and I was startled by the sharp gleam of his dark eyes beneath the bushy silver brows. 'Bit late to ask about that, isn't it?'

'We have received a report – I would say it is no more than rumour – suggesting we might look into the death of Mr Sheldon. We are aware he passed away sixteen years ago. We are busy people at the Yard and anxious to settle the matter and close the file as soon as possible. That is why I have taken the liberty of coming out here to Putney and troubling you. I apologise.'

Croft waved his pipe back and forth to dismiss my apology as unnecessary. 'Refresh my memory,' he said. 'What did it state on the death certificate?'

'I have it here, sir.' I took the copy Morris had obtained that morning and handed it to Croft.

He read it carefully and handed it back. 'Yes, cardiac failure, quite so. He was of an advanced age, you know. Although,' Croft permitted himself a smile, 'as one grows older, one is less inclined to admit any age is advanced. I am seventy-nine myself.'

'You surprise me, Dr Croft. You appear in excellent health.'

'Oh yes, I am. Well, given the usual aches and pains.'

'Do you recall if you had any doubt about the cause of death in the case of Mr Sheldon?'

Croft took his time before replying. 'I was confident in the reason I gave on the certificate there.'

I began to suspect that Croft would not volunteer information but he would answer questions. If I could find a way into the conversation, he would speak fairly freely. While I sat silent trying to see how I might do this and give a lead, without overplaying my hand, Croft decided to help me out.

'Tell me, Inspector Ross, are you by any chance acquainted with the comedy by the French writer, Molière, usually translated into English as *The Imaginary Invalid*?'

'I have not studied French, alas, Doctor. My wife may know it. She learned French as a girl. She had a French governess for a short time.'

The Imaginary Invalid? Suddenly I thought I saw his

reason for asking. 'Mr Sheldon was such a person? A hypochondriac?'

'I wouldn't go so far as to say that. But, just as with the character in the French play, he was very concerned with his health. I was required to call on him regularly. On one occasion he might fancy his pulse faint, on another his heartbeat irregular. He was plagued with headaches. His joints ached. His appetite had failed. His digestion was at fault. He either could not sleep or slept too much. He felt weak, lacked any energy. All of these things he was pleased to describe as his symptoms. It did no good to point out his advanced age; and such inconveniences come with that, as I mentioned to you just now in my own regard. Or that he took little or no regular exercise, hardly left his house, and ate unsuitably rich food. He would insist I prescribe some medication. Rhubarb pills or bismuth usually did the trick.'

'Were you surprised when you learned he had died? Had you attended him that day?'

'Not on that day. I had attended him a few days earlier. He had complained of shortness of breath. I suggested a light diet in order that he might lose a little weight, and a reduction in his consumption of wine and spirits. Although, to be fair, I would not have described him as severely overweight. I lectured him on general fitness and suggested a gentle walk each morning might help him regain some general measure of well-being. He was quite horrified at the idea. I listened to his heartbeat. It was not the heart of a man of twenty, admittedly, but I did not detect any severe irregularity. I cannot remember what I prescribed. It would have been some harmless panacea.'

I indicated the death certificate. 'But you confidently gave cardiac failure as cause of his death.'

'Eventually, Inspector, it is the case with all of us that our hearts stop beating and we die. Of course, the causes of our hearts doing that vary tremendously. When I thought through all the things he'd complained to me of, I decided that his heart must have been failing and this had led to his death – that and his age. I could also have said that he worried himself to death! But that would not be medically acceptable.'

'Do you recall the day he died? I realise I am asking you to think back sixteen years.'

Croft's pipe had gone out. He tapped the bowl against the wooden arm of the seat to dislodge the remains of the tobacco. 'I remember it very well, as it happens. It was in June, but it had been a very warm month, and on that day we were treated to a sudden thunderstorm and downpour.'

It was all I could do not to cry out aloud in triumph. Everything we learned supported Mills's tale. This went far beyond coincidence. Surely the assistant commissioner could not object to further investigation now? 'Yes, sir?' I prompted.

'The storm had barely passed and the rain ceased – I recall how the water dripped from the trees – when a servant arrived from Fox House, asking that I come at once.'

'A woman or a man?' I asked quickly.

Croft glanced at me with raised eyebrows. 'A man, I

fancy it was the gardener. He was in a state of alarm and requested I come as fast as I could. Mr Sheldon had collapsed. I hurried to the house where I found the entire household in a state of panic.'

'Where was Mr Sheldon?'

'Upstairs in his bedroom.'

'You are sure of that?' I asked in surprise. This was not what I'd expected. It did not tally with Mills's tale of Sheldon having died in the parlour. From elation I was plunged into uncertainty.

'Oh, yes, quite sure. I was conducted up there to see him.' Croft puffed at his pipe.

'It was not possible he had died elsewhere in the house?' I held my breath.

Croft eyed me. 'I suspect you have more information than you are willing to divulge, Inspector. I don't know whence you have it. But you are right. I was given to understand he had been found unconscious downstairs, before the parlour fire.'

Again I had to suppress an urge to exclaim, *yes*!

'It had at first been assumed he was sleeping,' Croft continued. 'But a maid had brought in some tea at the time he was accustomed to drink a dish, and been unable to rouse him. The gardener and stableman had been summoned to carry him upstairs. They had laid him on his bed. They had partially undressed him.'

Croft paused. 'Sheldon had continued to dress in the fashion of his youth. In fact, he bore a remarkable resemblance to His late Majesty King William the Fourth and I suspected it was his small vanity to play to it. He always wore a collar with high points and a silk stock, with a brocade waistcoat. All this had been removed and his shirt unbuttoned. I saw at once that he was dead. Grotesquely, they were attempting to revive the corpse with application of a mustard plaster to his chest. I made the usual checks for signs of life, of course. But clearly he'd been dead for over an hour or more. He was already cool, despite the hot plaster. I detected the onset of rigor in the extremities.'

'Were you surprised that they had carried a dead man upstairs?'

'People do not always behave logically, Ross. You must have had some experience of that in your work. When a death occurs unexpectedly, as in this case, it is not unusual to find the household in considerable confusion, and a reluctance to face the fact that the worst has happened. They did not wish to accept that he was dead, hence the mustard plaster. Let me add that I have more than once in my long career been called to view a dead body, only to have the corpse sit up and demand to know what I was doing there! So errors of judgement around death are not uncommon. They were clinging to hope – in vain.'

'You checked for the vital signs, Doctor, but you did not examine the body closely for anything else?' I asked.

'What else?' asked Croft, his sharp gaze resting on me again. 'Are you suggesting I missed something, Inspector?'

'I suggest nothing, sir. I merely ask for my own satisfaction.'

'There was no necessity for closer examination. I'd examined him some three or four days earlier. He was eighty-three, had complained for some time of advancing weakness and general indisposition. His style of living was self-indulgent. His heart had given out. I was quite satisfied that was the immediate cause of his death. I was pleased that his end had been so peaceful, sleeping before his own hearth, because he was a fine old gentleman, known for his charitable ways. His idiosyncrasy, if you wish, was his obsession with his health.'

'Thank you, Dr Croft, I'll trouble you no more,' I said, returning the death certificate to my pocket. 'I would only ask for your discretion in the matter of my visit. I would not wish the family to be troubled.'

Those sharp dark eyes beneath the bushy brows rested on me for a last time. 'I see no reason why I should trouble the family,' he said.

I left him to his pipe and his roses. The evening had drawn in while we'd spoken. The sky was flushed a dusky crimson. The roses seemed to me to glow in this light like large jewels. (I was growing poetic!) Their scent was enhanced. I envied Croft his retirement and hoped that when his time came – not for a long time yet, of course – that he passed away sitting peacefully in his garden, enjoying his pipe.

When I eventually arrived home, I found Lizzie awaiting me eagerly, demanding to know what I'd learned at Putney. Biddle had told them where I'd gone. It wasn't all he'd done.

'I'm afraid,' said Lizzie, 'that Constable Biddle has eaten your pork chops.'

'What?' All the way home the image of a plate of fried chops had filled my head. I had dwelled on it to disguise the memory of Croft's certainty that there had been no mystery regarding Sheldon's death.

'He looked hungry,' explained my wife, 'and we didn't know when you'd return. There is a portion of cold steak pie and plenty of cheese. Or, if you'd prefer something hot, I can cook you bacon and eggs.'

'The steak pie will do very well,' I said, sinking into a chair. 'But Biddle is becoming altogether too familiar a sight here!'

'You sent him with a message,' she pointed out.

'Next time I'll send someone else!'

Lizzie waited impatiently while I ate the pie. 'What did you learn?' she asked, as I set down my knife and fork.

I recounted all the conversation. 'He was more helpful than I'd anticipated; and I must say his recall was excellent. He even remembered the storm. Or perhaps it was because of the storm he remembered the day so well. So far everything has supported Mills's tale to a remarkable degree. I believed him at the time and, if possible, I believe him even more now.' I paused to sigh and shake my head.

'I have to confess that the optimism I felt when talking to Croft faded on my journey home. The good doctor was satisfied as to the cause of death. After sixteen years he won't change his mind and it would do no good if he did. If he'd had doubts at the time, well, things might have been different.'

'But why did they move the body?' demanded Lizzie

obstinately. 'Why all that piece of theatre with a mustard plaster? It is grotesque and can only have been in an attempt to fudge the circumstances of his death.'

'Croft didn't find it grotesque. He believed they were only unwilling to accept Sheldon had died. He's known "dead men" sit up. So have I. Dr Carmichael, who has carried out so many postmortems at police request, told me that he has twice in a long career begun an incision only for the "corpse" to let out a groan. Sheldon's household were trying to bring about resuscitation. No, no, it won't do. I am afraid, Lizzie, we have reached the end of our investigations. Even if the assistant commissioner agreed to my delving further into things, I don't know where I could now turn my attention. I don't think even your informant, Mrs Hogget, could help. Mills would be satisfied at the efforts we've made.'

'Well, something else may turn up,' said Lizzie, refusing to accept defeat. 'One door closes and another opens, don't they say?'

'Not in police investigations, my dear, or not often.'

'Pah!' said my wife robustly. 'You are only tired. Look how many doors have been slammed in your face – metaphorically speaking – since you first heard Mills's story. You haven't given up and I know you won't now. Something will turn up, you'll see. Keep your fingers crossed!'

There is a saying that one should be careful what one wishes for.

Chapter Nine

THE NEXT two days, although busy from the point of view of the Yard, found me concerned with matters of deception, burglary and other ways of theft, including demanding money with menaces. I also had reports of rape, bigamy and child abandonment: all the things that go on in great cities and small villages up and down the land, to a greater or lesser degree, and serve to erode any confidence a police officer ever had in his fellow man. I was forced to put Fox House out of my mind. But not the disappearance of Jane Canning and her daughter, Charlotte.

Mr Hubert Canning could not be considered a matter of routine, but his appearance had become almost as regular a feature in my life as any of the others.

I was expecting to see him, after reading the letter from my colleague in Southampton. I anticipated that Miss Stephens, following Hughes's visit, would have contacted Canning about his wife's disappearance, demanding to know what had happened to her great-niece. Sure enough, Canning erupted into my office in his usual manner, with that mix of outrage and pomposity I'd come to associate with him.

'This is disgraceful!' he announced, glaring at me.

'Do sit down, Mr Canning,' I invited him. 'Tell me, what is disgraceful?'

Canning plumped himself down on a chair pushed forward by the obliging Constable Biddle. He shook a forefinger at me. 'Don't pretend you don't know to what I refer!'

'Mr Canning,' I told him as calmly as I could, 'I am a very busy man. The whole of Scotland Yard is a busy place and the police force, as a body, is constantly being called upon for all manner of urgent matters. We are continuing to search for your wife and daughter. I do hope that we shall soon have some news of them. When we do, I'll contact you at once.' Canning opened his mouth but before he could speak, I continued, 'You will understand, therefore, that your continual appearance here does nothing to help and a certain amount to hinder.'

Canning's mouth opened and closed several times. His complexion darkened to an unhealthy purple and I was about to send Biddle for a glass of water when the visitor spoke.

'How dare you, Inspector Ross? How dare you?' he asked in a croak. 'I shall complain about your attitude. I shall make formal written complaint to the highest level! May I remind you that I am a taxpayer, a respectable citizen, of blameless reputation both in personal and in business matters. You are a public servant. I have been under considerable strain since the departure of my wife, taking our daughter. I should have thought that by now you could have found *some* trace of them! But do you go out looking for them? No. Instead, you contact another police officer, in Southampton, and he – he . . .' Canning spluttered in rage. 'He was so brazen as to call upon an elderly lady in poor health, my wife's great-aunt, springing upon her, with no warning, the distressing news – that I'd hoped to keep from her – and leaving her in a state of alarm and despondency. It is a miracle she did not collapse with the shock!'

'Inspector Hughes was surprised,' I said, 'that you had not already been in touch with Miss Stephens to tell her what had happened.'

'Am I speaking to a brick wall?' yelled Canning. 'I did not want the lady disturbed or troubled with this matter. I made it clear to you that my wife would not have gone to Southampton. Indeed, she would have no means of getting there.'

'The railway?' I suggested.

He looked taken aback, then shook his head. 'No, no, she would not have had sufficient money on her.'

Aha! I thought. 'The housekeeping fund?' I inquired mildly.

'Mrs Bell takes care of the housekeeping,' he snapped.

'Mrs Canning's personal allowance?'

'Mrs Canning's necessary expenses – her dresses and so forth – are taken care of by me. All bills are sent to me. I settle them.'

'Well, then, her – what is commonly called "pin money" – her day to day small expenditure, what of that?'

'Oh, well,' said Canning, beginning to look uncomfortable, 'she would have had a little petty cash for trifles

– little treats for the child, that sort of thing. But *you* claim to have seen Jane two days after she left the house. You tell me she was living under a railway arch! If so, it is clear she had no money or had spent all she had on her.'

So now it seemed Canning accepted it had been his wife I'd encountered that night. But I'd learned an important thing. Jane Canning had been allowed only the smallest sums of actual cash. Why? Not because Canning was mean, in the usual sense. No, because he had feared something of this sort – that she might leave – and he meant to ensure she could not.

'I think you have not been entirely frank with us, Mr Canning,' I said. 'I believe your wife has run away from your home of her own volition and you have known this from the beginning. It is not our job here at Scotland Yard to solve domestic disputes. However, it is our concern to find your daughter. To do that, we must find the mother. I'll continue to do everything possible, but I do not expect, Mr Canning, to have you here in my office haranguing me and failing to cooperate by not volunteering all the facts! I would remind you that if you had come to us at once and not waited two days, there is a strong possibility we would have found Mrs Canning by now. Certainly, when I encountered a well-spoken woman with a young child sleeping beneath the arches, I would have suspected at once it might be your wife. You see? It is not the fault of Scotland Yard that the trail has grown cold.'

Canning stood up. 'And I do not expect to be spoken

to in this manner by you, Inspector Ross! Be assured, I shall make a formal complaint.'

'You are free to do so, Mr Canning.'

Canning huffed at me, but found no more words. He turned and strode out.

'I thought the gentleman was going to have a fit, sir,' said Biddle.

'Not if it didn't suit his purpose!' I said crisply. 'Mr Canning is something of an actor, I fancy. His position is weak and he knows it. Off you go, Constable, I think you must have work to do.'

'Yes, sir,' said Biddle, hurrying out.

It was three days after my visit to Putney, and the day following Canning's visit, that I was summoned to Superintendent Dunn's office at mid-morning. Canning has made the formal complaint he threatened, I thought, as I made my way there. He has probably written to the commissioner. I braced myself and mentally marshalled my defence.

But Dunn was not alone when I arrived. He had a police sergeant with him, one totally unknown to me. He was a stocky fellow with a ginger moustache who stood rigidly to attention by Dunn's desk, his helmet tucked under his arm.

'Good,' said Dunn, as I came in. 'There you are. This is Sergeant Hepple from Wandsworth Division. He has been sent by Inspector Morgan there to request our help. They have a murder investigation on their hands, it seems.' Dunn gestured to Hepple to take up the tale.

Hepple turned to me and saluted with his free hand. 'A woman's body has been found by the river on the mud, sir—' he began.

'Jane Canning?' I interrupted in dismay, looking at Dunn.

'What? No, not her.' Dunn waved away my interruption irritably. 'That has been established. The sergeant will explain how and why.'

'The body was found at around half past eight this morning, sir, at low water just below Putney Bridge,' resumed Hepple. 'It was discovered by a bit of luck. The tide had turned and was coming back in. Low water last night was shortly before three. That meant high water this morning would be around a little before nine. You'll understand, sir, that the body had to be removed from the location where it was discovered because the water would soon have covered it. It is at present in temporary housing; not a proper mortuary but a nearby shed of some sort.'

'This is not an accident or suicide, some poor wretch leaping from the bridge?' I asked. 'The body could have been deposited there when the tide went out.' (Maria Tompkins had sprung to my mind.) 'Are we sure this is a murder?' I looked at Hepple.

'The outer clothing is muddied and damp. But her petticoat and, er, stays and so on, they are all dry and clean, sir,' said Hepple confidently. 'She has not been in the water. A doctor has attended and, in advance of a proper postmortem, has suggested she has been strangled.'

A murder, then, almost certainly. 'Is there any indication as to her identity?'

'Yes, sir,' confirmed Hepple. 'She is well known in the area, having lived there many years. Her name is Rachel Sawyer and she was employed as a housekeeper to Mr and Mrs Lamont at Fox House in Putney.'

I could not repress a gasp and turned to Dunn.

He was watching me with a gleam in his eye. 'I thought you'd be interested in this one and that you would be the best person to investigate it, since you already know something about that household! So take Morris and get over there. Sergeant Hepple here will conduct you.'

I turned to Hepple. 'The body is in a shed, you say? Who is guarding it?'

'One of our constables, sir. He won't let anyone near, other than the doctor, of course. He's a local man, a Dr Croft.'

'Dr Croft! I understood Dr Croft had retired from practice!' I exclaimed unwisely. From the corner of my eye I saw Dunn twitch an eyebrow at me in warning.

'Oh,' said Hepple, surprised, 'you know the doctor, do you? Yes, he's getting on a bit and doesn't see patients on a regular basis. But he's been of help to us a few times, acting as a police surgeon when needed.'

'I will sign off the cost of a cab as necessary expense,' said Dunn.

So it was that very soon after, I, together with Morris and Sergeant Hepple, found ourselves crammed into a four-wheeler, of the sort nicknamed a growler from the rumble of its wheels, and similar to that driven by Wally Slater. I wished it had been Slater's cab. That would at least have been clean. There was a strong smell of wine dregs coming from these squabs suggesting that the previous night some gentlemen had been conveyed home in it, after spending the evening carousing. Some women of the town had accompanied them – and it was not hard to detect that. The overpowering scent of cheap perfume mingling with the wine told me. Our discomfort was increased by our cramped conditions. None of the three of us could be described as of small build. Hepple sat facing Morris and myself, his helmet on his knees and pearls of sweat running down his face and collecting in his ginger moustache, which acted as a sort of sponge. From time to time he mopped it with a large red-checked handkerchief.

'Let us not waste the time,' I said to him. 'Tell us everything from the beginning. Leave nothing out.'

'Well, sir,' began Hepple, 'there's not a great deal as I can tell you that I didn't mention already, upstairs in the superintendent's office – at the Yard.' Hepple spoke the word 'Yard' with deep reverence. 'Around half past eight, some youngsters down on the mudflats came upon a woman's body. They were what they call "mudlarks", sir, hunting for anything left by the river as the level dropped. They went running up from the river towards the High Street to seek help and ran straight into the parish clerk of that church, who was on his way to open up the building for the day. He went with them to where the dead woman lay. The tide had already turned, as I explained, and he knew that it would not be long before that stretch of riverbed would be completely under water again. So he told the three boys – that's how many of them there were, sir – to stand guard and promised them a shilling apiece if they let no one near. The clerk made it clear they mustn't touch the body or the clothing or take anything away. He was worried they might search the pockets, you see, sir. Then he went to find someone in authority.'

The growler lurched and stopped. We heard our driver roundly cursing the coachman of a private carriage that had insisted on taking precedence, as it was entitled to do, over a hackney carriage. After a few moments we rumbled onward again.

'Because of the urgency – the body being at risk of being covered by water – he went to the house of a magistrate, who is a member of that congregation, and was the nearest person available.' Hepple coughed into his hand. 'That's Mr Harrington, sir. Mr Harrington sent one of his servants to Wandsworth police station for us. Then he went with the parish clerk back to the shore and organised the removal of the body – and in the nick of time, for the water was only inches from it by then. They carried her to a shed in the grounds of a house nearby. It's by way of a potting shed, sir. There is a workbench in there and it was cleared and the woman laid out on that. The parish clerk had recognised her by then and declared her to be Miss Rachel Sawyer. She is the housekeeper at Fox House – or was.' There was a pause and then Hepple added, 'I gather she was a woman of a sour disposition.'

'How do you know that?' I asked in surprise.

'Not from personal acquaintance with her,' Hepple said hastily. 'But I heard the parish clerk say it to Inspector Morgan, when we got there.'

There seemed to have been quite a crowd gathering around the temporary mortuary. 'Was Mr Harrington, the magistrate, still there when you arrived, Sergeant?'

'No, sir, he'd left, having business to attend to elsewhere. When we received the news at Wandsworth Inspector Morgan set out at once, ordering myself and Constable Beck to accompany him. When we arrived we found the parish clerk waiting very anxiously, as he had paid off the boys with the promised shillings, and sent them about their business. He was all alone with the body.'

'It is a great pity,' I said, 'that he sent away the boys who actually discovered the body and are important witnesses. We shall have to try and find them again.'

'Yes, sir,' said Hepple, looking embarrassed. 'I fancy Mr Morgan was very put out that they had gone. But the parish clerk was in a bit of a state and not thinking straight. We'll find the young scamps again, never fear. They will go telling everyone they know about it and word will get back to us. Like as not they will be setting up regular guided tours, getting people to pay them a penny to show where the body was and describe it.' Hepple cleared his throat. 'Anyway, Mr Ross, we took a look at the deceased and the parish clerk offered to go and fetch Dr Croft. I think the clerk was glad of the excuse to leave the body. He was still looking very queasy. So, Dr Croft turned up. He was alone, the clerk having made some excuse about work to do in his vestry. You will be able to speak to the doctor yourself, sir, as I think he is waiting until you arrive. Constable Beck was put on guard over the shed, I was sent to the Yard, and the gardener sent home.'

'Gardener? Where did he come from?' exclaimed Morris.

'He'd helped earlier with the removal of the body into the shed. He had been hanging about since then, grumbling, because he wanted to be about his work, and objected very strongly to the use his potting shed had been put to! He was told he couldn't go into his shed while the body was still there. But he still hung about grousing until we told him it would be some hours before he could use the place and we didn't want him under our feet.

'Mr Morgan sent for an experienced detective to come – which is yourself, Mr Ross, and the sergeant here with you – because Mr and Mrs Lamont are well known and respected locally and wealthy folk. They will want everything done proper. She don't appear to have done herself in – killed herself – since there is no sign how she could have. Besides, she was a respectable woman. Mr Morgan declared it must be foul play and Dr Croft suggested it might be a case of strangulation. Well, we don't see too many murders in that locality, you see, so Mr Morgan considered it a job for the Yard.'

Morris gave a groan. 'Has no one taken any statements?'

Hepple looked offended. 'Mr Morgan was of the opinion that you would wish to speak to the witnesses yourself, Mr Ross. That is to say, to speak to the parish clerk and the doctor. Mr Harrington has not been able to await your arrival. He has business in town, as I think I mentioned.'

The noise from the growler's wheels increased suddenly. We had rolled on to the wooden bridge across the river to Putney.

'We're here, sir,' said Hepple, looking and sounding mightily relieved.

We had arrived before the church and clambered down. The news had got about, not surprisingly. An eager crowd had gathered in the street and various individuals in it started to point out the new arrivals to each other. 'It's the detectives!' we heard and, 'It's the Yard!' A couple of young fellows raised a somewhat derisive cheer. I paid off the cabman and, with Morris, set off in the wake of Sergeant Hepple, our guide.

'I don't know about this, Mr Ross,' muttered Morris. 'The boys who found her have been sent away, the body has been moved, and I don't know how many people have been called in to look at it before we arrive. Now half of Putney has turned up to see the show! All we lack is a brass band.'

We had been following a path alongside the river, which was still high and lapping at the bank, although here and there a streak of fresh glistening mud at the very edge suggested it was already turning. I asked Hepple when low water was again expected.

'Around half past three this afternoon, sir, or a few minutes before.'

It wouldn't help us. The place where the body had been discovered earlier was several feet below the surface of the water. When the tide receded, any evidence would have been washed away forever. There was a brick wall to our right. Leaning against it was a bearded man wearing a moleskin waistcoat and red neckerchief, arms folded. As we approached him, he demanded in a surly tone, 'How long is it going to be?'

'How long is what going to be?' snapped Morris.

'Until you move that woman out.'

'What's it to you?' demanded Morris, who was clearly out of sorts by now.

'I want my scythe. It's in the shed.'

'Scythe?' Morris sounded taken aback. 'Who are you, then? The Grim Reaper?'

'No, I'm Coggins, the gardener, and I was all ready to cut the grass today. Mr and Mrs Williams will be coming home tomorrow. They've been travelling in foreign parts. They will want to see the garden tidy and that's my job, to make sure it's so. But I can't do it without my scythe and that constable won't let me into my potting shed.'

'Mr Williams,' Hepple informed us, 'is the owner of the property where the shed is – where the body is. But he's away, as Mr Coggins has said, until tomorrow.'

'And he won't want to find a body in his shed and the grass not cut!' shouted the gardener after us as we abandoned him.

It wasn't long before we were greeted by the sight of the legs and boots of several small boys. They had scrambled as far as they could up a brick wall and were leaning over the top, clinging on for dear life and eager for macabre entertainment.

'Here we are,' said Hepple in relief. 'Oy!' he added in a shout, 'You just get down off there!'

The boys all dropped to the ground, some landing on their feet and others in small heaps on the path and rolling around.

'Were any of you among those who found the body?' I demanded, as they sorted themselves out and examined their bruises.

Disconsolately, they denied it. So we chased them away and opened a gate in the wall.

The potting shed was situated at the lower end of the garden, shielded by some bushes. As we approached I sniffed the air and thought I could detect pipe tobacco smoke. We rounded the leafy barrier to find a stalwart uniformed man, presumably Constable Beck, standing with his hands behind his back. A little further off stood two men in conversation. One, bulldog-like in stance and appearance, must be Morgan. The other – the tobacco smell had already betrayed him – was Dr Croft. Of the parish clerk there was no sign. Beck looked relieved at seeing his sergeant.

'Go and stand outside that gate,' Hepple ordered him, 'and keep those youngsters from coming back.'

I held out my hand to Morgan and introduced myself. He, in turn, began to introduce Croft.

'Inspector Ross and I are already acquainted,' said Croft before Morgan could complete his introduction.

'Well, Ross, I don't think we anticipated seeing one another again so soon!'

Morgan frowned at this unexpected turn in events, so I thought I should say hastily to him, 'I had reason to call on the doctor a few days ago. Yes, Dr Croft, I had not thought we'd meet again – certainly not in these circumstances.'

'The body's in there,' said Morgan, pointing at the shed with some impatience.

Four of us, myself and Morris, Morgan and Dr Croft, all squeezed into the small shed. Much of the room in there was taken up by a wooden bench from which all the clay pots had been swept and lay about higgledy-piggledy, some on the floor, two or three broken, the soil in them scattered together with any cuttings. I could imagine the gardener's reaction to that when he finally got in here and saw what had happened to all his careful labour. In addition the shed held implements, including the scythe, spades, forks and so on. Thick cobwebs hung across the roof space and a spider watched us from the corner where he lurked awaiting his prey.

But an earlier killer had struck. The body of a woman in a dark dress lay stretched on the workbench. Light from a small window above fell on her. Death can sometimes lend a dignity, even serenity, to a face. Sadly this is not often the case in those who have died violently. Rachel Sawyer, even as a younger woman, had probably never been a beauty, or even passably attractive. The face down on to which I gazed was plain almost to the point of ugliness, with thick eyebrows, a lumpy nose and coarse skin. The potting shed surroundings might have appeared unseemly for another corpse. But Rachel had been born and had died in workaday surroundings well suited to her. Her mouth was opened to reveal her tongue pressed against her upper teeth. Her eyes were open, bulging and glazed, her complexion livid and greying hair disordered. I gently moved aside a few strands of hair to reveal her earlobe. It was pierced to take an earring but none adorned it. There was no sign the jewellery had been torn out roughly by someone in haste, either by her killer or another. Had she not bothered to fix earrings before leaving the house because she was in a hurry? Or had it been because she felt that early mornings were not the time of day for any kind of 'dressing up'?

'Well, Doctor?' I asked.

This was Croft's area of expertise and he squeezed between us to join me by the body.

'It is not I who will be conducting the postmortem,' he said firmly. 'However, I have taken a quick look, and there are marks on the neck I would consider pressure points. I therefore suggest manual strangulation, throttling, as cause of death. At this point it can only be an educated guess. If whoever conducts the postmortem finds the hyoid bone fractured, that would confirm it. Here, you may see it for yourself.' He pulled down her collar a little.

I leaned over the body to see where he pointed. Just above the collar and below the jaw, the throat appeared swollen to my untutored eye, and there were dull red bruises.

'Would she have struggled, fought back?' I murmured, more to myself than in a question to Croft.

Croft answered anyway. 'Not necessarily. If the attack came suddenly, the assailant had strong hands and gripped her throat tightly, she might have died quite quickly, unable to do anything. I will say no more. I will leave it to your pathologist.'

I looked over my shoulder towards Morgan. 'Nothing has been removed?'

'Not that I know of,' said Morgan. 'Nor did the parish clerk mention removing anything. He's gone up to the church, where he has business, if you want to find him.'

'Have a word with him later,' I murmured to Morris, who nodded. 'And we are confident in the identification of her as Rachel Sawyer?'

'The clerk knew her as worshipping at the church and I know her by sight, too,' said Croft. 'That is Miss Sawyer, the housekeeper at Fox House. There is no doubt about it.'

'How long would you say she has been dead?'

'Not long,' Croft said firmly. 'Rigor is beginning but is very far from complete. I would estimate she has been dead four to five hours. It might even be a little less. It is never possible to be exact in these matters.'

'The clothing was not disarranged in any way?' I glanced at Morgan.

'She was as you see her now,' Morgan said. 'The parish clerk has assured me.' He paused. 'Bear in mind the body was originally found by young rascals foraging along the river bank. The clerk saw no purse or reticule lying on the mud, and no jewellery could be seen on her person.' (Morgan had checked this point as I had done, and mulled over the possible reason.) 'The boys may have removed that before they fetched help. It is a great pity the clerk sent them away. We are doing our utmost to find them. But if they took anything of value, they won't admit it. If they try and sell it, well, we might hear of that.'

We all jostled and squeezed our way out again. Croft tactfully wandered off a short distance and busied himself with refilling his pipe.

'Well,' said Morgan quietly. 'I am completely at your disposal, together with Constable Beck there, but otherwise I leave this in your competent hands, Mr Ross.'

'I'll be grateful for Constable Beck. Has the coroner been informed?'

'I sent a message by telegraph to his office. The coroner may give instructions regarding moving the body. We can't leave it here.' Morgan indicated the potting shed.

'Ideally,' I said, 'I'd like Dr Carmichael over at St Thomas's to take a look at it. He's examined a few murder victims in his time. I am not questioning the judgement of Dr Croft and I think we are probably agreed as to death being caused by manual strangulation. But we are laymen in medical matters and Croft has expressed himself unwilling to carry out a postmortem examination. In any case, that wasn't his line of medicine. I'd like to hear what Carmichael has to say. I have just one more question. Has anyone informed the woman's employers?'

Morgan gave a crooked smile. 'Well, now, Mr Ross,

Putney has grown apace over the last twenty or thirty years, but at heart it is still a small and close community. I would be surprised if no one at Fox House has heard the news of a body being discovered by the time you get there. As to whether they'll know it was Miss Sawyer's body, that's another matter. By rights they shouldn't.' He lowered his voice. 'But the church clerk may have spread the word already.'

'Well, then,' I said, 'it seems my first call must be at Fox House, and I must hope the clerk hasn't been there before me.'

We all left the garden with the exception of Constable Beck, who glumly remained on guard over the body.

Chapter Ten

I SENT Morris to run the parish clerk to earth. After that, if possible, he should trace Mr Harrington the magistrate. He must get statements from them both; and anyone else who might have seen Rachel Sawyer alive that morning. Then I set off alone for Fox House. I had feared that I might be followed all the way by a retinue of spectators, but they had dispersed. I suspected Sergeant Hepple had made sure of this. I had received precise directions from him and before long found myself standing where the wretched Mills must have stood some sixteen years before, in the shelter of the trees opposite the house.

Lizzie had added her description to that of Mills, so that I felt I knew this place already. There it was, a long, low building of considerable age that did suggest it might once have been an inn. But the busy road on which it once had stood was now a quiet lane, seeing hardly any traffic. Even if Lizzie and her helpers had not encountered a walker, who might well have been Lamont himself, Wally's cab would have attracted notice as it jolted by. I glanced up at the roof. There was little wind today and the running fox turned slowly back and forth as the breeze played with it. I fancied I could hear a faint creak. The old weathervane had stood aloft many years; if I were the owner, I'd send a man up there to check its safety. The window to the right of the main door, I conjectured, that is the parlour. Standing there to peer inside, Mills saw murder done. Now another murder connected with this house had brought me to it.

I walked across the road, up the path to the door. The ghostly form of Mills, soaked with rain, seemed to walk beside me and I had to drive away the unsettling notion. The brass knocker resounded with a dull echo within.

The door was opened by a butler. Well, I thought, it would seem the Lamonts keep more staff than the Cannings. A butler, Rachel Sawyer as housekeeper (doubling as companion to the lady of the house) and a cook, as it had not been suggested that Rachel had cooked. There must be a housemaid and probably a kitchenmaid, as Bessie had been before she came to work for Lizzie and me.

I produced my card. 'I am Inspector Ross of the Metropolitan Police at Scotland Yard, and I would like to speak to the house owners.'

Unimpressed, the butler eyed me, read my card, and eyed me again. 'Mr and Mrs Lamont are at table, sir. It is lunchtime.'

Being accustomed to work through the day when on a case without pausing to eat, I had not remembered that others kept a more regular timetable. It must be well after twelve by now.

'I am very sorry to disturb them, please apologise on my behalf. But I must speak to them now, without delay.'

'On what business shall I say, Inspector?'

'Official.'

The disapproving butler took my card away to convey news of my arrival to his employers. He returned within a few minutes to ask me to step inside and wait. He then left again. My arrival was clearly the subject of some discussion. I took the opportunity to look around me. The interior of the house matched the date of the building and its probable early use as an inn. This central hallway was wide enough to accommodate travellers arriving with luggage, and the walls panelled with aged dark oak. There was a smell of cooked food. One of the small rooms opening off to the left must be the dining room. To confirm this I heard the murmur of voices and a faint clatter as if someone had dropped a knife on a plate.

The butler returned and told me Mr Lamont would be there in a moment and made to retire. I stopped him.

'I would like to see both Mr and Mrs Lamont, if that is possible.'

I wanted to see the impact the news had on both of them. Supposing, of course, they hadn't heard already and had time to compose themselves and agree a reaction.

The butler looked at me as though there would be no end to the social faux pas I would make. But he said he would tell them. Meantime, he showed me into a small room on the right-hand side of the hall, with a low-beamed ceiling: the very parlour through the window of which, some sixteen years earlier, Mills had with horror watched Isaiah Sheldon die.

I had hoped for this and, while waiting, studied the room. It was eerily the same as Mills's description, adding substance to his story. An oil lamp still stood on a small table by the window, and yes, there stood a grandfather clock! There was the hearth with chairs set either side of it, although no fire was lit today. But the copper coal scuttle was filled to the brim and ready if needed. The chairs looked new. The one in which Isaiah Sheldon had died had been removed. It would have had a sad association but, in any case, after sixteen years and with new and younger owners, it was no surprise the furniture had changed. Two or three small oil paintings hung on the walls, family portraits I guessed, and by run-of-the mill artists. One was of special interest. It showed a middle-aged man of business, of florid complexion, wearing a black coat and shirt with high collar starched into sharp points and stock. His waistcoat was of a rich brocade and he stood with his hand resting on a thick accounts ledger. He looked a decent sort of commercial John Bull. This must be the late Isaiah Sheldon when still engaged in the coffee trade.

The door opened to a rustle of petticoats. A woman came in, closely followed by a man. He stepped forward in front of her and demanded, 'I am Charles Lamont – this is my wife. May we ask your business, Inspector Ross? And why it is necessary to disturb both of us?'

He cut a handsome figure, perhaps forty-five years of

age, with dark hair and moustache. He had, perhaps unconsciously, struck a pose, one arm hanging straight down by his side. The other arm was crooked to reach inside his coat to a silk brocade waistcoat rivalling that of Sheldon in the portrait, a forefinger hooked into one of the little pockets. A heavy gold watch chain of the type called an 'Albert' was strung across his midriff. If any artist were engaged to paint him, I thought, that is very much the pose he'd choose. He spoke crisply and appeared indignant. But I'd interrupted his luncheon and could not blame him for being displeased.

The woman, who now stood a little behind and to one side of him, was watching me warily. The detective in me – who lives as a voice in my head – whispered: this is a woman who knows something. But what it is, and whether it concerns the events of today, remains to be seen.

Or is her apprehension (I replied silently to that voice) based on concern that the man's aggression – at present only simmering beneath the surface – may lead him to say or do something unwise? From what Dunn had told me of the man (learned from the assistant commissioner), Lamont was of volatile temperament.

'I am very sorry to disturb you both and at such an inconvenient moment,' I began. 'I have to apologise on two accounts, because I am afraid I am also the bringer of bad news.'

'What sort of bad news?' asked Mrs Lamont quickly.

Lamont turned his head slightly to cast her a glance; before turning back to stare straight at me, his thick black eyebrows raised. 'Yes, Inspector, what kind of bad news?'

'You have not heard that a body was discovered earlier today down by the river?'

'No,' said Lamont simply.

'Ah, I had wondered if one of your servants might have heard the news. That sort of thing quickly gets spread about.'

'I do not encourage the servants to gossip,' said Mrs Lamont, and pressed her lips tightly together. She was a handsome woman – perhaps once the beauty described by the appreciative Mills – but now her manner appeared severe.

'Why is this discovery – very sad, of course – of any interest to us, Ross?' Lamont asked.

'Because it has been identified as being that of someone in your employ, your housekeeper, Miss Rachel Sawyer.'

At that, with a little gasp, Mrs Lamont collapsed on to the carpet in a dead faint and lay there insensible.

That put an end to the interview for quite a while. Lamont ran to the door and shouted for assistance. Then he bent over his wife in concern and seized one of her limp hands.

'Amelia? Amelia, my dear?' He looked up at me, his features working in fury. 'Are you a complete fool, Inspector?'

To be fair, he had reason for his rage. But I am a practical man. There was a sewing table in one corner of the parlour, the sort with little compartments for thread and so forth. Lizzie has one. I went quickly to it, and riffled through the contents until I found what I needed.

I turned to Lamont and held up a pair of scissors. 'You had best cut the lady's laces,' I said.

'*What?*' His face turned purple.

'Come, come, man!' I snapped. 'If she can't breathe properly there will be great difficulty in bringing her out of a swoon!'

Lamont blinked, then held out his hand. I passed the scissors to him and tactfully turned my back.

After a moment or two I heard the lady give a faint moan and I can confess to you freely that I was very pleased to hear it.

'I'm sorry,' I said, swivelling to face him. 'I did warn you it was bad news.'

'Bad news?' Lamont struggled to control himself. He was still kneeling by his wife. He had rolled her on to her side and the back of her bodice was still unhooked. The scissors lay on the carpet and I assumed he'd cut the staylaces, as I'd suggested. Lamont glowered up at me. 'Your claim is nonsense, in any case. If a body has been found it cannot be that of Sawyer. She has duties in this house. She cannot – could not – have been anywhere near the river this morning.'

Amelia Lamont was stirring and appeared to be coming out of her faint. Help arrived at that moment in the persons of the butler and two maids. The maids patted Mrs Lamont's hands and urged her to speak. The butler, who with foresight had brought a jug of water, took it upon himself to sprinkle a little with great delicacy on the lady's face. I was irresistibly put in mind of a clergyman baptising a baby. Mrs Lamont was assisted by the maids, first to a sitting position, and then to her feet. She was half-carried, half-led from the room, the maids supporting her to either side. The butler would have followed behind with his jug of water, but Lamont called him back.

'Ask Miss Sawyer to come to the drawing room at once!' To me he added, 'We will settle this nonsense once and for all. There has clearly been a mistake. The body of which you told us cannot be Sawyer's.'

'Miss Sawyer does not appear to be in the house, sir,' replied the butler in tones of deep regret. 'I have not seen her myself this morning.'

Lamont muttered an oath and waved the butler away. The man departed with his jug of water.

Now we were alone, Lamont turned his full fury on me. 'I asked you earlier why you needed to see us both. Now I ask you again. If this wretched woman *is* Sawyer, why could you not have broken the news to me and left me to break it to my wife? Could you not foresee what a shock it would be to her? This whole scene has been a disgrace! Improper, embarrassing and totally unnecessary. I shall complain most forcefully to your superiors.'

I couldn't reply that I had needed to see her reaction for myself. It had told me an important fact: that she had not known about the body or, if she had, certainly not known that it might be Rachel Sawyer's. As for his threat to complain about me at the Yard, if he chose to do so, he might find he had to join a queue of aggrieved persons, bringing up the rear behind the governor of Newgate, the home secretary, the commissioner of the

Metropolitan Police and Mr Hubert Canning, taxpayer.

'I understand your dismay,' I told him. 'Unfortunately, in inquiries of this nature, the usual conventions have to be discarded.'

'Inquiries?' he asked sharply. 'You have brought us the news. You claim to know the identity of this unfortunate woman. Even if it is Sawyer, of which I am still not convinced, then neither my wife nor I was aware she had left the house. How can we help you any further? Where is – where is the body?'

'At the moment it is temporarily housed in a potting shed in the garden of a house near to the spot where she was found.'

'Potting shed?' cried Lamont.

'The body had to be moved to prevent the rising river level covering it. She was found on the mud.'

'Sawyer threw herself into the river? Good grief, why on earth should she do that? She was a level-headed woman and devoid of any imagination. She gave no indication of being suicidal. She lived here in comfort. What on earth could have prompted such a desperate act?'

'No, Mr Lamont, you misunderstand. You will appreciate that there has been no time for a proper post-mortem examination nor for the coroner to rule on the body, but we have reason to believe we are dealing with a case of murder.'

'Murder?' Lamont shouted. 'No, that is impossible! Who would kill her and why? She was . . . nobody of any significance, a housekeeper for many years in this house.

Murders don't happen in Putney, Inspector, or certainly not in respectable households!'

'Sadly, Mr Lamont, I have to inform you that murder in respectable households is surprisingly well known to the police.'

Lamont spun on his heel and walked to the window where he stood, his hands clasped behind his back, staring out at the trees on the further side of the road. 'There is no doubt?' He spoke without turning, his tones now muted.

'It doesn't appear so, sir. The woman is dead. Two people have named her.'

'They could both be mistaken. Some errand may have called Sawyer away early. She may yet return.' His voice was flat and carried no conviction.

I did not try to answer this and my silence ended his resistance to the news.

'Who found her?'

'Some mudlarks. I am afraid this means considerable disruption to your household. Miss Sawyer's movements must be traced in detail, what time she left the house, whether she was alone, went directly to the river bank, spoke to anyone in the vicinity and so forth. It would have been early this morning. Can you think of any reason why she should have been down by the river at that hour?'

'Of course I can't!' he snapped. 'There *is* no reason why she should be there.'

'But she is not here, where she might be expected to be,' I reminded him gently.

Lamont blinked. 'Who are the two people who identified her?'

'The parish clerk of St Mary's church and also Dr Croft.'

'Croft? Is he not retired? He must be as old as Methuselah.'

'He was the nearest doctor to hand, so they fetched him. I understand that Dr Croft is in his late seventies, retired indeed, but not quite as old as the Biblical personage you mention.'

'Well, well . . .' muttered Lamont, scowling.

'I'm afraid I need to ask you, as her employer, if you would assist us by coming with me now to identify her in addition to the two gentlemen I mentioned. Usually, it is a relative or a close associate who makes the identification and it's as well to stick to the rules in these cases.' I paused. 'And you can satisfy yourself that there has been no mistake.'

'You want me to go down to this garden shed?' He sounded resentful. I couldn't say whether it was the notion of viewing Rachel's corpse or doing so in the humble surroundings of a potting shed that disturbed him most.

'Yes, sir. But I need first to ask your other staff if any of them saw her earlier. It is very important we establish when she left the house.'

'Wait here!' ordered Lamont and walked out of the room.

I was reminded of Canning, who had been similarly anxious to prime his employees before I questioned them.

Lamont was gone some minutes. When he returned, he was accompanied by the ubiquitous butler and a waif-like child, about twelve or thirteen years of age, dressed in an over-large grey gown and apron.

'Johnson will explain,' Lamont said briefly, with a gesture towards the butler.

'Miss Sawyer customarily ate breakfast alone in her sitting room,' the butler said to me. 'She required only tea and toast and it was taken up to her, on a tray, by Harriet here.'

The waif gave me a look of panic.

'Don't be afraid, Harriet,' I urged her. 'What is your position in the household?'

'I wash up, sir,' whispered Harriet.

'Harriet is the skivvy,' said the butler.

Interesting, I thought. No housemaid carried the housekeeper's breakfast tray up to her, as might be expected. The task was given to the lowly skivvy.

'You took Miss Sawyer her breakfast tray this morning as usual?'

'Yes, sir.'

'What time was this?'

'Seven o'clock, sir, as usual.' Harriet was almost inaudible. 'Hot water goes up at half past six. Breakfast tray at seven.'

I wanted to ask her to speak up but worried that might frighten her even more. 'Did she speak to you?' I asked encouragingly.

'Yes, sir, she said, "Put it on the table." She meant the tray, sir. So I did – and I left.'

'She gave no indication she was going out? How was she dressed?'

'As usual, sir.' Harriet looked bewildered.

'Was she wearing a cape or shawl or a hat – anything that suggested she was just about to leave the house?'

'No, sir.' Harriet's pale face unexpectedly brightened. 'She was wearing her balmorals, sir.'

The girl was more observant than the earlier part of the interview had suggested. Rachel had not been wearing her usual indoor shoes, but the stout ladies' walking boots made popular by Her Majesty on her Scottish holidays. I cast my mind back to the corpse lying on the bench in the shed. I had not paid particular attention to her footwear. I should have done so.

'Did you see Miss Sawyer leave the house, Harriet?'

A shake of the head. 'It's awful busy in the kitchen in the morning, sir.'

'No one saw her leave,' intoned Johnson. 'I have inquired of Cook and the maids. I myself did not see her at all this morning.'

'She did not usually appear in the kitchen in the mornings?'

'Not before eleven, sir. She would then come to discuss the luncheon with Cook.'

'So you were all surprised in the kitchen when she did not appear as usual at eleven?'

The butler looked affronted at the idea that anything might surprise him. 'Cook had things well in hand, sir. Mrs Lamont sometimes required Miss Sawyer for other duties. It occasioned no surprise.'

I was reminded of Admiral Nelson's famous words, on putting the telescope to his blind eye, 'I see no ships!' In this well-trained household, the presence of the police was an unacceptable intrusion. None of the servants would have seen anything that morning. Avenues of inquiry had already been blocked.

'One more thing, Harriet,' I said to the kitchenmaid. 'When you went back to fetch the tray, had Miss Sawyer drunk her tea and eaten her toast?'

'Yes, sir, but only eaten one piece of toast. She left the tray outside her door as usual. I just picked it up and took it back to the kitchen.'

There was no more to glean from Harriet. I nodded to the butler and said, 'Thank you.'

Johnson looked relieved and gave Harriet a little push to usher her back to her dirty dishes.

'Bring me my hat and cane, Johnson,' Lamont ordered him. 'I am just going out with the inspector. Tell Mrs Lamont I will be back by four?' The query in his voice was addressed to me.

'I would hope so, sir,' I said. I'd hate to disturb his tea table as well as luncheon.

When we were outside the property, I asked Lamont: 'Is there some little-used route from here to the river? I walked here along the High Street and up Putney Hill to an inn called the Green Man. I then struck off across the heath. Is there another way, one that would avoid the High Street and most of the houses?'

Lamont stared and tapped his chin with the silver head

of his cane. 'There is a footpath that skirts the rear of the properties near the river; and comes out where there is open land on the banks. You think that is the way Sawyer would have walked?'

'I am interested in all the usual ways of reaching the river from here. As I said, I walked here the most obvious way. I'd like to see the other. My sergeant will be making inquiries in the High Street and around to find out if anyone saw Miss Sawyer there very early this morning. I don't want to cover the same ground.'

Lamont looked at me thoughtfully before turning and leading the way across the road and into the copse.

'Can you think of any reason that would have led to Miss Sawyer leaving the house to go anywhere without letting anyone know, so early in the morning?' I asked as we followed a narrow path between the trees.

'None,' he said briefly. He swished his cane at a clump of nettles. 'I have told you so already. Her private life, if she had one, was her own business. I doubt if a woman so dull had a private life.'

It was important I did not reveal to him that I already knew something of his household. So I asked him now, 'Has Miss Sawyer been a long time in your employ?'

'Yes.' He paused and then realised I was waiting for him to elaborate. 'Fox House was my wife's family home. She lived there with her late uncle, and inherited it on his death. Sawyer was already employed there and remained.'

'She had been the housekeeper to Mrs Lamont's uncle?'

'No, she was a housemaid in his time.' Lamont did

not like this conversation and I was beginning to get the impression he had not much liked Rachel Sawyer.

'What would have been Mrs Lamont's maiden name?'

'Sheldon!' said Lamont curtly. 'What has this to do with Sawyer's body being found this morning?'

'Fox House was also Miss Sawyer's home,' I said to him. 'I am very interested to learn how long she'd worked there and anything at all about her.'

'Seventeen years!' snapped Lamont. 'And, before you ask and since you are so anxious to know every detail, my wife and I have been married fifteen years.'

So Rachel had been merely a housemaid at Fox House, and for only a year when Isaiah Sheldon died. It seemed to me most odd that Amelia Sheldon had promoted her to housekeeper. Rachel could have had no real experience for the job, other than dusting and making beds. She had gone from that, in a single leap, to directing all the other staff, dealing with tradesmen, making all manner of domestic arrangements – and being a sort of companion to her mistress.

'Did Miss Sheldon – as she was when she inherited the house – keep on all her late uncle's staff?'

'No, only Sawyer.' Lamont was now clearly uneasy. 'My wife was very fond of Sawyer. That is why she fainted when you revealed to us – in a brutal manner – that her dead body had been discovered.'

All this confirmed what Wally Slater and Lizzie had gleaned. 'It was very useful to you, no doubt, that Mrs Sheldon had someone like Miss Sawyer on whom she could rely.' This was really needling the man and I waited to see how he'd reply.

He stopped short and turned to face me. 'You may as well know, Inspector Ross, that I found Sawyer a tiresome woman and I made sure to have as little to do with her as possible. I would have liked to dismiss her but my wife wouldn't hear of it. She had become very dependent on Sawyer and, as she needed some female company, it suited her to have the woman there. I didn't suit me particularly but I should stress that, as housekeeper, Sawyer acquitted herself well. She was, I do believe, devoted to my wife. My wife and I have no children. If we'd had a young family, my wife's interests would have been different and Sawyer might not have wished to stay. However . . .' He shrugged and started to walk on very quickly, swinging his cane.

We had crossed the heath and begun to walk downhill, keeping our silence. I could see buildings ahead. Now Lamont touched my elbow.

'This way!' He pointed his cane and led me along a narrow footpath to the rear of some gardens. I conjectured we would occasionally be visible from the upper windows and at other times shielded by trees and fencing. The path took a steeper downward angle. A gull swept overhead. We were not far from the river. Without warning, we suddenly stepped out into an open grassed area with a few trees, and I found myself gazing across the brown water at a procession of barges making their way up river. I consulted my watch. It had taken us a good half-hour, striding out at a brisk pace with the occasional brief pause to talk, unimpeded by traffic and downhill most of the way.

I was now convinced this was the route Rachel Sawyer would have taken just after seven that morning. (Harriet had taken up the tea and toast at seven. Rachel was already wearing walking boots. She had taken a couple of minutes to drink the tea and eat one slice of the bread, but not to finish the rack of toast.) It would have taken Rachel, with her shorter woman's strides but wearing serviceable boots, slightly longer than it had taken us. If she had gone to meet someone near the river, the rendezvous must have been set for around a quarter to eight. The early hour and the secretive way she'd left the house indicated the very private nature of the meeting. She and the other person would not want to be observed and this spot was a likely one agreed for the meeting. I turned my head and looked back. None of the properties we'd passed would have an uninterrupted view of the location. Rachel's killer, if he had chosen it, had chosen well.

A little later we stood in the potting shed, still guarded by the dependable Constable Beck, and gazed down on the dead face of Rachel Sawyer.

Lamont's face bore an expression of disgust. He glanced at our surroundings. 'Surely she cannot be left here? What of the owners of the property?'

'Arrangements are in hand to move the body. I would prefer it taken across the river for postmortem examination. It may be, however, that it is taken to a mortuary chapel or some such place here in Putney and the pathologist will come out here to examine her. That's not certain and depends on the coroner.'

'She'll be as stiff as a board if you don't get on with it,' Lamont said callously.

His tone shocked me and I'm not easily shocked. I said nothing.

'Her clothes are muddy,' Lamont said next. 'Are you sure she did not attempt to drown herself?'

'Muddy is not wet,' I told him. That reminded me to examine her boots. I did so, watched with interest by Lamont. The boots were dusty and the soles had some soil clinging to them. But there was no trace of river mud. The boys had found the body on the mudflats and the clothing had mud on it. So, after killing her, the murderer had moved her body, either dragging or carrying it down to the river where a stretch of mud had not yet been covered.

Yes! I thought. The killer had timed this well. Did that indicate a premeditated murder? Had he planned that the water spreading out across the mud would cover the body and destroy evidence? She might have floated or been swept away. If she were later washed ashore, or spotted half-submerged, it would be thought a drowning like Maria Thompson's. If only the police could have been there before the river covered the site. There would surely have been deep footprints, perhaps a long furrow in the mud showing where the body had been dragged to its resting place. I must ask about that. It was imperative we find the boys who discovered the body. They might have observed something. The parish clerk might have noticed such a mark in the sludge, although he seemed to have been in something of a panic. Harrington, the magistrate, might have kept a cooler head.

'Must we stay here any longer?' demanded Lamont with an irritated gesture at our surroundings. 'I am anxious to return to my wife. This is a time I should be by her side.'

'Of course. Thank you for coming, sir. One last question – do you know if Miss Sawyer has any relatives who should be informed?'

'I have no idea. I never heard of any. My wife might know. But Sawyer never asked leave to go visiting anyone. Nor did anyone, to my knowledge, ever come to see her.'

We were outside the shed now, and I saw Morris approaching.

'Ah,' I said to Lamont, 'here is my sergeant.'

Lamont eyed Morris up and down. 'He is in ordinary clothing, as are you.'

'We are members of the plainclothes division of the criminal investigation department, sir.'

'I suppose it's better than having uniformed men swarming all over the place!' he muttered.

Morris raised an eyebrow at this discourtesy, and Constable Beck was heard to mumble something we luckily could not catch.

'I still need to talk to Mrs Lamont,' I said to Charles Lamont. 'Especially as she had such a long and close acquaintance with the deceased.'

'Then you will have to come tomorrow,' retorted Lamont. 'She is in no fit state to talk to you today. Come tomorrow, about eleven in the morning – before luncheon!' he added in a parting shot.

'Who is that gentleman, then?' asked Morris, as Lamont disappeared into the distance.

'The dead woman's employer.'

'Could he tell us anything, Mr Ross?'

'Not much, not yet. Whether he knows more than he says is another matter.'

Chapter Eleven

I DECIDED to take Superintendent Dunn's offer of the cost of a cab to Putney as expenses to mean a cab in both directions. So Morris and I, having walked across the bridge to Fulham, soon found a free conveyance and started back for the Yard.

I told him what I'd learned as we jolted along. 'She was murdered somewhere on the river bank near to where she was found. Her outer clothes were muddied but her boots surprisingly little, and her undergarments were dry. So she had been lying on the mud but she had not walked on it. She was dragged or carried to the place she was found. We must send a couple of experienced men over there as soon as we get back – see to it, Morris. They must search the banks and open area carefully. There may be some clue indicating a struggle, some broken or trampled vegetation, or the killer may have dropped something. We can hope for that, but I don't really expect it. The best thing would be if someone saw her, preferably in the company of another.'

'No one that I talked to saw her,' replied Morris. 'I found that parish clerk and he told me pretty well what

Sergeant Hepple told us. He also apologised for dismissing the boys who found the body. He thought they would be under our feet, in the way. He's never been involved in a murder investigation before and he didn't think the boys' testimony would be needed. I also managed to speak very briefly to Mrs Harrington – the wife of the magistrate who ordered the body taken to the shed. Her husband had left word with her that he will call at the Yard, perhaps late today. He has business until then. I made extensive inquiries in the High Street and along the river bank, but no one remembered anyone resembling Miss Sawyer so early in the day. She was well known to tradesmen. If she'd walked down the High Street, any time before eight o'clock, I do believe she'd have been noticed by shopkeepers as she passed by.'

'I am fairly sure she did not walk down the High Street, but took pains to avoid being observed.' I told him about the path Lamont and I had taken.

'Ah,' said Morris. 'I wonder what she was up to?'

'I am wondering why this obviously planned murderous attack took place *now* . . .' I mused, half to myself.

'Now, Mr Ross?' asked Morris.

I was obliged to explain. 'See here, Morris, Rachel Sawyer had been employed as housekeeper and companion to Mrs Lamont at Fox House since the death of Isaiah Sheldon, sixteen years ago. She was not a newcomer, having, I have now learned, previously worked there as a housemaid. In all that time, there does not appear to have been anything against her other than that the other servants didn't care for her much – nor, by his admission, did her employer, Mr Lamont, though even he thought her competent. Certainly, Sergeant Hepple heard the clerk tell Inspector Morgan that Miss Sawyer was a woman of sour disposition. That is hardly cause for murder.'

'Jealousy on the part of another servant?' suggested Morris. 'If she'd been made not only housekeeper but also a sort of companion by Mrs Lamont before her marriage.'

'Indeed she had and, from what Lamont said to me, I gather Mrs Lamont wouldn't hear of Rachel being dismissed. But a jealous servant who waits sixteen years to exact revenge? No, no. It raises two questions in my mind, Morris. First, why now, after so many apparently uneventful years, did Rachel Sawyer become involved in something that led to her murder?'

'Something new had come up,' offered Morris. 'She'd got involved with someone outside the household, perhaps?'

'Then we must find out who it was. Second, why did Mrs Lamont choose to keep as a sort of confidante, as well as housekeeper, such an unsociable person? Lamont says his wife needed female company. Very well, but surely, she could have found a companion more agreeable and suitable to have close than a former maidservant of, presumably, little education or worldly interests. What did they talk about together? Fashion? Hardly. Mrs Lamont is a well-dressed female, but Rachel Sawyer's garments, as we saw them, were, frankly, dowdy. Did the two women discuss books? I don't suppose Rachel ever read one. Travel? If the Lamonts travelled, I can't see them taking Rachel with them. Yet Lamont describes his wife as being very fond of Sawyer and dependent on her. What had those women in common, Morris?'

Morris frowned. Then his expression cleared. 'The late Mr Sheldon, sir.' He saw that I looked surprised and added, 'Well, Miss Sawyer worked for him and then worked for his niece, the present Mrs Lamont. He's the link, as it seems to me.'

'You never let me down, Morris,' I said. 'You are quite right.'

'Thank you, sir. But it still doesn't exactly explain it. I can't get over how an ordinary housemaid could make the jump to housekeeper and companion, just like that. It doesn't happen, Mr Ross. You have to work your way on up the ladder, as it were, on the staff of well-to-do households. They're very particular about that sort of thing below stairs!'

'No – it shouldn't have happened and now we know about it, it explains the attitude of the present staff towards Rachel Sawyer. They weren't employed in Mr Sheldon's day, but they would know that Rachel had made that leap, and it offended them to have her directing them as housekeeper when, in their minds, she was no more than a housemaid.'

We had reached the Yard. As our cab rattled away, I added to Morris, 'There is something else, too.'

'Yes, Mr Ross?'

'Bless me, I can't tell you,' I was forced to admit. 'It was something in that house, something that took my attention but then – I don't know. I've forgotten what it was and why it struck me. It was that wretched woman fainting like that. It destroyed my concentration.'

'Likely as not, that's why she did it,' observed Morris. His years as a police officer have sadly made him sceptical.

I went to inform the superintendent of my progress and sent a message over to St Thomas's hospital for Dr Carmichael, advising him that the coroner would soon be asking him to carry out a postmortem examination, at a place yet to be established but probably in Putney.

That matter at least was settled quickly. The magistrate, Mr Harrington, arrived at the Yard with apologies for not having been able to await our arrival in Putney.

'We are obliged to you for coming in, sir,' I assured him.

He was a tall, lean man, perhaps sixty years old, formally clad in a black coat. He sat down and rested his hat on his knees and his gloves on his hat, his movements precise. When satisfied, he looked up.

'This is a shocking business and I wish I could tell you something to help you trace the culprit, Inspector Ross. But I fear that is unlikely. I realise that the body having been moved will hinder your investigations. But there was no choice, as I hope you understand. I am not a police officer, of course, but a simple Justice of the Peace. However, it was clear to me that to save the body from inundation, the unfortunate woman must be moved at once, so I took it upon myself to give the order.'

'I do understand, sir, and am grateful that you were able to move it to a safe location so nearby.'

'It will have to be moved again from there today. I suggest the undertaker's premises in Putney. If you agree, I can arrange that immediately on my return,' Harrington suggested. 'I understand Mr and Mrs Williams are about to return home and they won't want to be greeted by a corpse in their potting shed.' The magistrate paused. 'I will offer them my excuses for using their premises in such a way. Williams is a reasonable fellow. I am not sure how his good lady will take the news.'

'Thank you. Please add my regrets and tell them I'll call on them as soon as I have a moment, to apologise in person. Meanwhile, I'll inform the coroner and the pathologist of the location. I would like you to describe, if you would, the scene when you first came upon it. Any little detail, however trivial, will help us.'

Harrington nodded. 'I have given it much thought. The parish clerk to St Mary's had brought me the dreadful news. He was very agitated, as might be expected. Bodies have been washed up before, from time to time, along that stretch of the river, but not in recent months. When we arrived back at the scene, we found some boys, three of them, standing by the body. They were the discoverers of the corpse, and one of them had originally taken the news to the clerk. Fortunately he had happened to be at the church. He'd asked them to stand guard and they had done so efficiently.'

'Did you see anything on the mud, any disturbance that looked unusual?'

'It was very disturbed. The boys had been tramping about in it and also been digging in it, seeking valuables of any nature. The clerk had added his own footprints. I did notice, however, that a long rut, as I think I might describe it, had been scored across the mud between the body and the bank.'

Bless you, Mr Harrington! I thought. 'Would you say this rut might have been caused by the body being dragged across the mud?'

'I might. I hesitate to say so for sure.' Harrington was not a man to speculate. 'I explained to him that she must be moved at once to avoid the encroaching river. We called out to a labourer we saw walking along the river bank. He proved to be the gardener in the employ of Mr Williams, on his way to work. He came across and helped us carry the poor soul to the potting shed. The house has a gate facing the river, so it seemed the ideal place, with ease of access. We did not have to carry her far and the family was away.' Earnestly, he added: 'We had to get her out of sight before too many people began using the area. We should have had a mob around us in no time.'

'I dare say,' I offered, 'that the gardener didn't much like the plan.'

Harrington gave a wry smile. 'He protested that he was responsible for his employer's property and it would cost him his place. I overruled him and promised to appease Mr Williams. The truth, I fancy, is that, like many gardeners, the potting shed is his refuge as well as a place to keep his tools and seedlings! He was mortally offended at our commandeering it.'

Harrington gave a wry smile, and then grew sober. 'It

was when we began to lift her that we had a closer sight of her, and that's when we recognised her. The parish clerk was already in a highly nervous state, and when he realised this was someone he actually knew, I am afraid the poor fellow went quite to pieces. I managed to calm him down.'

'Did you see anything lying on the mud that might have belonged to her?'

'No,' Harrington shook his head. 'But the water had already almost reached the body and anything of that sort might have been covered already. I had become somewhat muddied during the process of moving her. I had business in town and so had to hurry away immediately home again to change my clothes. I have learned that after I left the clerk dismissed the boys. I should have reminded him to keep them there, as they discovered her.'

'Inspector Morgan at Wandsworth is hopeful of finding them again,' I consoled him. 'You say you knew Rachel Sawyer—'

He interrupted me, raising his hand. 'Not well, only in that I have long been a churchwarden and knew her as a member of the congregation. Other than her name and that of her employers, I can tell you nothing. She did not appear to have any friends in the congregation. I never saw people stop to chat to her after the services.'

'How about her employers, Mr and Mrs Lamont? Are you acquainted with them?'

'Again, in my role of churchwarden only. Although many years ago I did know Mrs Lamont's late uncle, Isaiah Sheldon, quite well.'

'Oh? I have heard his name . . .' I managed to say casually.

'I expect you will have done, if you have spoken to anyone in the Putney area,' Harrington told me. 'He was a noted local philanthropist and much missed. A very fine old gentleman who had made a fortune in the coffee trade.'

'Yes, I have heard of his generosity. But he's been dead some time, I fancy?'

'Oh, it must be fifteen years at least, even more.' Harrington nodded. 'He died suddenly and it was a shock to all. Mind you, he was of advanced age.'

'He'd been in failing health?' I was afraid the casual tone might start to sound forced. Mr Harrington was no fool.

'I understood the doctor had been calling on him. It often happens that a man of his age might fail suddenly, I dare say. When I say it was a shock, I did not mean it was so much a surprise, because he was in his eighties. I meant that those charitable enterprises that depended on his support were temporarily left without a generous benefactor.'

'Mrs Lamont took up where her uncle left off, perhaps?'

Harrington treated me to a perceptive look. He had begun to see there was a trend to my questions. 'I do not think so, Inspector Ross, but I have no detailed knowledge.'

He stood up and set his hat carefully on his head. 'I can tell you no more, Inspector. But if I think of anything I shall, naturally, get in touch at once.'

Elizabeth Martin Ross

Frustratingly, I could not return to Putney. I understood why. But to stay at home and twiddle my thumbs was intolerable. I had to find something else to occupy me.

'I intend to go to Dorset Square this afternoon and visit Mrs Parry,' I told Bessie. 'Would you like to come too? You'd like to see your old friends below stairs, I expect.'

'I can't say as they was particularly friendly to me, when I was working there,' retorted Bessie. 'But I don't mind a bit of a gossip.'

Visiting my Aunt Parry, as she liked me to call her, was not something I enjoyed much, but it was a duty. She had been kind enough to take me in as her companion when I had been alone in the world, without a roof of my own or any fortune. Companions tended to pass through Aunt Parry's household in a steady procession. I doubt I would have lasted very long, either. However, Ben arrived on the scene, rather like the knight in the old tales, and rescued me. But to ignore Aunt Parry now would be unforgivable. So Bessie and I set off for Dorset Square by a succession of omnibuses. It is not a comfortable way to travel and the risk of gaining a flea or two as a friend very high, but I didn't think I could really justify a cab again. The trip to Putney and back with Wally had made quite a dent in my housekeeping budget.

Bessie scurried off down the basement steps to the kitchen. Simms, the butler, showed me into Aunt Parry's drawing room – where I found a surprise waiting for me.

She was not alone and the visitor was male. He got to his feet at my entry and greeted me with a broad grin.

'Frank!' I cried. 'I thought you still abroad!'

When I had lived in Dorset Square as Aunt Parry's companion, her nephew, Frank Carterton, had also lived there, preparing to go out to our embassy in Russia in a diplomatic role. This had been a source of great concern to Aunt Parry who was convinced he would be eaten by bears. Since then, Frank had moved on to China, where Aunt Parry imagined even worse fates. But it seemed he'd escaped all dangers.

'I arrived back in England ten days ago,' Frank explained to me. 'And very good it is to be here – to see Aunt Julia again . . .'

He turned a smile on Mrs Parry, who basked in it. I had read the expression but never before seen anyone actually do it. It was as if a ray of sun had fallen on her face.

'Dear Frank,' she cooed. 'Oh, Elizabeth, you can have no idea what a relief it is to see my nephew here again, safe and sound. What I have suffered by way of worry since he left for the East, you cannot imagine. It was bad enough when he was in Russia, but in China . . . So far away, so – so *foreign*!

'I lived very comfortably there, Aunt Julia. I wrote and told you so,' protested Frank.

'My dear boy, of course you did. You wanted to allay my fears. But I was not fooled. You were suffering terrible hardship, I know it.'

Frank caught my eye and winked. A career in the

diplomatic service has not cured you, Frank Carterton! I thought. You are still incorrigible.

'Rice!' exclaimed Aunt Parry suddenly. 'Nothing but rice, it must have been intolerable.'

'Truly, Aunt Julia, I ate a varied diet and not only rice.'

She was not prepared to listen. 'The Chinese do such dreadful things to people. I have read of it. Death by a thousand cuts!'

'That is a misinterpretation often heard here in the West,' protested Frank. 'They do, indeed, have some unpleasant ways of execution. But the death by a thousand cuts refers to the manner in which the corpse – after death – is dismembered into many small pieces. It's a way of underlining the punishment. It inhibits the spirit, making it very difficult for it to reassemble itself in the afterlife.'

'Whatever it is,' said Aunt Parry firmly, 'it does not sound the sort of thing that would ever happen in Britain. Now then, as Elizabeth is here, we shall have tea. Do ring the bell, Frank.'

'Are you without a companion, Aunt Parry?' I asked. There was no sign of the usual depressed female presence.

Aunt Parry threw up her hands. 'You remember Laetitia Bunn?'

'I do remember Miss Bunn. I thought her very pleasant.'

'She married a curate!' snapped Aunt Parry. 'No thought for me. You girls are all the same. You are always running off and getting married. It will do her no good.

Her husband has no influence to obtain a living of his own and they will starve. Yes, Simms, we'll have tea now. Are there any scones? I did particularly ask this morning for scones.'

'Crumpets, scones, seed cake and éclairs, madam,' said Simms gravely.

'Oh, good!' Aunt Parry clapped her podgy hands together. 'We should be able to manage with that.'

Frank cast his gaze ceilingwards.

Our tea party proved very jolly. Frank had set himself to be entertaining, something he was very good at, and Aunt Parry devoured an extraordinary amount of the good things sent up by Mrs Simms, the cook. She punctuated her mouthfuls with little cries of pleasure, although it was not always clear whether on account of Frank's anecdotes or the cakes.

Shortly after Simms had carried the remaining crumbs away, however, Aunt Parry fell silent and once or twice nodded.

At last she gathered herself together and stood up, with some effort. 'My dears, you will excuse me? I am unaccountably a little sleepy. I think I will go and rest. So nice to see you, dear Elizabeth. My kindest regards to the police inspector.'

When we were alone, Frank asked, 'Well, Lizzie? How are you really? And Ross? Still keeping us safe from desperate criminals?'

'We are both very well, thank you. Yes, Ben is doing his best. By the way, Aunt Parry seems to believe we don't chop up dead bodies in Britain, but the unclaimed bodies of the poor are routinely sent to the schools of anatomy. They are often unclaimed only because there is no legal claimant – not because no one comes forward. It can cause great distress when illegitimate children, for example, are refused a parent's body to bury. Many of the poor still believe that a dissected body won't be able to rise up at the Last Trump.'

'Dear Lizzie,' said Frank, 'you are the only lady I have ever met who would introduce that as a topic of drawing-room conversation. I am so glad to find you unchanged!'

He leaned back in his chair and looked thoughtful. 'There are some other changes here. I'd been away for so long, I think I had forgotten just how much Aunt Julia eats. Well, she always did enjoy a good table. But, is my memory at fault, or is she really eating even more?'

'Because you've been away, you probably notice it,' I told him. 'I think she has put on a little weight, however.'

'A string of medical men over the years have told her to keep to plain fare. This going off to have a nap in the afternoon is something new. She never did that when I lived here.' Frank looked worried.

'I've not seen her do that before, either,' I admitted.

'I am fond of her, you know,' Frank said suddenly.

'I know you are,' I assured him. 'She is devoted to you. She really did worry about you all the time you were abroad.'

'Hm, well, she may not have to do that much longer,' was the enigmatic reply.

'Are you not to return to China, Frank? Will you now be off to some other exotic place?'

'You may as well know that my career in the diplomatic may soon be over. Aunt Julia is keen that I go into politics. I am to stand for parliament.'

'What?' I gasped. 'Oh, sorry, Frank, that sounded impolite. I am sure you – you would do very well as a member of parliament, but is this truly going to happen?'

'She has been manoeuvring frantically for months, ahead of my return from Peking, to find me a safe and available seat. She knows an awful lot of influential people, and for a while she has been calling in her markers – if you'll excuse my using a gambling term. It is common knowledge that there will be a general election before the end of this year. As it happens, a suitable seat will become vacant. The sitting member has let it be known that he will retire at the next election, due to his age and infirmity. It seems I am to submit my resignation to the Foreign Office and stand in the vacant seat as candidate for the Liberals, with a good chance of getting in.'

'I wish you all the very best of luck, Frank,' I said, not knowing quite what else to say.

'It has meant a good deal of lobbying on my own behalf,' he admitted. 'In the short time since my return, I have had to meet no end of people whose good opinion I need to win. Time has passed in a blur. I've sat at so many dinner tables I really don't remember the names of all the hosts! I was even taken to meet Mr Gladstone so that he could cast his eagle eye over me.'

'I am speechless, Frank,' I said honestly.

'So was I, very nearly, on that occasion. Anyhow, it is agreed now and a candidate I shall be.' Frank paused.

'Some of the conversation at the dinner tables I mentioned was very interesting, all sorts of anecdotes told. Your husband's name was mentioned on one occasion.'

'Ben's?' I almost shouted in my surprise and horror. 'Oh, Frank, was it because of Mills, the murderer?'

'The details of the matter weren't discussed. But I understand,' Frank said with a grin, 'that the home secretary was hauled from his bed in his nightshirt. I should like to have seen it. Oh, come, Lizzie, don't look so downcast! Ross hasn't wrecked his career. His persistence and devotion to his duty were admired. I was told the story only as an illustration of the realities of public office. Any good citizen and voter who has a grievance feels entitled to take it to his member of parliament. One is liable to be bothered at any hour of the day and one's private life is at the mercy of public duty. Even someone in such high office as the home secretary is not exempt. If I am to go into parliament, it is something I shall have to expect and have to accept. That is the only reason Ross's name was mentioned.'

A thought struck me, making my heart sink. 'Frank? You haven't been trying to help Ben, have you? I realise it would have been kindly meant but Ben—'

'My dearest girl,' said Frank. 'I'm in no position to help, as you describe it. I told you about it in case you'd been worrying. I don't even know what it was all about. It's up to you if you want to tell Ross.'

'No . . .' I said thoughtfully. 'Not yet awhile, at least.'

'Oh, I know your husband doesn't approve of me. But honestly, I have not been meddling.'

'I am glad because I don't like to keep things from Ben,' I told him. 'Not permanently, anyway.'

'Also, if I go into parliament,' Frank gave a sigh of resignation, 'I suppose I shall have to find a wife. The voters like a married man, I'm told.'

'I hope you won't marry someone just for that reason!'

'What reasons are left to me, since the lady I wanted to marry turned me down?'

'Frank!' I warned him. 'Don't start speaking of that. You did not really want to marry me. It was some madcap notion you took into your head for a while when I lived here.'

'Lizzie dear.' Frank's tone was mild, but I caught an unaccustomed note of steel behind it. 'Kindly allow me to know what I wanted.'

'I am sorry,' I said, 'if you were very disappointed. But Mrs Parry would never have permitted it and your career – in the diplomatic or in parliament – would have been doomed from the start.'

I didn't mention that she would almost certainly have cut him out of her will, as well.

'Now,' I told him. 'I really should be going. I must send word down to the kitchen to Bessie to get herself ready.'

'That funny little scrap who used to work here?' asked Frank, reaching again for the bell pull. 'You still employ her?'

'Bessie is indispensable,' I told him firmly.

'You will call again, won't you? Before I sink in a sea of politics? I should like to see you again, Lizzie.'

He asked this in a perfectly calm and friendly tone, but it presented me with a problem, even so. I am the first person to admit I don't call on Aunt Parry as often as I should. If I should suddenly start calling more often while Frank was staying with her, Ben wouldn't care for it one bit. I don't mean that Ben does not trust me. However I know he doesn't trust Frank.

Inspector Ben Ross

I had thought that, when I arrived home that night, I would have enough startling news to fill the evening. Lizzie listened to what had happened that day and looked alarmed.

'Ben, this couldn't have anything to do with – with my going to Putney with Wally Slater and Bessie, could it?'

'At the moment I can't see that it can be anything but a sad coincidence. I don't think your visit would have influenced today's events, or that anyone at Fox House knows of it. Clearly Rachel Sawyer had her secrets and until we find them out, we won't know why she died. I was surprised to see Dr Croft at the scene, however. But I asked him to be discreet about my earlier visit to him and I am pretty sure he will have been. There is so much we don't know and . . .'

That irritating sense that I couldn't remember something I'd seen that day came into my head again. I must have scowled because Lizzie asked the cause. I explained. 'It's such a stupid thing. If it were important, surely I'd remember?'

'If you don't try so hard to remember, then you will,' said Lizzie simply.

'Let us hope so. Anyway, I shall be paying a call on Mrs Lamont tomorrow morning. That may jog my memory. Lamont suggested I arrive at eleven. I shall present myself on their doorstep at half past ten. It is not for him to say when I may conduct inquiries!'

'I have a little piece of news, too, Ben,' said my wife. 'I paid a call on my Aunt Parry.'

'Oh, how is the lady?'

'Well enough, but she left us, as soon as the tea table was cleared, to take a nap. I've never known that. She didn't sleep in the afternoon when I lived in Dorset Square with her. She didn't rise from her bed until lunchtime so there was no need. Frank thinks—'

'Frank?' I fairly yelped. 'Do you mean Carterton is back?'

'Yes, I was surprised to see him, too. He is giving up the diplomatic.'

I didn't say that I'd always wondered just how Carterton had been of help to his country in that field. He'd always struck me as indolent and a wastrel. All right, I confess I have always felt some jealousy towards him. I know he had his eye on Lizzie from the start, when she entered that house, although Lizzie won't believe it. Aloud, I asked, 'And has he any plans about what he'll do next?'

'He is to stand for parliament,' said Lizzie.

I must have sat there gaping like a landed trout. 'Carterton?' I managed to croak at last. 'Has he any chance of getting in?'

'Very good chances, I understand. There will be a vacant seat, and Frank is to contest it for the Liberals. The present member is to retire. But the seat is still considered a safe one. Frank has been introduced to Mr Gladstone, and all sorts of other people, in readiness.'

I would have slept fitfully that night anyway, my mind on the murder of Rachel Sawyer. This news ensured I hardly slept a wink. When I did, my dreams were filled with a nightmare vision of this country's affairs being governed by a House of Commons packed with Frank Cartertons.

Chapter Twelve

I MADE an early start the next morning, crossing the river a little after nine. I wanted to pay a call first at Wandsworth police station and consult with Inspector Morgan. If Constable Beck were still available, I might also take him with me to Fox House. A uniformed man, waiting outside while I interviewed the lady, might impress upon the Lamonts how serious a matter a murder investigation is. At the moment they seemed to view Rachel Sawyer's death as a nuisance. I felt a moment's pity for the dead woman. No one grieved for her. Perhaps I was wrong. I might yet discover, when I spoke to Mrs Lamont, that she was feeling the sudden loss of her housekeeper and companion more keenly than so far suggested. She had swooned away on my first visit. That might just have been the result of receiving such shocking news . . . or too-tight lacing. However, fainting away is as good a ploy as any to dismiss an unwanted visitor. I was still undecided when I entered Inspector Morgan's office.

'Ah, Ross,' Morgan greeted me cordially, rising to his feet and holding out his hand. 'Hot on the trail? Excellent.

We might be getting somewhere, eh?'

I thought he seemed very cheerful and wondered why. I explained that I was on my way to Fox House to interview Mrs Lamont.

'We have been busy here, too,' Morgan informed me. 'We've tracked down your mudlarks!'

So that was the reason for his glee. I was pleased, too. 'I'd like to talk to them as well,' I said.

'Indeed you shall. I'll send out Beck to round them up and bring them here. It will take an hour or so, but we do know where to find all three. They are of one family. The father is not unknown to us. He is a brawler when drunk and a petty thief when sober.'

That destroyed my plan to take Beck to Fox House. But talking to the boys was more important. I said so.

Morgan grew thoughtful. 'I don't know what they'll tell you. I have already questioned them and asked them whether they'd removed any item found at the site. I didn't ask if they'd robbed the body because I'd hardly expect them to confess to that! I merely asked if, by chance, they'd seen something of value, as they'd been searching for such items. They said – all three – they hadn't. I expected no less. They are accustomed to a police officer arriving at the door to arrest their father for theft, their mother as well on occasion. She specialises in stealing washing put out to dry by neighbours. But you may have more luck talking to them.'

Tracking down the boys was a good start. I felt quite optimistic as I made my way to Fox House. The disapproving Johnson did not appear surprised to see me there earlier than eleven o'clock. The butler was by now clearly resigned to my lack of any social graces. He went to announce me and returned to lead me to a small back parlour.

I had hoped that we'd talk in the main front parlour, the scene of Isaiah Sheldon's death, but it was not to be. The little back room was empty and modestly furnished. I felt I'd been demoted. I was not a guest of any consequence. I was only a shade above someone admitted by the tradesmen's entrance.

A few minutes after Johnson had left me there, a click at the door announced the arrival of Amelia Lamont.

She was alone. That surprised me because I'd expected Lamont to come with her to stand guard in case I said anything to send her into another faint. She seemed composed and invited me to sit down.

When we faced one another, and she had arranged her skirts, she spoke first. 'You wish to talk to me about poor Rachel.'

Now that her husband did not obstruct my view, I was confirmed in my first impression that Amelia Lamont was a very handsome woman. She had fine large dark eyes and a smooth, wrinkle-free skin. Her thick chestnut hair was twisted into a knot at the nape of her neck. I wondered if she was indeed really also a murderess.

This morning Mrs Lamont had not dressed in mourning black and I'd not expected it. However close she might have been to Rachel Sawyer, the dead woman had been an employee. Mrs Lamont wore a gown of glazed cotton, a discreet reddish-brown plaid in pattern, with modest braid trimmings. To the bodice was pinned one of those Scottish brooches set with the 'jewels' often called cairngorms after the mountains where that sort of quartz is found. It set the right note. Her hands, folded in her lap, wore only a wedding band on the left, and a small cameo ring on the right. She had herself well under control and would not faint on me today. But my aim was to trouble that calm or I'd learn nothing. It was a pity I hadn't been able to bring Beck. It might have helped to have him pacing up and down outside in his big boots.

'It was distressing news I brought you yesterday,' I began. 'I am sorry for the shock it caused you. I hope you are fully recovered?'

She inclined her head in acknowledgement of my apology. 'I am quite well, thank you. It is hard to accept the news about Rachel, but I must.'

'I do need to talk to you about Miss Sawyer, ma'am. I understand it will be distressing. But it is a dreadful murder I am investigating here.'

She winced as if I'd stuck a pin in her but said nothing.

'Miss Sawyer had been with you a long time, since before your marriage, I understand.'

'Yes.' Amelia Lamont's voice was very quiet. 'A very long time.'

'I wonder if I might ask what will seem a very personal question?'

Her lips moved almost to form a smile, but it was not one of good humour. Like the earlier wince, it was nearer a grimace of pain. I began to think I'd been wrong in suspecting she'd faked the faint on my last visit. Mrs Lamont was deeply distressed, though hiding it as a woman of her upbringing and background would. But what was the cause of that distress?

'I am sure you will do so, Inspector Ross. Isn't that why you are here?' she asked.

I managed a deprecating gesture. 'It is my lot, Mrs Lamont, to intrude on people's grief and trouble them with such questions. Rachel Sawyer was, I believe, a housemaid here in the days when your uncle was alive. Your husband told me so.'

She nodded.

'I also understand that, after the death of the late Mr Sheldon, you dismissed all the household staff except Rachel Sawyer. I am wondering why you chose to keep her on.'

'You have been talking to others and not only my husband,' she said. 'The staff had all – with the exception of Rachel – worked for some years for my uncle. The pattern of the household was set as if in stone. It was clear it would be almost impossible for me to make changes. I decided to engage my own servants and train them as I wanted. Rachel had only worked here for a year, slightly less. She was more malleable. Also, I liked her.'

'Yet she must have been a young woman of undistinguished origins and little education. You made her your housekeeper and, I understand, something of a personal companion.'

Mrs Lamont dealt with what should have been a tricky

question easily. 'Rachel's parents had kept a small lodging house. She was not without education, as you seem to think. She read easily, wrote a fair hand and could reckon up numbers at considerable speed. She had kept the accounts of her parents' business. I felt she deserved better than to be a housemaid.'

'Why had she left her parents, since she was obviously of great use to them?'

'They had died within a month or two of one another. There had been debts. She had been obliged to sell everything and was alone in the world, no other family.' Mrs Lamont paused. 'It was a situation with which I had great sympathy, having once been in a similar circumstance myself.

'Rachel applied to be taken on the books of an agency supplying domestic staff. It was from this agency my uncle had engaged her.' Amelia Lamont paused. 'My late uncle had many charitable interests. He was well known for his generosity. He was of Quaker upbringing; although no longer a member of that Society. He had become a staunch member of the Church of England. But he had kept many of his Quaker principles, including an interest in practical projects to improve the lives of the poor. The domestic agency of which I spoke sought to place respectable young women, like Rachel, who had fallen on hard times. He had engaged staff from them before.'

'I understand, of course,' I said. 'But it seems unfair to me that the other staff, who'd served your uncle well for a number of years, were all dismissed.'

'They all found employment elsewhere. To have worked at Fox House was a good reference.'

'There was an elderly valet to your uncle—' I began.

She flushed and interrupted me. 'Inspector Ross, you seem to have made detailed inquiries about me and I suspect you have been listening to gossip. I cannot see this has anything to do with Rachel's dreadful death.'

Mrs Lamont had had time, since the day before, to consider the questions I might ask and prepare her answers. I had expected that. But she hadn't expected me to know of her shabby attempt to deprive the valet of his annuity.

I raised a placating hand and did not pursue that direction of questioning. It was true it had nothing to do with the murder and she was right, someone had listened to gossip. It had been Wally Slater and not I, but she did not need to know that. My mentioning the valet had served the purpose. It had rattled her composure.

I supposed I could ask for the name of the domestic agency from which Rachel had come. But their records – if the agency still existed – probably wouldn't go back seventeen years.

'Did Miss Sawyer often go out early in the morning?'

'It is possible. I usually did not see her much before mid-morning. She would come to discuss the menu for lunch then, although not always. Sometimes that had already been arranged with the cook the day before. If I wanted to see her before that time, I'd let her know the evening before. But I generally don't go out so early myself. I rise later, usually at nine, and come down to breakfast at ten. If I was not paying or receiving calls, Rachel would sit with me in the afternoons. If my husband were out of an evening, then Rachel joined me in this parlour. In that way, you might say she was a companion. But she did not sit at table with us.'

There had been rules governing Rachel Sawyer's admission into her employers' company. It had been strictly only as necessary. She had not to show her face otherwise. What a miserable existence, I thought. Although others would say that Rachel had done well, living in a comfortable home with some authority over other staff.

My mind turned to Charles Lamont. I had described him in detail to Lizzie and she was sure he must have been the man she'd seen from the cab, striding back towards Fox House. 'Mr Lamont goes out for a morning stroll perhaps?' I asked.

'Yes, often, usually after breakfast.'

'He didn't go out yesterday before breakfast? I ask because it's possible he might have glimpsed Miss Sawyer as she left the house.'

'If he had done that, he would have told you so yesterday!' Mrs Lamont said sharply. 'And he did not. Also, generally, he walks on the heath. He does not often walk down towards the river. He would not have seen Rachel in any case.'

'I see. Do you have any idea at all why Miss Sawyer left the house so early and walked all the way down to the river?'

'I cannot imagine any reason, Inspector. Obviously,

that is what she did. But it is a complete mystery to me why she chose to do so.'

'You will now need to engage another housekeeper,' I remarked. 'Will you also take someone who can act as companion – to replace Miss Sawyer?'

'Another housekeeper, certainly, although I suppose Cook is capable enough for the moment. I might raise her to be cook-housekeeper, and not engage another. As for a companion, I shall have to give that some thought. I am sure our domestic staff arrangements are of little interest to you, Inspector Ross, and you make only conversation.'

Now she had neatly stuck a pin in me, metaphorically speaking!

I would get no further today with any questions. I had learned quite a lot. The reason Mrs Lamont had given for choosing to keep on Rachel Sawyer alone of all her late uncle's servants was plausible. It made sense of the idea to make her a housekeeper, if she had previous experience running her parents' lodging house. But I was still not satisfied. I thought of the dead woman laid out in the potting shed, her coarse features and dowdy dress. What on earth had a wealthy, strong-minded, educated woman like the one facing me found likeable about the one-time maidservant? Likeable enough, that is, to make her want to share her afternoons, and sometimes evening time too, with her? What on earth had they talked about? Had Amelia Lamont simply been desperately lonely? Had she no friends? Had the marriage to Charles Lamont not proved a success? Where did he go when he went out of an evening? I thought I knew the answer to that: he went to the gaming tables. He'd married a wealthy heiress. How much of that fortune was left?

I thanked Mrs Lamont for giving me her time and left. As Johnson was about to shut the front door on me, I asked him, 'Is Mr Lamont not at home this morning?'

'The master has business in town today,' I was told before the door was almost slammed on me.

I left the house at a brisk pace but when I was some way off – and well out of sight – I stopped and waited for fifteen minutes. Then I made my way back as unobtrusively as possible. I did not go to the front door this time, but slipped down the side of the building to the rear. I could see the kitchen door was open. A clattering of pots was audible from within. After a few minutes, Harriet the skivvy emerged, carrying a bowl of dirty water. She threw it in the general direction of some bushes.

'Harriet!' I called as loudly as I dared, because I did not want to be heard by anyone else in the kitchen. She looked up in surprise. I quickly put a finger to my lips before beckoning to her.

She came trotting up, still clasping the bowl in her thin arms. 'Yes, sir?'

'I have a question I'd like to ask you, Harriet. You took the hot water up to Miss Sawyer every morning at half past six?'

'Yessir.'

'Do you take hot water upstairs to anyone else, to Mr and Mrs Lamont?'

'Yessir, but not so early. I take up the master's at eight and the mistress's at a quarter to nine.'

'At different times? Do Mr and Mrs Lamont not share a bedroom?'

'No, sir. They have rooms next to one another.'

'And when you take up the water, do you carry it into the room – as you did for Miss Sawyer?'

'I take the jug into Mrs Lamont's room, sir. Mr Lamont's room I don't go into. I leave the water on the little stand outside in the corridor. Then I knock on the door and call out to him that it's there.'

'And does he answer?'

'No,' said Harriet simply. 'He knows it will be there. He don't bother answering.'

'Thank you, Harriet, here . . .' I pressed a florin into her hand.

'Blimey, sir,' she said. 'Thank you!'

'No need to mention our conversation to Mr Johnson or any other member of the staff, Harriet.'

'My lips is sealed!' declared Harriet with gusto.

Chapter Thirteen

BY THE time I returned to Wandsworth the excellent Constable Beck had rounded up the three boys. He lined them up in front of me. They were clearly brothers, by name Albert, Edward and Arthur Smith. The Smith family might survive by scavenging and petty crime, but they were clearly patriotic and royalist to the core. I wondered if her gracious Majesty would appreciate the Smiths naming their offspring after her husband and sons.

Despite the fine names, all three urchins were of scrawny, unwashed and ragged appearance. Otherwise they were as alike as peas in a pod, differing only in height. The tallest brother Albert's clothes were obviously handed down, patched and well worn to begin with. Edward probably inherited the cast-offs of his elder sibling and gave them another good wear. By the time the sorry garments reached the smallest, the unfortunate Arthur, they were almost in shreds. None of them wore shoes. They all had pinched faces with pointed chins, large grey eyes and straggling hair that might have been fair, if it had been cleaner, but appeared now a dirty brown.

Albert Smith, at ten years old and so by virtue of size and seniority the appointed leader of the little gang, spoke up first.

'We ain't dun nuffin',' he said. His brothers nodded agreement.

'I'm very pleased to hear it,' I told them. 'I wanted to see you all because I need to talk to you about the morning you found the body.'

'We found 'er. We never took nuffin' off 'er!'

The earliest lesson they had probably learned at their mother's knee, or by their father's belt, was not to talk to the police. To get them relaxed and chatty wouldn't be easy, as Inspector Morgan had already found out.

'Did you have breakfast this morning?' I asked.

Albert had not expected this question and hesitated. 'Yus!' he said at last. His brothers glanced at him in clear, if unspoken, disagreement.

'But it is past midday, so you must be hungry again now,' I suggested.

'We might be,' said Albert cautiously, after sizing me up. He recognised a deal in the making.

'We'll go out and I'll buy hot meat pies,' I said. 'I passed a stand selling them just down the road on my way here.'

'Cor . . .' breathed Arthur, the youngest at six years of age, staring at me in awe.

'One each!' stipulated Albert. I suspected Albert had the makings of a businessman and would soon branch out from salvaging odd items from the mud.

I led my little troop of ragamuffins out of the station, under the bemused eye of Sergeant Hepple, and down to the hot-pieman's pitch. I ordered four pies. They smelled appetising and I didn't see why I should have to sit hungry and watch the Smiths eat. I was not in uniform, after all. A uniformed officer is not allowed to eat on duty.

'None of them wiv the burned crust!' Albert ordered the pieman.

We took our pies, burning our hands, to the nearest scrap of patchy grass and sat down beneath a tree. I didn't suppose Dunn would have approved my sitting with three urchins and mopping gravy from my chin. I told myself that, in this district, no passer-by would know me and report my undignified behaviour.

For a few minutes there was silence while we ate. When the last scrap had been disposed of, and the three Smiths heaved sighs of satisfaction, the mood had changed. Albert recognised the food had to be paid for. In man-to-man tones, he announced, 'I shall 'ave to consult wiv me bruvvers.'

'I'll just take a turn round and come back in five minutes,' I told them.

I left them crouched in a huddle and strolled round the tiny patch of green, keeping an eye on them. They wouldn't run away. Beck had found them twice already and would find them again. Nor would they wish to do anything to incriminate them or bring the police to the family home.

When I returned, the huddle broke up and Albert declared, 'We'll tell you about finding the body.'

I nodded encouragingly. 'Go on.'

'We'd been looking in the mud since the tide went out. We was working our way along, see, starting under the bridge, because folk lean on the parapet chatting and not looking what they're doing, and they drop stuff off it. But there wasn't much. So we moved on to the bank above the bridge. That's not where she was lying dead.' He paused to make sure I understood.

'I follow you,' I told him. 'Go on.'

'There wasn't a lot there, either,' continued Albert disconsolately. 'Nuffin' worth anythin' much. People don't drop stuff off the boats like they did. Used to be, when a few of them excursion steamers had been up and down, afterwards you'd find all sorts on the mud when the water level dropped. Anyway, by that time the river was rising fast. So we thought we would just look under the bridge one more time, then take a look along the stretch below the bridge. Not that you find so much there. Where the river runs through the middle of London, that's where you find the good stuff. But the city gangs have got the rights to it and it's no use us turning up. The local boys would chase us off. We have to take what pickings we can find down here.'

'So you moved to the bank below Putney Bridge,' I encouraged him, as he seemed inclined to expand on his grievances, as all traders do, complaining about rivals, poor turnover, the general situation in the country being against the honest businessman and so forth.

'There she was,' said Albert simply. 'Teddy saw her first, didn't you, Teddy?'

Edward, aged eight and the middle brother, responded to this version of his name with a vigorous nod.

'Flat as a pancake, she was,' he informed me. 'Lyin' on 'er back and staring up at the sky.'

'How did you think she got there? I mean, what was your first impression?'

They looked vague. 'Fell off a boat?' suggested Teddy.

'Might've chucked herself off the bridge,' observed Albert. 'Or that's what we thought, first off. Then we got a bit nearer and saw her clothes was dry. I said to my bruvvers, "She's not been in the water."'

'And I said,' Teddy chipped in, "Well, she's goin' to be in the water soon, because the river will cover 'er up!"'

'So I left me bruvvers there, and ran off to tell someone,' Albert continued. 'I found the old feller from the church and I told him. I don't mean the vicar.'

'You mean the parish clerk,' I said.

'Right. He come down to look at 'er and I thought he was going to faint away. He turned a funny colour. We said, "Look, the water's rising and she's going to be under."'

'So he told us,' Teddy took up the tale again, 'to wait there and guard the body. That's what he said, "Guard the body, boys, and you shall have a shilling each." We thought that was pretty good, seeing as we'd found so little that day.'

From the corner of my eye I saw the smallest brother, Arthur, shift awkwardly.

'The parish clerk . . .' said Albert, rolling out the title

with due solemnity, 'come back wiv the magistrate! That give us a nasty turn. I wouldn't 'ave gone and got him if I'd known he'd do that.'

'You all know the magistrate, then?' I asked.

Glumly, they nodded.

'Old Harrington, it was. He said there was nothing for it but to move the poor unfortunate, although strickly speakin', the body ought to be left until the police come. But the river wouldn't allow that. So, there being not enough time to fetch a constable, they shouted out to some geezer walking on the bank. He come across to help them move 'er. The ole clerk give us a shilling each, like he promised, and told us to clear off. So we did.'

'Thank you,' I said. 'That was a very fair account.' They looked relieved. 'As far as it went,' I added. They stopped looking relieved and became apprehensive.

'You know what evidence is?' I asked.

'Yes,' they muttered together.

'You know what a serious matter murder is?'

They nodded furiously.

'That poor woman had been murdered.'

'We heard that,' said Albert, 'but we didn't know it then, did we?'

'No!' Teddy and Arthur supported him.

'Of course, you didn't know it then. But you know it now. That makes a difference. It means that anything you may have found on the mud near the body, for example, would be important evidence. If such a thing was to turn up later anywhere – let's say, if anyone tried to sell it –

the police would get to know about it. That could mean very serious trouble.'

'We wouldn't rob a body!' Albert scowled at me.

'She'd haunt us,' whispered Teddy hoarsely.

They might not rob a dead body now, but give them a few years and I fancied they would no longer fear ghosts and be made of sterner stuff.

Aloud, I said, 'I am not suggesting that you did. I only ask you if you are quite sure you didn't perhaps chance to see something worth picking up. Perhaps you didn't see it at once, or even until after the clerk, the magistrate and the third man had carried the dead woman away. In that case, I would understand that you didn't hand it over to one of those gentlemen. But it would need to be handed over now to me. So, let me ask you again. Did you find and pick up, or even see and not pick up, anything at all? Think carefully.'

There was a pause and then Albert and Teddy turned their heads in unison and looked at Arthur, who stared back defiantly.

'You still got it?' asked Albert.

'Yus!' said Arthur sullenly.

'Then hand it over.' Albert held out his hand.

'I found it and it's mine!' argued Arthur with spirit.

'Oy! Just do like I say, right? Hand it over or I'll screw yer head off!'

I had a feeling this threat had been issued many times before because Arthur did not look particularly scared by it. But it marked the end of his resistance. He foraged in his ragged garments and produced some small object that he passed to his eldest brother.

Albert held out his hand, palm open and flat. On it nestled a small, yellow object.

'We reckon it's gold,' he said. 'We was going to sell it. But what wiv all the fuss and rozzers all over the place, we didn't.'

I took the object. It was a cufflink. 'Yes,' I said, 'I think you are right and it is gold.'

'It wasn't near the body.' Albert was anxious I should mark this important point. 'It was right over by the bank.'

'Between the body and the bank? Or further along?'

'Between the body and the bank. There was like a long scrape in the mud. It was lying in the middle of that.'

He dropped it! I thought in exultation. The murderer dragged the body across the mud and in so doing the cufflink was torn from his shirt, but he didn't notice it. He will have noticed the loss soon and be worried he lost it at the scene. But he'll be hoping the water covered it before it was found.

I turned the little object so that the sunlight caught the flat surface of the lozenge that made up one half of the linked pair. It was engraved. I peered more closely and saw that it was a monogram. I distinguished two letters entwined as an L and a C. Or better, a C and L. I would like to view it through a magnifying glass to make sure, but I did not think I was wrong. Now, why was I not surprised? I peered again at the reverse of the monogrammed side. There were marks, the stamps of an assay office and what were probably the initials of the jeweller, so tiny I would really need a magnifying glass. But they would give us the year the links were made and, if we traced the jeweller, he might be able to tell us for whom.

'How about a reward, then?' asked Albert, ever the entrepreneur.

I let them go, after telling them they would be required to return later to Wandsworth station and make statements. These would be written down and they would have to make a mark in place of a signature. Albert told me loftily that he could write his name, thank you very much! His brothers, he admitted, couldn't.

'Little blighters,' said Inspector Morgan when I returned to give him the news.

'Don't be too hard on them,' I begged. 'They seldom find anything of such value and they have handed it over.'

Morgan snorted. 'If they had told either of their parents of their find, we should not have it now!'

'I think,' I told him, 'that they've learned early that if they find anything of real value, they keep it to themselves. If not, any money it's sold for will be spent at the nearest public house.'

I set off back to Scotland Yard on foot. I knew Dunn would not sign off too many rides in a hackney cab. It was lucky I did, because as I stepped on to the bridge I saw coming towards me a familiar form. Charles Lamont was returning from whatever business had taken him into central London.

He was very dapper, as he'd been on the previous occasion we'd met. He swung his walking cane and strode out briskly. He was not wearing the country suit he'd worn the previous time we'd met. He was city-dressed, in a black frock coat and tall silk hat. But the luxuriant moustache made him instantly recognisable.

He had also recognised me and did not look pleased. We met in the middle of the bridge.

'Well, Ross?' he began. 'I take it you have spoken to my wife and satisfied yourself that there is no way she can help you. I trust you will not bother her again.'

'Yes, I've spoken to Mrs Lamont. She was very composed both when I arrived and when I left. She has explained to me how she came to keep on Rachel Sawyer after dismissing all the other members of her late uncle's household.'

Lamont looked discontented. 'I cannot see how it is of any interest to you to know why my wife kept Rachel Sawyer in the house. She did so, and that's enough, surely?'

'We police officers like to cross the "t's" and dot the "i's",' I told him pleasantly.

That gained me another scowl. 'I cannot see why, but I suppose you know your business.'

'I hope so, sir.'

Lamont took his time to study me. The wind blew quite strongly down the length of the Thames and across the bridge. I hoped he wouldn't lose his top hat. My own round bowler hat was wedged firmly over my head. I realised I must look the complete officer of the law in comparison with this dandy.

'I do not want my wife troubled unnecessarily over

this,' he said suddenly. 'No doubt you cast about for inspiration, but you won't find it in our parlour. I told you, my wife was fond of Sawyer. I found little to recommend the woman, other than a competence for household accounts. But Amelia – Mrs Lamont – was accustomed to have her nearby. This has been a matter of great sadness to her, Ross, and I hope you are keeping this in mind.'

'Yes, sir. I, too, hope not to have to trouble either you or your wife unnecessarily. But, as with all investigations, it depends on the progress we make.'

Now the breeze caught at his hat and he grabbed the brim to prevent it flying off his head and away into the river. 'Do you make progress, Ross?'

'Yes, I think so. I have now spoken to the boys who found the body.'

'Oh, the urchins? Someone had to find her, I suppose. They are what are called mudlarks, are they not? Scavengers on the shoreline?'

'Yes, sir.'

'One wonders what they find,' Lamont observed. 'A few coins, I suppose, and broken scraps of metal. The annual Boat Race between Oxford and Cambridge Universities begins just by here, you know. Then great crowds come down to see the rowers away. Many of them are fashionable people. All of them know to beware of pickpockets. But in the excitement they are careless of small items: coins, little articles of jewellery. Immediately the crowd has departed, the poor descend on the area to comb it. Any valuable thing dropped would be found almost at once. The rest of the year, well, I can't imagine what the urchins turn up.'

'For the very poor,' I told him, 'it is amazing what they can find of value to them. There are dealers to be found in London who will buy almost anything, from metal scraps to a dead cat for its fur. As it happens, something of interest to me has turned up; that is, something been found – down there.' I pointed in the general direction of the river bank on the Putney side.

'Oh?' Lamont's strongly marked black brows rose in query.

'But I don't want to say too much about it, you understand,' I told him. 'It is a small item and it might prove irrelevant.'

'Yes, indeed,' said Lamont, after a moment's silence. 'Well, good hunting, Inspector Ross!'

He saluted me with his cane and strode away, still holding the brim of his hat.

I continued on my way to the Yard.

Morris appeared as soon as I stepped inside the building.

'We make progress, Sergeant!' I told him cheerfully. I produced the gold cufflink and held it out. 'This, I fancy, will lead us to our man.'

'Yes, sir,' returned Morris, peering at the object. 'There has been progress in other matters, too, Mr Ross.'

'Oh, how so?'

'A message has arrived from Southampton, sir, by the telegraph. It's from Inspector Hughes down there. Mr Dunn requests that you go to his office immediately.'

'Ah, there you are, Ross!' exclaimed Dunn, on my entry. 'About time, too.'

'I walked back from Putney, sir.'

'I should hope so. The public purse cannot be always paying for you to ride about in cabs like a gentleman. So, how did you get on?'

I explained the recent developments to him. He listened carefully and we discussed the possible implications.

'Hum,' he muttered. 'We shall have to wait and see. Leave the cufflink here with me and I will see about deciphering the assay marks and what you hope are the maker's initials. Dr Carmichael has conducted the post-mortem examination, by the way, and sent over his report. He confirms that the woman was strangled manually. He could find no sign that she struggled or fought. He suggests the assailant was both strong and determined, and suggests that the element of surprise should not be discounted.'

'That was more or less Dr Croft's theory,' I said.

But Dunn was already moving on. 'Now then, on the other matter, that of the missing child, Charlotte Canning. You've spoken to Morris, I suppose? He told you of this?'

He picked up a scrap of paper from his desk and held it out.

I took it and read the telegraphed message. *Missing female and child here. Suggest come at once. Hughes.* I set down the message on his desk. 'I should go tomorrow, sir.'

'So that will be another expense, train tickets for you

to go down to Southampton and bring the Canning woman and her daughter back to London,' Dunn grumbled. 'Morris had better go along, too. He is a family man. At this rate, Ross, you are using up your expense allowance for the entire year! Moreover, I would remind you that if you had only taken the woman in charge when you found her sleeping as a vagrant under the arches, together with a very young child, all of this might have been avoided.'

'At least,' I pointed out to him unwisely, 'we now know that Canning didn't murder his wife and child.'

'Go, Ross!'

I went.

Chapter Fourteen

'THIS IS going to be a difficult business, Mr Ross,' observed Sergeant Morris as we boarded the train for Southampton the next morning. We had already attracted some curious glances and murmured speculation from all around us. Both Morris and I were in plainclothes. But the public recognises officers of the law, especially in a pair of solid fellows with no luggage, and making little conversation, who travel with purpose in their expressions.

'I hope,' continued Morris, 'that the female in question, Mrs Canning, won't be in floods of tears. A little girl, also . . . it's going to look very strange, if I may be so bold, sir. Two big fellows like us, chivvying along a sobbing female and child. It wouldn't surprise me if we will not be attacked by the crowd.'

'Sergeant!' I protested. 'You are taking a pessimistic view without any reason.' Morris looked at me. 'Very well, you have some reason,' I admitted. 'But Mrs Canning will not, I trust, be in tears all the way to London. As for the child, you are a father, Morris. Use your paternal skills. It's why the superintendent wanted you to come with me.'

'It's hardly our business,' said Morris with unlooked-for obstinacy. 'Of course the lady shouldn't have taken the little girl away from her home without the child's own father's permission. But to send two officers from Scotland Yard to arrest the lady? It's not like we don't have that murder out at Putney to attend to, sir.'

'Morris, I am well aware of all this. I don't need a lecture. If the mother had simply taken the child and gone at once to Southampton by train, as we are doing now, and if, having arrived at Miss Stephens's home, either Mrs Canning herself or Miss Stephens had informed Hubert Canning immediately, it would be another matter. Canning would have boarded a train and gone at once to retrieve his daughter. The issue would have ended in a divorce court or been settled privately. The police would not have been involved. But that is not what happened, I would remind you, Sergeant! Canning came to us and declared his wife and child missing, and so they were.'

'Yes, sir,' said Morris. 'In my view, sir, Mr Canning had come very close to wasting police time. He told us they'd been abducted by a gang of criminals!'

'He was mistaken. I don't need to point out to you, Morris, that my own position in all of this has been much criticised. I left the woman under the arches . . .' I drew a deep breath. 'I'd be obliged if we let the matter drop until we get there, is that understood?'

'Right-o,' said Morris, folding his hands and leaning back in his seat.

Other people clambered into our carriage and that settled the matter.

* * *

I had been looking forward to meeting Inspector Hughes who had given the impression, from our correspondence, of being a sensible fellow. He was on the short side for an officer, probably just the minimum height, but stocky in build, with black hair and a round, good-natured face, and a soft Welsh lilt to his voice.

'Well, now,' he said, when we were all seated. 'This is the way of it. I don't have Mrs Canning locked up in a cell. It did not seem the best thing. She is with Miss Stephens, her aunt, and the little girl also. I don't think there is any fear of them absconding. Mrs Canning is in no fit state, nor the child. She walked here from London, you know.'

'Walked?' I could not keep the dismay from my voice, 'what, all the way? What about the child? She could not have walked.'

'No, Mr Ross. Mostly, the mother carried the child on her back, which slowed her progress and made it more difficult. They existed by begging along the way. Mrs Canning arrived at her aunt's home in a state of exhaustion. Miss Stephens put them both to bed at once, and sent for a doctor. She next sent a message to me. By the time I arrived at her house, I should warn you, Miss Stephens had also engaged a lawyer on her niece's behalf. Miss Stephens is not young, but she is a very energetic lady, and one who knows her own mind. I did mention to you, Ross, in my letter, that I fancied Miss Stephens might feel some responsibility for her niece's present predicament. I won't call it guilt. But she did urge the marriage and it turned out badly, it seems.'

'Engaging a lawyer to argue Mrs Canning's cause will cost them dear,' I said. 'But it is probably the most prudent thing from her point of view.'

'The lawyer in question is a Mr Quartermain. He is not charging any fee, as I understand it. He is a local man and is giving his services as a friend. He is acquainted with Miss Stephens through the charitable works the lady has engaged in over the years.' After a pause, Hughes added, 'Very fortunate, you might say.'

'It is a great pity,' I muttered, 'that they did not consult Mr Quartermain when the marriage was being discussed in the first place.'

'Wise after the event, Mr Ross, wise after the event,' replied Hughes placidly. 'I, myself, married one of my cousins. I didn't gain any family I didn't already have! That wasn't the reason I chose my wife, of course. But at least I knew what I was getting. Well, now, it only remains for you and me – and the sergeant here – to go to Miss Stephens's address. You can talk to the lady and make arrangements to take her and the little girl back to London with you.'

The fresh sea air was an invigorating change to London's soot and fog. The gulls wheeled and shrieked above us. Morris had stopped looking as if the end of the world was nigh, and appeared to be enjoying his walk. Hughes asked me if I'd ever visited the area before. I told him that both Morris and I had once been called upon in a professional capacity to hurry down to this part of Hampshire, albeit just across

Southampton Water, in the area of the New Forest.

'The Shore House murder, eh?' said Hughes. 'I wasn't here myself at the time, but I have heard of that case.'

Miss Stephens lived in a neat terraced house not far from the sea front promenade and the ancient grey city walls. I could have guessed this was a maiden lady's abode. The lace curtains were crisp and as white as snow. The minute scrap of ground between the house and the pavement was set with a row of potted geraniums, standing on pristine gravel. The windowpanes gleamed with much polishing, as did the brass doorknocker.

'You had better wait outside, Morris,' I said. 'The presence indoors of three of us would be overpowering. Besides, we don't want to be interrupted, and, should a crowd gather – which might happen – you can send them all on their way.'

'Oh, the neighbours have had plenty to talk about since Mrs Canning arrived,' said Hughes. 'They will all have been expecting us and be watching from behind the curtains!'

Our rap at the door summoned a middle-aged, capable-looking maid who ushered me inside quickly. But not fast enough to prevent the neighbours spotting the activity. Even if they hadn't already done so, they couldn't miss Morris standing rigidly outside with his hands behind his back.

We waited in a parlour of daunting neatness for a very few minutes before we heard a rustle of skirts and the two ladies appeared.

I was truly very shocked at the sight of Jane Canning.

She wore what appeared to be a well-washed gown, perhaps one left behind when she had originally moved to London. She was as thin as a wraith and her skin burned as dark as a gypsy's from exposure to the sun on her long journey by foot to the south coast. Her features were so drawn she appeared quite ten or fifteen years older than I knew her to be. I remembered the photograph I'd seen in which she had been a new mama with her baby on her lap; and the earlier one obviously taken at the time of her marriage. This hardly seemed the same woman. She looked at us with nervous inquiry in her eyes.

'I am very pleased to see you safe and sound, Mrs Canning,' I said to her.

'I am very pleased that it is you who has come, Inspector Ross,' she replied. 'You were kind to me that evening.'

Hughes, who did not know of our encounter beneath the arches at Waterloo, looked surprised and glanced at me.

'Perhaps not as kind as you would have me,' I told Jane Canning. 'I should not have left you there alone, with your daughter.' I turned to Miss Stephens. 'I am pleased to make your acquaintance, ma'am.'

Miss Stephens was as I might have imagined the owner of this spick-and-span little house to be. She was a spruce and surprisingly handsome woman. Despite her age, her hair was still quite dark with only streaks of grey in it. She stood as bolt upright as a guardsman and fixed me with a gimlet eye.

'You should know, Inspector Ross, that my niece arrived at my door in a lamentable condition.'

Jane looked down at the carpet.

Miss Stephens continued. 'She had worn out her shoes completely on the long walk here and arrived barefoot. Her clothing was in rags. The maid did not recognise her, on opening the door, and thought it a beggar. My niece had to remind her who she was. Sarah – the maid – let out a shriek and I came running. I had never thought to see such a sight, I can tell you.'

I thought Jane about to dissolve in tears at hearing her miserable appearance so bluntly described.

'Perhaps Inspector Hughes has already told you,' rolled on Miss Stephens, 'that I have engaged the services of Mr Quartermain, the lawyer?'

'Indeed, ma'am, he has. But I must still take Mrs Canning and the child back to London with me today. I have spoken to the nursemaid, Ellen Brady,' I added to Jane. 'I think I have a fair idea what led to your leaving St John's Wood.'

'It was foolish of me,' she said. 'But I was panicked. I thought my husband and the doctor meant to send me to an asylum.'

'Hah!' cried Miss Stephens. 'They ought to send him to an asylum.'

'I just walked out of the house with Charlotte,' Jane continued. 'I had some idea I might find employment and support us both. But the money I had with me was so very little. It paid for only one night's lodging in a very unpleasant and dirty place. The landlady there was – she guessed what might have happened, that I'd run away. I mentioned to her that I hoped to find employment and she said – she said that a young woman such as myself had always one sure way of earning money. I knew what she meant.'

'Scandalous!' snapped Miss Stephens.

'I left the place immediately the next morning and did not dare to try and find anywhere else. I spent what I had on food. I had virtually nothing left when you saw me that evening. I knew that, sooner or later, Hubert would go to the police. I realised I had only one place I could hope to go, and that was to Aunt Alice and beg her to take us in. I had no money for any form of travel. I had to walk.'

'It is a miracle she got here,' said Miss Stephens.

I didn't disagree with her. 'And now I must ask to see the child, Charlotte Canning,' I said to Mrs Canning.

Jane spoke quickly before her aunt could reply. 'I'll fetch her,' she said and left the room.

Now that we were alone for a moment, Miss Stephens said fiercely, 'I wish that wretch Canning had never set foot in Southampton! He led my niece a miserable existence. Oh, I don't deny, and nor does Jane, that she had a comfortable house to live in, and servants, and he paid her dress bills without a quibble. Mr Quartermain tells me that all that will go strongly in Canning's favour. The fact that he almost made her a prisoner in the house will count for nothing. Then that incompetent medical man he brought in to examine Jane will give his sorry opinion: that she ought to be sent to some kind of special clinic. He'll state as much, as a so-called expert in such matters, to any judge. They will believe him. It will be almost impossible to get justice for Jane, but Mr Quartermain – and I – will not give up without a fight!'

'I am glad to hear it, ma'am,' I said. 'But I must still take them both back to Mr Canning.'

'I shall accompany my great-niece,' declared Miss Stephens.

This rather took the wind out of my sails. 'Well, ma'am, you need not fear that your niece will be treated by us with anything but courtesy. Sergeant Morris, who is waiting outside, has five or six children and one grandchild. He is very good with the little ones.'

'That is neither here nor there. I am not worried about you or your sergeant. I am worried about that fiend, Canning. You mean to return to London by the railway?'

'Yes, it is not too long a journey.'

'Then you cannot prevent my accompanying you. The railway exists to carry the public. I am a member of the public. I shall be in possession of a valid ticket. I shall go with you.'

I heard Jane Canning speaking in a low encouraging tone and a moment later a little girl peeped into the room.

'Hullo, there, Miss Charlotte!' encouraged Hughes. 'I think you remember me, eh? I came to see your mama.'

Charlotte sidled in, her mother close behind her. She, too, was as brown as a berry but otherwise appeared in a reasonable state. Most of the scraps of food begged by Jane along the way had obviously gone to feed her daughter. The child was dressed in new clothing.

'This is Mr Ross, Charlotte,' said Jane to her, pointing at me.

But while Hughes was a known figure and accepted, I was not. Charlotte turned and buried her face in her mother's skirts.

'We are all packed and ready,' said Miss Stephens briskly. 'We have been expecting you.'

Jane held her daughter's hand. At her aunt's words, she must have given an involuntary jerk, because the little girl looked up at her mother in alarm. Jane bent and whispered in Charlotte's ear and stroked the child's hair with her free hand.

I had never before regretted having become a police officer. But I can honestly say that for a moment then, I did so.

We all set out as a little party to walk to the railway terminus. Our progress had to be at the pace set by the child, so it was leisurely. It was further slowed by the large numbers of other walkers all about us. But it was a fine day and to anyone observing us we must have appeared no more than a set of visitors, mopping up the sights. Morris carried Jane's small bag of belongings and Hughes nobly carried the not-much-larger portmanteau of Miss Stephens. We must have progressed about half the distance when something altogether unexpected happened.

Whilst not being a firm believer in Fate, I do not dismiss it altogether. What else could have brought Lizzie and me together after so many years? What of the long-ago sudden summer storm that drove Mills to seek refuge – and made him a witness to a murder? Or, come to that, was it only fickle chance that James Mills, the young student, was walking by the river when his eye was taken by a pretty girl in a punt, being propelled along by a stranger? Yet that stranger, a lifetime later, would be the cause of Mills going to the gallows.

Now Fate – or Chance – took a hand again. As I had been taking my time to look about me, I couldn't help but notice how many of the people were heading in the same direction as us, and all seemed to be carrying baggage in one form or another. Teams of sweating horses hauled trams crowded with passengers and their belongings. I mentioned the busy state of the area to Hughes.

'Well, such coming and going is normal,' he replied. 'There is the railway terminus close by here, of course, but also just ahead of us is the Victoria Pier. A regular paddle steamer service crosses from there to Le Havre, and to the Channel Islands as well.'

I think it was the mention of the Channel Islands that put Charles Lamont into my mind and, as it were, focused my eye as well as if I'd had a telescope. I have often wondered since if but for Hughes's words I would have noticed him among so many hurrying figures all carrying bags and bundles. But it was as if Hughes were a conjuror, for there was Lamont striding out some forty to fifty feet ahead of us, bag in hand. Even so, it was hard to believe I was not imagining him.

'Morris!' I called out. 'Isn't that Charles Lamont up ahead? Tell me I'm not mistaken.'

'Bless my soul!' exclaimed Morris. 'That's the fellow well enough.'

'We must stop that man and arrest him!' I urged the astonished Hughes. 'See him? That smart-looking fellow marching along!'

As I spoke Lamont, perhaps alerted by some sixth sense that he had become an object of interest, turned his head and we saw his fine moustache. That dispelled all doubt. His expression, as he registered my presence, was quite comical at first in its disbelief. Then it turned to horror. He flung away the portmanteau he carried, and ran.

'He is a suspect in a murder case in London. He's trying to flee the country!' I called to Hughes. 'Come on, Morris!'

If Hughes had been going to object, the sight of a fleeing man took care of his qualms. A man running from officers is a man who must be stopped.

We all pounded forward, abandoning the astonished ladies. I raced past the bag Lamont had flung down; noticing as I did that some opportunist was already grabbing hold of it. The same had happened to Lamont's hat. It had fallen off and, caught by the wind, bowled through the air to drop neatly into the arms of a dockside idler. But we could not stop for any of that. Lamont ducked and weaved through the throng, taking full advantage of the fact that the same crowd impeded us in our pursuit.

In any other packed location some public-minded persons might have joined the chase. Someone did raise a cry of 'Stop, thief!' But no one else was prepared to abandon their bags as Lamont had done. This was a gathering of respectable pillars of society: the sort that leave tangling with the criminal classes to others. Only a few ragamuffin children, there to offer to carry bags or show people the way to the boat (both offers best refused), ran alongside Lamont – and they were cheering him on.

I do believe the fellow might even have escaped us, but to his misfortune and our good luck he came up against an unexpected obstacle. A pair of weather-beaten seafaring fellows, crew of the paddle steamer perhaps, came rolling out of a public house just as he reached the doorway. Lamont had chosen that moment to glance back and, not having his eye on the way ahead, cannoned into them. We saw how he swore at them and tried to push them aside. But they objected to such impoliteness and caught at his arms. He struggled furiously, kicking out at them.

We arrived just in time to prevent Lamont being on the receiving end of some rough treatment and to take him into custody.

As we came face to face, his first words were, 'My wife knows nothing of this!'

Chapter Fifteen

WE RETURNED to London not as a party of four including the child, as anticipated, but as a party of six. Lamont was handcuffed to Morris and simmered in a sullen rage. Both women regarded him with some alarm. The shackled man was also causing much whispered comment all around, so Morris removed himself and his prisoner to a different carriage while I travelled with the ladies. I had telegraphed ahead to Superintendent Dunn to let him know of developments. Thus when we arrived at Waterloo Station in the early evening I was not surprised to find him waiting for us at the barrier.

Dunn raised his hat politely to the ladies and introduced himself. Then he turned to Morris.

'There is a prison van waiting outside. Take your prisoner over to Bow Street and lock him in a cell there, Sergeant,' he ordered. 'We can deal with him in the morning.'

When Morris and the scowling Lamont had left us, Dunn turned briskly to the business in hand.

'I shall accompany you, Ross, to St John's Wood, with the ladies. I have a growler waiting for us outside.'

We stepped out into the area before the station just in time to see the 'Black Maria' with Lamont inside it being driven away. Dunn was pointing in the opposite direction. Why was I not surprised to see Wally Slater's ex-prizefighter's features crumpled in what was supposed to be a smile? He was waiting beside his cab. It was drawn up away from the regular cab rank and bore a hand-printed notice reading 'reserved'.

Wally whisked the notice out of sight into the pocket of his coat. 'Good evening, gentlemen and ladies.'

'To St John's Wood, cabbie,' ordered Dunn. 'Tell him the exact address, Ross.'

For a moment I feared Slater – who must have seen Lamont loaded into the Black Maria – was about to deliver some observation on our apparent success. But he merely replied, 'Right-o, gents, leave it to me and Victor.'

The early evening traffic was busy and it took us a while to reach our destination. Charlotte, exhausted by the long day and the train journey, had fallen asleep cradled in her mother's arms. Jane looked down at her sleeping child, her expression sadly resigned.

Miss Stephens, observing the chaos that was normal for central London at that hour of the day, observed, 'This is very disorganised. Cannot it be better arranged?' Apart from that, no one spoke until we were almost at our destination. Then Miss Stephens addressed Dunn.

'Is Mr Canning expecting to see my niece and his daughter tonight?'

'He has been informed, ma'am,' replied Dunn.

'Well, we must face up to that. There is perhaps some

modest but well-appointed hotel in the area? I do not think Mr Canning will wish to have me under his roof tonight. As for Jane . . .' She glanced at the mother and sleeping child. 'I do not think my niece will wish to spend the night in the same house as Mr Canning, or that he will want her there. But I suppose we shall be obliged to leave the child with him?'

'Certainly for the moment, ma'am,' said Dunn politely.

Jane said very quietly, 'If Hubert will allow it, I would like to stay with Charlotte.'

The door was opened to us by Mrs Bell, who must have been waiting impatiently for our arrival. There was no sign of either of the housemaids. Mrs Bell stared at us stonily before inviting us to enter the house. We trooped into the hall. Then, at one and the same time, Hubert Canning came out of the parlour into the hall, and the nursemaid, Ellen Brady, running down the stairs, erupted on to the scene.

'Praise be to the blessed Lord and all his saints! Haven't I prayed for this moment? To see the darling child safe and sound – and you, too, Mrs Canning.'

Charlotte stirred but did not fully wake. Hastily Jane placed her daughter in Ellen's arms and ordered, 'Please take her upstairs and put her to bed in the nursery, Ellen.'

Ellen bore her charge away. Although he'd been expecting his wife and me, Canning had probably not been expecting Dunn. Certainly, from his shocked expression, he had not anticipated seeing Miss Stephens with us. He turned back into the parlour, and we all followed. Mrs Bell closed the door after us, but I was sure she waited outside in the hall, hoping to overhear what was said.

'I am obliged to you, gentlemen, for finding and returning my daughter,' said Canning stiffly to Dunn and myself. He had taken up a position before the hearth, feet spread and hands behind his back. He turned his head towards the elder lady. 'I had not anticipated seeing you, Miss Stephens.'

'You did not think I would allow Jane to return, with the little girl, under police escort without coming too?' she retorted. 'That would have been most remiss of me.'

Canning flushed and muttered, 'Yes, quite so.' He had been careful not to look at his wife in all this time. Now he turned to her, open hostility on his face. 'You, madam, have disgraced me and disgraced yourself. You may go wherever you will. You will not remain under this roof.'

'Jane and I,' said Miss Stephens loudly before either Dunn or myself could reply, 'will take rooms in a suitable hotel nearby. Mr Quartermain will arrive tomorrow and we shall consult with him.'

'Who the devil is Mr Quartermain?' roared Canning, his complexion turning dark red and his Vandyke beard quivering.

'Mr Quartermain is a lawyer I have engaged to act on my niece's behalf,' retorted Miss Stephens.

'Have you, egad? Well, ma'am, you may engage as many lawyers as you wish. My daughter remains here with me, under my roof, and in my protection.' Canning swung round to face Dunn and myself. 'I don't know what the procedure will be now with regard to yourselves.

I do not wish any charges to be pressed against Mrs Canning with regard to her behaviour and her abduction of my daughter. That would cause too much gossip. I want – I need this to be kept as quiet as possible. I, too, shall take legal advice first thing in the morning. I don't believe I need trouble the police any further.'

'Well, sir,' said Dunn calmly, 'we shall need to trouble you a little more. But that can wait until tomorrow. Then, perhaps, you might care to present yourself at Scotland Yard, together with your legal adviser.'

'Whatever for?' cried Canning.

'There is the matter of your having made a false report, sir. You claimed your wife and child had been kidnapped by unknown agents; something you knew not to be true. You did not explain to us the precise sequence of events that had led to your wife leaving. Considerable police time and resources have been expended. However, we can discuss that tomorrow. I shall see the ladies safely settled into a hotel. Goodnight, sir.'

Outside, as Slater was helping the women into the growler, Dunn said to me in a low voice, 'You can leave Canning to me. When he turns up with his solicitor tomorrow, we shall probably issue him a stern warning and leave it at that. He has been a nuisance but it would be difficult, if not impossible, to bring any serious charge against him. It will now be all up to the lawyers to decide the future of the Cannings' domestic arrangements – and the little girl. You had better concentrate on the Putney murder. Will you go there tonight and inform Mrs Lamont we have her husband in custody?'

I opened my mouth to reply, but Slater had returned. I asked him if he knew of any small, respectable hotels in the area.

'I know just the place, gents,' he informed us. 'Leave it to me.'

We joined the women inside the growler. Jane was weeping softly.

'I shall not see my daughter again, Inspector Ross. She will be so frightened when she wakes tomorrow and I am not there – and don't appear.'

Her aunt patted her arm. 'There, there, my dear. The nursemaid appears to have a real affection for the child. You need not fear for her wellbeing. Let us wait and see what Mr Quartermain has to say when he arrives in London tomorrow.'

A great deal seemed to be riding on Mr Quartermain. I hoped he did not let his clients down.

The hotel to which Wally Slater drove us appeared eminently suitable, so we left the two women there.

'Well, Ross?' Dunn asked as we returned to the waiting growler.

'I would prefer,' I said, 'not to go all the way to Putney tonight. The light is already fading and by the time I get there, it will be dark. Lamont told me his wife knows nothing of all this, but I am not so sure. I believe they are in it together and the whole thing goes back to the murder of Isaiah Sheldon, all those years ago. Let Mrs Lamont wait and worry a little. I'll go there first thing in the morning.'

'Very well, I'll leave it to your judgement as you have

met the woman already. Get this cab to take you home. You have further to go than I do. I'll walk, or take another cab if I see one.'

'There is one thing, sir,' I said with some trepidation.

'Well?'

'I should like to take my wife with me tomorrow, when I go to interview Amelia Lamont.' I held my breath. What I asked was, to say the least, irregular.

'Why?' asked Dunn with remarkable calm, but with a sharp eye on me.

'Mrs Lamont is a wealthy woman of good social standing in her community. We have Lamont because he tried to flee the country. She was not with him. She is, presumably, still sitting at home in Putney, utterly respectable to all eyes. Many people might believe her the wronged party, the deserted wife, the woman who foolishly married a villain. We cannot simply bring her in and question her as we might do a—'

'A common criminal?' suggested Dunn, a dry note in his voice.

'That's just it, sir. It is one thing for me to believe she *is* a common criminal: a murderess who killed a member of her family . . .'

'Not yet proved!' warned Dunn.

'I shall get the evidence! Moreover, she and her husband have conspired, I do believe, in the death of Rachel Sawyer, and I'll get the truth out of the pair of them. But you are right in what I think you were implying. We cannot treat Amelia Lamont like a brothel madam or petty thief. She is a clever woman, in the world's view blameless, whom the public will find hard to believe so wicked. So I need someone with me who will understand such a woman, that is, understand how her mind might work far better than I. Another woman might notice things in the behaviour of Amelia Lamont, or in her general demeanour, that might not strike a male observer. I would value Lizzie's keen eye.'

I was about to add that Mrs Lamont had fainted on me once and, if the faint had been a trick, it was one I thought she was less likely to repeat before a female witness.

But Dunn spoke. 'Very well, but discretion, Ross. Above all, discretion!'

He strode away, perhaps before he could change his mind.

I heaved a sigh of relief. 'To my house, Wally,' I said to Slater.

'Get you there in no time, Inspector Ross,' the cabbie assured me. 'Giddyup, Victor!'

Elizabeth Martin Ross

It had grown late by the time Ben had finished recounting everything that had happened that day. I was happy to hear that Jane Canning and her daughter were safe, but could only feel deep sympathy for poor Jane. I was sure her fears that she would be parted from her child were well founded.

Ben told me that he had requested permission of Superintendent Dunn to take me with him to Putney in the morning, though I would be an observer only. I was astonished that Dunn had agreed to let me go with Ben, provided I kept quiet. I told him, rather indignantly, that of course I wouldn't interrupt. I knew that Ben had asked for me to be allowed to go because he was so worried about the interview with Amelia Lamont. So we fell to discussing the murder of Rachel Sawyer, and how best to approach Mrs Lamont.

'She doesn't know we have Lamont in custody,' Ben warned. 'I shall have to tell her that first. I don't know if she'll fall flat on the carpet, as she did before, or go into hysterics. I don't know if you will need to bring her round, or calm her down, or both, Lizzie. I just don't want Johnson, the butler, coming in with his jug of water!'

It had grown late, but who could sleep with so many unanswered questions still buzzing about in both our brains? Perhaps we could not find the answers, just sitting and talking, but perhaps we might find what my father often called 'the end of the string'. I quoted this to Ben, who asked what it meant.

'Why, that events are connected and if we start with one end of the string and follow it along, we'll come to the end of it eventually.'

'Your father was an optimist,' Ben said.

'He was a very practical man, a doctor. If a patient came to him complaining of assorted symptoms, he had to follow those to the source of the problem.'

'I have been trying to deal with three patients at once, if you want to put it that way,' said Ben. 'I have returned Charlotte Canning to her father. I have Charles Lamont in a cell. Now I have to tackle Amelia Lamont and I remain horribly afraid she may be the trickiest.' He sighed. 'I just wish I could remember what it was I saw, on my first visit to Fox House, that has lodged in my mind like a splinter in the skin.' He tapped his fingers irritably on the arm of his chair. 'I had hoped, on my second visit there, to be shown into that parlour again, the one in which Isaiah Sheldon died. Then I might have noticed whatever it was again, and I'd have known what train of thought it started. But I was shown into the back parlour and had no opportunity.'

'All right,' I suggested, 'tell me again what you observed on your first visit, during the few minutes you were alone there before Lamont and his wife came in.'

Ben leaned back, closed his eyes, and said, 'I saw what James Mills saw, when he looked into the window sixteen years ago. That is what struck me: how little it had changed, if Mills's description is accurate. I think his description must be exact because it was all so recognisable. Oh, there were new chairs, either side of the hearth, but they stood where Mills claimed the previous chairs had been.'

'So, what did you see?' I persisted. 'The butler had shown you into the room. He'd left you, closed the door?'

'Yes, Johnson closed the door on me. I was there alone for perhaps five or six minutes. Let's see, if I stood with the door behind me, the window was to my right. There was an oil lamp on a small table by it, just as Mills described there being. The grandfather clock he mentioned still stood against the far wall. To my left was the hearth, with a chair set either side of it. No fire in the hearth when I was there, of course.'

Ben paused. 'I did question that when Mills told his tale. Why, I asked, was there a fire on a day there had been a summer storm, suggesting sultry weather? But I think I had the answer from Dr Croft. Isaiah Sheldon worried about his health. The day had been warm leading up to the storm, but once it broke and when it had passed, the temperature would drop. Sheldon feared the sudden change might be injurious to his well-being.'

'Mr Sheldon may have been a charitable and generous man,' I said thoughtfully, 'but he must have been rather difficult to live with, always worried about imaginary ailments.'

'Croft said he suspected, when he was called to attend that day, that Sheldon had worried himself to death. But otherwise Croft did not suspect foul play.'

'He wasn't looking for foul play,' I said.

'No . . . no, you are right, Lizzie, we see what we look for.' Ben thumped his fist on the chair arm. 'What did I see, Lizzie?'

'You were telling me,' I reminded him. 'You got as far as the hearth. There had been a fire on the day Sheldon died, but not when you were there.'

'No, the weather is too mild at the moment and the Lamonts don't fear chills as old Isaiah did! There was a coal scuttle nearby, well full and ready for when it turns colder of an evening. It was good sitting-room coal,' Ben added with a wry smile. 'Not cheap poor-quality stuff. I know about coal! Once a miner, always a miner, Lizzie. I took a good look at that coal scuttle.' He leaned back. 'Mills's first thought, when he saw a young woman enter the room, was that she'd come to make up the fire. But then he saw she was a young lady, not a housemaid.'

A tingle ran up my spine. 'Oh, Ben . . .' I whispered.

The same notion had struck him. He sat bolt upright in his chair. 'But as we now know, there *was* a housemaid working in that place, someone whose job it would have been to make up the parlour fire.'

'Rachel Sawyer,' I gasped. 'Ben, surely it was Rachel Sawyer! Listen, Johnson, the butler, closed the door behind you when he went to summon his employers because he did not want you to overhear anything they said to him, or he to them. But if Amelia had *not* closed the door behind her when she came in . . .'

'She didn't!' Ben jumped up from his chair and began to turn up and down our small parlour in agitation. 'Mills told me so. He said, when the young lady left, after committing a terrible murder, she closed the door behind her . . . *the door she had left open on entering.* She left the corpse alone before the fire.' Ben clapped his hands. 'Rachel Sawyer was on her way to the parlour with a scuttle of coal. Through the open door she saw Amelia smother the old gentleman. That is what *must* have happened. Rachel could have raised the alarm, told the world what she'd seen! But she didn't—'

'Because,' I interrupted, 'she knew she could blackmail Amelia, now a wealthy heiress, for the rest of her life. That is why Amelia made her housekeeper. That is the reason for the peculiarly close relationship between those two women. Rachel Sawyer held Amelia Lamont in the palm of her hand.'

Ben stopped and frowned. 'But did Charles Lamont know about this?'

'Perhaps not at the beginning,' I said. 'But later Amelia must have confessed it to him, surely? Lamont didn't like Rachel. Left to himself, he would have dismissed her. Something prevented him from doing so.'

'His wife depended on Rachel, he told me that,' Ben said.

'It's not enough. There had to be more, Ben. At some point Lamont learned that Rachel Sawyer knew what Amelia had done.'

'But they both put up with the situation, intolerable as it must have been, for so many years,' Ben mused. 'Then, something changed, a new element . . .'

My heart sank. 'Oh, Ben,' I said, 'I do believe it must be because I went asking questions about Isaiah at St Mary's and quizzed the parish clerk. I was so interested in the headstone when we finally found it – and Amelia Lamont found me studying it. Did my actions that day lead to the murder of Rachel Sawyer? She was a blackmailer, we now think, and surely an unpleasant person, but to think I set in train . . .'

Ben came quickly to me, stooped and grasped my hands. 'No, Lizzie, you are not responsible for Rachel's death. It may have puzzled Amelia to know you had been asking about her uncle. And, yes, she has a guilty conscience – supposing her to have any human feelings at all! But you were just a woman who was curious. You had no official standing. I think it was my visit to Dr Croft that changed everything. I was a police officer asking about the death certificate and that was serious!'

Ben released my hands and stood up. 'Yet I asked Croft not to tell the Lamonts of my visit and he gave me to understand he would not. I was sure he would not. After all, it would spread the rumour that he might have mistaken the cause of death. But they must still have learned of it.'

'We shall find out tomorrow, Ben,' I said, doing my best to sound confident.

Chapter Sixteen

Inspector Ben Ross

I HAD arranged with Slater the previous evening that he should return to my house early in the morning to take us to Putney.

Bessie watched us roll away with downcast face. She would dearly have loved to be of our party, but accepted that was impossible.

'Mrs Lamont will recognise me I am sure,' Lizzie warned, as we rattled along.

'So she will, but it may even help us. She will know that we were on to her even before Miss Sawyer died. She will be further disconcerted and any story she has prepared might no longer serve her purpose.'

'I'm still afraid that Rachel Sawyer died because I went to Putney.' Lizzie turned her head to look out of the window. We were not far from the bridge. 'What if that turns out to be true?'

'Don't worry about it. Your presence in that churchyard alone did not set events on their course. That started long ago, when Rachel Sawyer and Amelia Lamont struck an unholy bargain. It could only end badly. Sooner or later there would have come a moment when the strain of that strange relationship became intolerable. The Lamonts and Miss Sawyer would have quarrelled and parted. It might not have come to murder because, after all, sixteen years had gone by. Rachel, as a dismissed housekeeper with a grudge, probably wouldn't have been believed if she'd chosen to speak of Isaiah's death. Nor would she have been able to explain why she had not spoken earlier. That it did come to murder, as I said last night I am sure it was because of my visit to Dr Croft. So if anyone is responsible, it is I. I'd still dearly love to know how the Lamonts learned of it! I can't believe the doctor told them.'

'Perhaps he didn't,' Lizzie pointed out.

'Perhaps. At any rate, Miss Sawyer did not die because Mrs Lamont found you prowling round the burial ground.'

I hoped Lizzie believed me, but she did not look convinced. The fact was that, for all my reassuring words to her, there was a nugget of truth in what she had said. I also carried a degree of guilt for the death of Rachel Sawyer. Even more, I felt responsible for my wife's unease. I should not have left it to Lizzie to verify the details of Mills's story. It had been a police matter from the start. If anyone had gone to Putney and looked around that churchyard, then I should have done it. I don't say I would have had nearly the success she had had. I might have found nothing. Even that elderly parish clerk might not have been so willing to give directions to the grave of

Isaiah Sheldon to a sturdy fellow like me – with an air of being there on business. A respectable lady, with a maid in tow, had appealed to his gallantry.

So Lizzie had the satisfaction of knowing she had carried out an excellent piece of detection on her visit to Putney. But now she had to live with the results of it: and there was no satisfaction to be had in that. A police officer knows one cannot sweep away the results of a serious crime as tidily as a maidservant sweeps a carpet free of the spent tea leaves she has scattered down to pick up the dust. The worst result of official interference is when an innocent is harmed. Rachel Sawyer had not been an innocent victim. She had set the seeds of her own destruction. I hoped that Lizzie would remember that. But, in the end, even I could say that Rachel Sawyer had died because I had passed on a tale told me by a man on his way to execution. It had salved Mills's conscience to tell it; but left with a troubled heart the person dearest to me.

It would seem we – or at least the police – were expected, for the door of Fox House flew open as we approached it and the butler all but dragged us inside. He had looked puzzled at the first glimpse of Lizzie, but still slammed the door to shut out the world and anyone passing who might observe us.

'Madam is in the drawing room,' he said before I spoke. 'This way.'

So Amelia Lamont was expecting me. Had her husband somehow managed to get a message to her?

We stepped into the front parlour – dignified by Johnson with the title 'drawing room' despite its small dimensions – and heard the door click behind us.

Mrs Lamont stood before the hearth with her back to us, staring down into the unlit hearth.

'Good morning, Inspector Ross,' she said, still without turning.

'Good morning, ma'am. I have brought my wife with me. I hope you do not object to her presence?'

Amelia turned and saw Lizzie and looked astonished. 'But I know you!' she exclaimed.

'We met very briefly in the graveyard, by your late uncle's headstone,' Lizzie said.

Mrs Lamont appeared nonplussed at this new development. Then she decided to leave further inquiry about that for the moment and indicated one of the chairs by the hearth. 'Please sit down, Mrs Ross.'

Lizzie sat down and Mrs Lamont, after she had gestured vaguely around the room to indicate I might pick any of the other chairs, took the armchair facing Lizzie. I brought over a chair standing by the window and so we formed a tidy little conversation piece.

Amelia Lamont looked wretched. Her complexion was blotchy and her eyes red-rimmed. Before I could speak, she said simply, 'He has left me.'

'Yes, ma'am,' I said.

With the fingers of her right hand she began to turn the wedding band on her left third finger. 'I shall not see him again,' she added in the same dead tone.

I felt Lizzie glance at me. 'Well, Mrs Lamont,' I said.

'You should not be too sure of that – although if you see him, it will not be in circumstances you would wish. It will be in the dock.'

Amelia looked up at me in surprise. Then fear flickered in her eyes as she realised what I meant.

'We have him in custody,' I added, to underline the point.

She gave a long, low sigh. 'How?'

'He was arrested at Southampton, near the ferry station, when trying to leave the country.'

'Then it is all over and there is nothing left,' she said.

'Why did he flee?' I asked.

She looked at me in surprise. 'Why, because he believed you knew what he had done, and why he felt he must do it. When he met you on the bridge he believed you were hinting you had found some evidence. Later we learned you had returned after leaving the house on that last visit here. You sneaked back and spoke to Harriet in secret. You asked about the morning routine; whether Harriet had taken the hot water into Charles's bedroom and seen him, on the morning Rachel died. She told you she had only left it outside the door. You asked because you believed he'd slipped out of the house and followed Rachel. Had Harriet seen him, that would have given Charles what you call an alibi, do you not? But she had not.'

'Harriet confessed that to you that I'd returned to talk to her, did she? I am surprised,' I admitted.

'She was too long about the errand she was on. When she returned to the kitchen, Cook scolded her and then she confessed you had delayed her, asking her questions. Cook called Johnson and told him . . . and Johnson saw that it was his duty to tell Charles, when he returned home. But Charles had already met you on the bridge and was sure you had found the cufflink, after your cryptic references.' She heaved another sigh. 'Charles wished to take all the blame on himself and protect me. That is why he fled.'

'Did you plan together to murder Rachel Sawyer?'

Sudden animation flooded her face. 'No! I swear I did not know what Charles intended to do! When you came to tell us Rachel's body had been found, it was as if the ground collapsed under my feet and I plunged down into some gulf. Nothing could have been more horrible. I guessed at once that Charles was responsible and it was more than I could bear. I didn't grieve for Rachel; I grieved for *us*, for Charles and for myself, because I knew that – that the police would not rest until they had Charles in chains. If he had told me beforehand, I would have begged him not to attempt anything so reckless. But Charles was always a gambler.' Her voice faded on the last words.

She rallied at once however, leaning forward to ask urgently, 'Why did you come asking questions of Dr Croft? Showing him my uncle's death certificate? Asking about that awful day? Why did *you*, Mrs Ross – ' she turned to Lizzie – 'why did you ask the parish clerk about my uncle and to be shown his grave? The clerk said you told him you inquired on behalf of a gentleman who could not come himself. Was it on behalf of the police? Did your husband send you?'

'No,' Lizzie said, 'it was my own idea.'

'But why?' Amelia almost shouted in bewilderment.

I feared she was becoming hysterical and it was time for me to take charge of this interview. 'Did Dr Croft tell you I had called on him?'

'No, no.' She shook her head. 'He said nothing to us, which made it all the more suspicious. It was that half-witted maidservant of his. She was so alarmed by the arrival of a Scotland Yard inspector at the door, she went round every house in the neighbourhood, telling all the other servants. Eventually, the gossip reached our kitchen and Johnson, who told us. What made you seek out that certificate? Why did you ask so many questions? And there was another man, too, making inquiries. Johnson learned of it. He was a rough-looking fellow who appeared in the taproom of one of the alehouses and was very interested to hear about Fox House in the old days. Did you send him?'

Mary, Croft's maid, must have lingered to eavesdrop. But it was for me to ask the questions. I pointed now at the cold hearth. 'There is no fire lit there today. But on the day your uncle, Isaiah Sheldon, died, the fire was lit, was it not? Even though the day had been very warm for June and there had even been a thunderstorm?'

Amelia was looking at me as if Old Nick had popped up from the Underworld to sit in her front parlour. 'How can you know that?' she whispered.

'I do know it. How? That can come later. The task of keeping the fire in good order was given to a maid at the time, Rachel Sawyer. That is why she came to the open door, and that is why she saw what happened here that day. Is that not so?'

Mrs Lamont's face had drained of all colour and I really feared she was going to faint away again.

Lizzie had noticed her distress. She left her seat, pulled a stool into a position beside Amelia's chair, sat down on it and then reached out and took Amelia's hand. I thought the woman might pull her hand away. But instead I saw how her fingers tightened on Lizzie's.

She turned to look at Lizzie and asked, 'Tell me, Mrs Ross, have you ever had the sad experience of being young and alone in the world, without parents or fortune?'

'Indeed, I have had such an experience,' Lizzie told her.

'Then you will understand my situation when I was a very young girl.'

It seemed as if Amelia Lamont might continue to talk only to Lizzie in a private tête-à-tête. I cleared my throat loudly to remind her that I was there in an official capacity and anything she said would be taken as a statement to the police.

She turned back to me, casting me a glance that showed no interest at all in my presence or in what I might learn. 'It is all over now,' she said. 'It doesn't matter *now*. Charles has gone. Without Charles I have nothing.' She drew a deep breath. 'In my case, both of my parents died within forty-eight hours of one another. There was an outbreak of cholera. It took people so quickly and it left me an orphan at thirteen. My father had not been the success in his business attempts that

Uncle Isaiah had been. He had left considerable debts. The house and all the furniture was sold off, my mother's small amount of jewellery, the dishes we ate off, the clothes hanging in the closets. I was left with what I stood up in. Thirteen years old!'

'My father was a doctor,' Lizzie told her sympathetically. 'He saw the cholera.'

'Uncle Isaiah stepped in,' Amelia continued. 'Although he and my father had not been close because there was such a great difference in age between them. My grandfather had been twice married. My uncle was the son of his first wife and my father born to the second marriage made much later. Uncle Isaiah also considered my father improvident, foolish in his investments and heedless of advice my uncle had given him. However, he brought me here to Fox House to live with him.'

'He was a kindly man,' I said.

'Oh, yes, Inspector Ross, indeed he was! As I grew up here I saw how his kindness stretched far beyond Fox House and me.' A dry smile briefly touched her lips but did not reach her eyes. She released her grip on Lizzie, held up her left hand and began to number off the fingers with the index finger of her right.

'Orphanages. Gospel missions in far-flung places. Lying-in hospitals for poor women. Public libraries for mill towns in the North. You cannot imagine the number and variety of good causes that came here, begging bowl in hand. All received something.'

'Not only a kind but a good man.'

'So I believed for several years while I was growing up

here. But then I began to see it differently. I realised, by the time I was nineteen, that I had become indispensable to his comfort. What Rachel later became for me, so I was then for him. I ran his household, young as I was. I dealt with problems among the servants; decided on the menus, saw that the grocery bill was promptly paid. I was also his companion. I played cards with him after dinner every night of the week except on Sundays. He was particularly fond of bezique. Sometimes, especially on rainy days, I would sit and read aloud to him until my voice almost gave out. Always such dry stuff, the newspapers, in particular the business news and anything to do with the coffee trade. Or it might be from a book of sermons by some long-dead parson . . . or from the translated essays of Montaigne. He did not care for fiction, and thought it light-minded.'

She paused. 'When I was twenty I met Charles Lamont. It was at a garden party in midsummer. All around me was colour, chatter, laughter and life – so different from here at Fox House, always so dark, so lacking in any humour or anything resembling trivial chat.' She fell silent again for a moment, remembering those long, dull days. 'I was speaking of the garden party. In the middle of all that gaiety was a newcomer to the neighbourhood, the most handsome man I'd ever seen. He had noticed me and asked someone to introduce us. That was Charles Lamont. I fell in love.'

The last words were spoken so simply and yet they said it all. I saw Lizzie look at me.

'We began to meet,' Amelia was saying, 'whenever and

wherever we could. He wished us to become engaged. I suggested he speak to Uncle Isaiah. He said he would do so willingly, but there was a problem. He had lost most of his money in some misfortune.'

Again Lizzie glanced at me but Amelia did not seem to notice. Yes, I thought, a misfortune on the run of play in some card game, or a horse that straggled in last of the field! But Lamont had had time to inquire about Isaiah Sheldon. He'd discovered he was wealthy and this young woman, gazing at him so adoringly, was Sheldon's only living relative. He had found every gambler's dream: an heiress, or one who soon would be rich. Wasn't Isaiah Sheldon an old man?

'By now,' Amelia was explaining, 'I was within weeks of my twenty-first birthday and would not need my uncle's permission to marry. But without his financial help, it would be impossible. I decided to ask him to help us, Charles and me. After all, my uncle had helped so many other people. Why not us?

'I remember our conversation very well. I sat here, where I sit now, and he sat over there facing me. That was his accustomed chair by the hearth, with his back to the door to avoid draughts. His great concern was his health. He was always fancying himself ailing and Dr Croft would be sent for. After – after my uncle died, I had both the chairs burned and bought these you see now. I explained that Charles and I wanted to be married. He asked me why Charles had not come himself to ask for my hand. I told him of Charles's misfortune in losing most of his money. I stressed it was a temporary setback and he would recover. I asked Uncle Isaiah to make a financial settlement on me the day I turned twenty-one. It was so near.

'He chuckled. I can see and hear him now!' Her voice grew vehement. 'He laughed at me! He said, "What's this, m'dear? You want me to give you a dowry so that you can marry that rascal?" I protested that Charles was no rascal. "You are too young and inexperienced in the world to know your own mind," my uncle said. "Especially in so serious a matter. You hardly know the fellow. It will do you no harm to wait. If he truly cares for you, he will understand that, and he will wait."

'I could not hide my dismay. I begged him. I said I asked for only enough to enable us to set up a modest home together. My uncle asked, "Why do you want another home? You have a very comfortable home here with me. Come, come, in a month or two you will have lost interest in this fellow, Lamont. You are not in love, my poor child. You have a girlish infatuation for a dandy with a glib tongue. You are a sensible child at heart and in time you will see him for what he is. Or you will have met someone else and fallen for a new beau. Let's have no more talk of your leaving Fox House and no more talk of money! After all, my dear, I am an old man and frail. One day soon you will inherit all I have. Perhaps then, if you are still set on marrying Lamont, you will do so."

'I had to tell Charles that I would inherit it all, but before that day, I would be given nothing. Charles assured me he would wait for me to be free and independent. In fairness, he said, perhaps my uncle wasn't being so unreasonable. He was over eighty. "I don't wish your uncle dead," he said, "but it will not be long before you are mistress of your own future."'

Amelia uttered an exclamation of annoyance. 'Charles didn't know Uncle Isaiah! He continually talked of being a frail old man, but he was as fit as a fiddle.' She pointed at the oil portrait I'd noticed on my first visit. 'That is my uncle, hale and hearty when younger. He was still the same at eighty, other than for his white hairs and a stiffness in the hip, believe me. Yet my uncle himself frequently declared he was at death's door. Dr Croft was always coming to the house. He tried telling my uncle that a little less wine and fewer roast dinners, a little more exercise, would cure all his aches and pains, his heartburn, sleeplessness . . . all the "symptoms", as my uncle was pleased to term them.'

She fell silent.

'You became afraid,' I said, 'that Charles Lamont would not wait for you if Mr Sheldon showed no sign of dying. There were other pretty girls, some with independent fortune, and he was a handsome fellow.'

'Oh, it was worse than that,' Amelia said quietly. 'One evening, a few weeks after our conversation, Uncle Isaiah and I sat at yet another game of bezique. Without warning, he said, "I have been investigating the background of that rogue Lamont. He is a gambler, up to his eyes in debt, a wastrel. You will never marry him on my money! It is my duty to do all I can to prevent you throwing yourself away on him. The scales would soon fall from your eyes if you did marry him. Well, I'll put a stop to it, not only now, but after my death. I intend to order my lawyers to draw up a new will. I shall leave you a respectable sum in trust. I would not leave you to starve, but you will have to live modestly. The bulk of my money will go to the many excellent charities I have supported in the past. Tell Lamont this. That is my decision. I will not change it. It is for your own good, my dear, and one day you will thank me for it."'

The next words were clearly the most difficult for Amelia Lamont to speak so far. 'I was afraid of losing Charles,' she said very quietly. 'I knew that without Uncle Isaiah's wealth we could never be married. He was not able to visit his lawyer about the will the following day because there was such a thunderstorm. Before it broke, the air had been heavy. I had had a headache all day and felt wretched in every way. Uncle Isaiah, needless to say, did nothing but complain. His joints ached. He had difficulty in drawing breath. He thought perhaps he should send for Dr Croft again. He insisted that the fire be lit in here while the storm still raged because, he said, now that it had rained, it would turn chill very quickly and a sudden change of temperature was well known to be injurious to anyone in such delicate health as himself. I came into this room and saw my uncle asleep. The next day the weather would be cooler. Nothing would prevent a visit to the lawyer. I had to act.'

'You took up a cushion and you placed it over your uncle's face,' I said. 'You smothered him.'

She gazed at me with such hopelessness. 'So Rachel did speak to you, after all. We were so afraid that she would when we heard that inquiries were being made about my uncle's death. After all this time! Charles feared that Rachel might seek to save herself by telling everything. I told him I did not think she would. She had too much to lose. But Charles had never liked or trusted Rachel.'

'No, Mrs Lamont, Rachel Sawyer did not speak. There was another witness.'

'No, no!' she retorted with sudden energy. 'That is impossible!'

'A gentleman who had been paying a visit in Putney that day was riding back into London. He was caught in the storm and tried to find shelter here. He could make no one hear at the door, so came to that window, over there.' I pointed. 'Through it he saw what you did.'

'But – but nothing was said at the time! This gentleman you speak of, why did he keep silent?'

'He had his own reason for being discreet about his visit to Putney. But he felt he could not go to his grave without speaking – and recently he gave a full account.'

She fell back in her chair. 'I thought only Rachel had seen. She was on her way here with the coal scuttle, as you guessed. I had omitted to close the door and she saw everything. She said I had nothing to fear from her. She wanted only a better life. She was capable, had run her parents' lodging house, had some education, knew about dealing with tradespeople. She was not content to remain a maidservant. If I would give her the position of housekeeper . . .' Amelia made a gesture of resignation. 'I agreed. It was like Faust's pact with the devil. We could never be free of her. She would come and sit with me like a companion. She would accompany me when I went out on minor errands. It all served to remind me that I could never be without her. Charles hated her from the first and would have sent her packing, so I had to tell him why she must stay, what I'd done. We have lived with this for the past sixteen years. I swear to you I did not know Charles meant to kill her. But to be free of her at last . . .'

'I must ask you to come back with me to London, Mrs Lamont,' I said.

'Yes, of course. Only let me tell them to bring my hat and shawl.' She stood up.

'My wife will assist you,' I said politely.

Lizzie, slightly surprised, got quickly to her feet.

But Mrs Lamont waved to her to be seated again. 'It is a matter of moments.' She walked out of the room with a steady step. I heard her call out for Johnson.

'Go, anyway!' I urged Lizzie.

Lizzie followed her out and a few minutes later Mrs Lamont returned, with Lizzie, dressed in her outdoor clothing.

'Then let us be off, Inspector Ross,' she said briskly.

Her manner was now composed and in complete contrast to what it had been throughout our visit, but I could only feel very uneasy. In those very few moments before Lizzie had joined her in the hall, what had happened?

Chapter Seventeen

IT TOOK some time to return to London and for Amelia Lamont to be taken in charge. I had then to go to Scotland Yard and inform Superintendent Dunn of everything that had happened that morning. Only then could I once more address the matter of Charles Lamont.

He had spent the previous night in the cells at Marylebone Magistrates Court, where he would have had some noisy, drunken and insalubrious company. He had appeared before the bench that morning and been remanded in custody. I had hoped that he had had time to reflect on his situation and I might find him less arrogant. I did not expect to find him cooperative, that would be too much, but at least facing up to reality. Unluckily, I was not his first visitor.

'His lawyer's here, sir,' said the officer at the desk. 'He came about an hour ago.'

'How the devil did he get here so quickly?' I muttered.

'Can't tell you that, Mr Ross. But he was very insistent. I had to let him talk to the prisoner immediately.'

As he ceased speaking, a door behind us opened. I turned to see a tall, thin and distinguished-looking gentleman in black enter. His stately demeanour and air of authority indicated the higher ranks of either the Church or the Law. The absence of a clerical collar – and the leather satchel of papers he carried under his arm – suggested the Law. He treated me to careful study before asking, 'You are perhaps Inspector Ross, the arresting officer?'

'I am, sir.' I could not help but feel, as I answered, that I stood on the witness stand and this gentleman was about to dissect my every word.

'My name is Pelham and I shall be representing Mr Lamont's interests, should the matter come to trial.' He paused. 'I understand you have also arrested Mrs Lamont, is that correct?'

'We have, sir.'

'Then I shall be representing her also.'

'You may be confident that the serious nature of the charges will ensure that both Lamonts stand trial, Mr Pelham,' I told him. 'May I ask how it comes about that you have been called in by your clients so quickly?'

'Certainly, Mr Ross. Mrs Lamont had been expecting you to call on her at home this morning. Her butler had been instructed, ahead of your arrival, that should you take *her* into custody, he was to contact me at once with the news. She learned from you, during your visit, that Mr Lamont was already in police hands. Therefore she amended her instructions to the butler accordingly, to include both her husband and herself. Johnson, the butler, came to find me the moment you had left the house with Mrs Lamont, to tell me both Lamonts were in police custody; and my services were needed urgently.'

So that was why she had been so composed on leaving the house with me that morning! She had already put in place a contingency plan. She needed only a moment alone with Johnson to confirm his instructions; and tell him that Charles Lamont, too, would need legal representation. She had obtained that precious moment by leaving the parlour promptly before I could ask Lizzie to go with her. Lizzie had arrived in the hallway seconds too late. The ever-loyal Johnson had obeyed to the letter. Amelia Lamont was a clever woman.

'Then I assume you will now be going to speak with your other client?' I asked.

He permitted himself a dry smile. 'Indeed I shall, Inspector Ross. No doubt we will meet again soon. Good day to you.'

Lamont was seated at the rough deal table in the centre of the small cell. He had not shaved that morning, but still managed to look the dandy, for all his rumpled coat.

'Pelham says you have arrested my wife!' he accused me, as soon as I appeared and before I could speak.

'We have,' I said.

'More fool you,' was his reply. 'She is quite innocent of any wrongdoing. You have been over-zealous, Inspector Ross, not to say extremely rash.'

'Indeed?' I took the seat opposite him on the second chair that must have been brought in for the use of the lawyer. I put my hand in my pocket and took out the cufflink concealed in my fist, then put it on the table and withdrew my hand.

Lamont looked down at the trinket. 'That little thing,' he said thoughtfully. 'You believe that to be mine?'

'It bears your initials and is stamped eighteen carat gold with the initials of the maker. It should not be difficult to find the goldsmith. He will remember making – or engraving – an individual object like this and for whom he carried out the work. It will be in his records. The link was found close to where Rachel Sawyer died.'

'Do you say?' He still wore that bemused expression. But his mind was working fast. His next words showed he had decided to abandon any pretence the cufflink was not his. 'I wondered what had become of it. I can't imagine how it got to where you say it was discovered. Who found it?'

'A scavenger on the mud,' I told him.

'Ah, yes, I have seen those young ragamuffins at their work. Such a boy's account is open to question. He might have come by it elsewhere and in compromising circumstances. He would be hopeful of some reward if he told the police he found it at the scene of an investigation.' He made a dismissive gesture with his hand. 'So, you see, I do not need to deny I lost the link. It was some time ago and I was very put out. I hunted for it everywhere. I still have its partner, of course, so it was in my mind to ask for a replacement to be made. I didn't get round to it. I have no idea how the lost one found its way into the pocket of a young ruffian. He, naturally, will claim to have found it.'

I returned the cufflink to my pocket.

He watched me as I did, then said, 'It does not mean I killed the woman. Why should I?'

'She was a blackmailer. She had witnessed a crime committed by the lady who would become your wife. That crime was murder and it enabled Amelia Sheldon to inherit everything from her uncle, Isaiah Sheldon, and to marry you. You had no money. I suspect you have always been short of money. You are known to be a gambler. Again, it is not difficult to learn what kind of reputation as a gambler you have.'

'You have a fertile imagination, Inspector Ross. My wife's uncle died sixteen years ago. The doctor at the time, Dr Croft, was well acquainted with the late Mr Sheldon and had no qualms about signing the death certificate.'

'Rachel Sawyer was a witness to your wife's actions,' I said. 'Only a housemaid at the time, she obliged your wife to make her the housekeeper and, in short, look after her for the rest of her life.'

'So, you deduce, I suddenly decided to kill the woman *now*? You suggest I allowed my wife to be blackmailed for so long and did nothing about it before?' Lamont gave a scornful snort.

'There had been a recent development for which you were unprepared. You and your wife had discovered that – after so many years – questions were being asked about Mr Sheldon's death. Soon the only remaining servant from Isaiah Sheldon's household might well be interviewed, too. You did not trust Rachel Sawyer. Under police questioning she might confess. You panicked, I think.'

'You still cannot charge my wife with the death of her uncle,' Lamont said very patiently as if I were a slow pupil. 'There is no witness who can come forward and testify to that. However Rachel Sawyer died, why and at whose hand, does not change that. She cannot testify now to anything.'

'There was another witness,' I said.

That shook him. The confident, almost casual, manner dropped from him for a moment.

'Who?' he asked sharply.

'There was a gentleman returning from Putney to London at the time. While attempting to seek shelter from the storm at Fox House, he witnessed what happened through the parlour window.'

Lamont had recovered his composure. 'Then the gentleman in question should have raised the alarm at the time – if he did see what you claim.'

'He had his reasons for not doing so. But he has made a statement about it now.'

'It will not stand up under questioning.' He narrowed his eyes. 'Who is he?'

This was not something I was willing to divulge at the moment. But Mr Pelham would find out soon enough, examining the evidence against his client. My heart sank. Lamont was right to be so confident. Rachel could not be questioned and neither could Mills. Pelham would realise at once that Mills's statement to me, made in such desperate circumstances, could easily have doubt cast on it by an able barrister.

But one thing Lamont could not deny.

'You panicked again,' I said, 'after I met you on Putney Bridge and you realised I had the cufflink. It was made worse when you found out I had been talking to Harriet, the kitchenmaid. I was concentrating on you – and you fled. In so doing, you demonstrated your guilt. Perhaps you hoped that by your flight you would distract our attention from your wife.'

Lamont held up his hand as if to silence me. I waited. 'That is something I must know, Ross,' he said. 'How the devil did you come to be waiting for me at Southampton? No one knew I planned to take that ferry. I did not know it myself until the previous night. My wife could not have told you. I had not confided in her.'

'Sometimes Fate favours Justice,' I told him. 'I was in Southampton on an entirely different matter – a police matter, but nothing to do with the murder. I chanced to see you, bag in hand, making for the Victoria Pier and the ferry.'

'Did you, indeed?' he murmured. 'Well, a coincidence is not evidence. It is not a crime to leave the country. I had not been charged with anything at the time, or even brought in for questioning. You had called to see us with news of an employee's death and asked me to identify the body. I had done so. As far as I was concerned, that was the end of my usefulness to you and I was free to do as I wished.' He shrugged. 'If you mean to tell me that my poor wife labours under the delusion I killed Sawyer, then let me tell you that she is mistaken.'

'The charge does not depend on what your wife says!' I snapped.

Lamont leaned towards me and smiled. 'Come now, Ross, you are an officer of some experience. If you wish to claim I killed Sawyer, you must ascribe to me a motive.'

'But I have already spoken of your motive,' I reminded him, 'your wife's crime, witnessed by Rachel Sawyer. You both believed the circumstances of his death were to be reinvestigated. It threw the pair of you into a considerable confusion. Would Miss Sawyer remain steadfast or would she also panic and admit what she'd seen, all those years ago? You had to make sure of her and there was only one way, in your view, to do that.'

'Ah!' Lamont leaned towards me and jabbed a finger at me triumphantly. 'But that is only *your theory*, Inspector Ross. How do you propose to show that Sawyer saw anything at all at the time you say she did? You cannot. The wretched woman is dead. In the absence of this eyewitness you say saw a crime happen, you cannot charge, let alone convict, my poor wife.

'But neither can you charge *me*, because my motive – as you believe it – does not exist unless my wife is first convicted of the murder of her uncle.' The smile with which he accompanied this statement was almost beatific.

Now he even chuckled. 'You are an experienced officer and you mean to tell me you would place such a case before a British jury? Sixteen years after the alleged event and with the doctor still alive who signed off the death certificate? Surely Croft cannot now change his mind about something that raised no doubts in him at the time. Sawyer, the witness on whom you would rely, cannot speak. Oh, yes, you say there is another witness, but you are curiously silent about him. I suspect that is because you do not think his testimony will impress a jury. No, no, Ross. You have built a house of cards and a British jury will bring it tumbling down. A court will never convict my wife. Therefore, you will have no case against me.'

I had underestimated my opponent. The wretch was almost laughing aloud at me now.

'Mrs Lamont has confessed!' I managed to say through gritted teeth.

'Has she, indeed? Let us consider the wild statements you say my unfortunate Amelia was unwise enough to make. My departure was decided upon at the last minute. My intention was to go to Guernsey and look into the matter of some family property on the island. I was tired of having the police around the place and the whole of Putney gossiping about my affairs, so decided on impulse to go. I did not tell my wife before leaving because she would have begged me not to. She was nervous of being alone in the house, but for the servants, after Sawyer's sordid death. I intended to send her a telegraph message when I reached Guernsey.

'Amelia was naturally thrown into complete disarray when you brought the news that I was under arrest. She did not know what she was saying when you interviewed her. She was in a state of shock. When she is calmer, she will retract the whole thing.'

He paused and added, 'Oh, I understand your own wife was present when Amelia made this alleged confession. A jury might find that extremely convenient for you and place little weight on your wife's corroboration. I think you will never see *my* wife convicted, Inspector Ross! Nor should she be, of course,' he added, a little too quickly. 'She did not kill her uncle. I did not kill Sawyer.'

He leaned back, pursed his mouth beneath that luxuriant moustache, and added, 'I did not like having Sawyer around. She was over-familiar in manner; and almost offensively plain. But she was an excellent housekeeper.'

'I have a feeling that both Lamonts will walk free,' I told Lizzie that evening. 'Dashed if they don't!' I had been plunged in deepest gloom since my encounter with Lamont that day.

'Surely,' Lizzie argued, 'Lamont won't be able to explain away his attempt to leave the country by some taradiddle about a property in Guernsey? I was present, remember, when you told Amelia Lamont that you had him in a cell. That was bad news enough. But even before you told her of his arrest, when she turned round and saw us both standing there in her parlour, her first words were, "He has left me." Her anguish was genuine, I would swear to it, and it was not due to his leaving against her wishes, as he would now have you believe. It was because he'd slipped out of the house and away for ever leaving her to face the police alone. She was destroyed by his desertion. Even the sight of me with you was of little interest to her, because the man for the love of whom she'd committed such a dreadful crime all those years ago had abandoned her. "Charles has gone and there is nothing left!" Don't you remember?'

Lizzie paused. 'I can't help but feel sorry for her,' she added very quietly. 'It was all for love of Charles Lamont.'

I bent to grasp her hands. 'Lizzie, listen to me! Never be tempted to feel sorry for a murderer. It is the most terrible of crimes. A life taken cannot be restored. Anyone can feel wretched, miserable, be exploited or misled. It does not justify turning to violence. Perhaps a person can act rashly if they find themselves threatened or they seek to protect a child . . . In the heat of the moment, in desperate straits, any one of us might seize a weapon and strike out. But not everyone can kill in cold blood. That woman stood over a sleeping man of eighty, who had rescued her from penury, and pressed a cushion on to his face.

'I do not mean to let her get away with it – nor for Lamont to evade justice.' I paused to think it over. 'The ridiculous excuse he gave me today – that he suddenly felt the need to look into family business in the Channel Islands – is nonsense, as you rightly said. I don't think any jury would believe it. A jury would see it for what it was: a sudden dash to escape arrest. He is by nature rash and given to panic. That is why he murdered Rachel Sawyer.'

Lizzie frowned. 'I wonder if he left his wife a note? He

hadn't seen her to tell her his intention to leave. So, in the morning when she found he was gone, she might have run to the police to declare him missing and raise the alarm. But she didn't. He knew he'd gone for good. He must have written a letter of some kind for her to find, some sort of excuse for his desertion.'

'Then she will have destroyed it,' I said automatically.

But Lizzie was shaking her head. 'I don't think so, Ben. It was the last communication she had from him and – if he'd got away successfully – it would remain his last few words to her, just as if he'd died. I think she will have kept it. If it wasn't in her possession when she was arrested, then it is still in that house. If it were up to me, I should organise a search of her room – perhaps she has an escritoire, one with a secret drawer or two. They are very common pieces of furniture. No lady wants her maid reading her most personal correspondence. That's where I'd put such a note and that's where she'd put it for safety – where no other person could happen on it and read it.'

It was a fair point. I needed any and every piece of evidence.

I tried not to give in to a dawning optimism. I still thought that Amelia would have destroyed any note of farewell; cast it into the fire . . . except that there was no fire lit that day! Optimism popped its head up again. Hadn't I taken Lizzie with me to Putney because I wanted her to judge Amelia's mood?

'I'll send Morris over there first thing in the morning,' I told her. 'Yes, I'll tell him he is to break open any cupboard or drawer he finds locked and if he finds any letter – or anything suspicious – to bring it to the Yard. In for a penny, in for a pound, as the saying goes! From the start of this business I have managed to upset just about everyone I've encountered and put my foot wrong so often, one more time can't make it worse.'

Chapter Eighteen

THE FOLLOWING morning early Morris went off on his mission to Fox House. I could imagine with what rage Johnson would watch the place being ransacked; as the butler would no doubt describe the police search in the inevitable complaint.

Amelia Lamont was now my priority. I intended to interview her as soon as I'd discussed the state of the investigation with Dunn. But before that, Mr Pelham arrived in my office.

He stood before me, in his black clothes, like some long thin bird of ill omen. 'Mrs Lamont is ill!' he announced.

'How ill?' I asked disbelievingly.

'She has quite collapsed. Her nerves have given way under the stress of her husband's predicament.'

'And her own, perhaps?' I suggested.

Pelham moved his head in a curious sideways motion, tilting it to one side. It made him even more resemble a crow inspecting a piece of carrion. 'Mrs Lamont has withdrawn the confession you claim was made to you. It was purely verbal, the result of a state of near hysteria, made in extreme and highly irregular circumstances. The only other person you say heard it was your own wife. Mrs Lamont will not sign any written statement relating to it.'

'Withdrawn it, eh? Well, that's not so easily done. Far from hysterical, she was perfectly clear when she made it. She spoke at some length, giving all the details. There was another witness to the crime, apart from Rachel Sawyer. Mrs Lamont will be asked again today—'

I was not allowed to finish.

'There is no question of you interviewing the lady today.'

'Has the police surgeon seen her?' I asked.

'He has and he agrees that she is in no fit state to be subjected to lengthy questioning. Moreover, she is a delicate female of good family and a prison cell is a most unsuitable place for her to be housed, sordid and unhealthy. I intend to make application on her behalf for her to be released pending further inquiries. There can be no reason for her not being allowed to return to her own home. If so released, there is no suggestion she would commit any crime or interfere with any witnesses, especially since . . .' Pelham favoured me with a particularly unpleasant sneer, 'despite your assertion that there is another witness to the crime you accuse her of, you seem singularly unwilling to name him, or produce him.'

I knew then, from the flicker of triumph in his pale eyes, that Pelham had found out the identity of my 'other' witness; and the circumstances in which he'd given his account. He was confident he could persuade a judge and jury to disregard as evidence the statement dictated to me by Mills that night in Newgate. No wonder I had found Lamont so confident that neither he nor his wife would ever be tried.

Pelham accepted my silence as having scored a point. He stood up. 'Mrs Lamont, if freed, will remain in Putney. She will not go anywhere else.'

'Unlike her husband!' I heard myself snap.

Pelham merely twitched an eyebrow. 'If it is necessary for you to speak to her again, you will be able to do so at her home – or in my presence. I cannot see how the police can object.'

With that he marched out, leather satchel under his arm.

I sent up a silent plea that Morris was successful in his search because it seemed very likely that Pelham would succeed in getting an order for his client's release from custody. If Mrs Lamont returned home her first action would be to destroy any evidence that might be of use to us.

The Fates must have been playing a furious game of dice that day. Pelham had not long left, and I had just returned from informing Superintendent Dunn of the latest developments, when Biddle appeared and told me two men were desirous of seeing me.

'Who are they? What is it about?' I asked testily, still put out by my encounter with Pelham.

'It's in relation to the Putney business, sir. It's a Mr

Williams and a man he says is his gardener.'

Williams . . . Williams . . . the name was familiar but I could not put a face to it. Then I remembered. Mr Williams was the owner of the house and gardens where the potting shed was; the shed that had served us as a temporary mortuary for the body of Rachel Sawyer. My heart sank. No doubt he had returned home to the unpleasant news of the use we'd put his property to; and was here to complain.

A clumping of feet on the wooden stairs heralded the appearance of two persons as unlike one another as was possible. One, well dressed, was small, slight, very pale in complexion, with a pointed nose and eyes that blinked short-sightedly at me. He was as like a white mouse as any human could be. The other man, in complete contrast, was burly, sunburned, dressed in working attire, and glowered at me. I recognised him at once as the gardener we'd encountered at Putney.

I addressed the small pale gentleman. 'Mr Williams, I think I know why you are here and I do assure you, that had there been any other available location to which the body could have been removed at such short notice – and in such urgent need—'

Williams waved both hands at me in an agitated manner. 'No, no, Inspector Ross, I beg of you! It was indeed very unfortunate that you had to put the body in the shed in my garden. But Mr Harrington, the magistrate, who, as I understand it, oversaw the transfer of the body from the mud to the shed, has explained it all to me. Mrs Williams was at first very upset at the news. She feared it would make our entire household notorious in the neighbourhood.'

'Both you and your wife were away at the time, I believe,' I told him hastily, 'I am sure people won't think . . .'

He leaned forward. 'But they don't!' he said earnestly. 'At least, not in the way my dear wife feared. She thought no other lady would call on her in future. That no one would accept an invitation to dinner. That we would not be invited to any respectable house again.'

'And this hasn't happened?'

'No,' said Williams frankly. 'We are – or our home is – indeed quite famous in Putney at the moment. But far from being scandalised, everyone seems fascinated. We see a constant stream of callers at our door and they all want to be shown the potting shed!'

'Human nature, Mr Williams, I am afraid,' I told him, trying to disguise the relief in my voice.

'The reason I am here and that I have brought my gardener, Coggins here, along with me, is quite different.'

I turned my attention to the gardener. His face had darkened as his employer described the many visitors to the potting shed and I saw that the sudden fame of the humble building did not suit him at all. Nor, I suspected, did he like so many visitors trampling over the lawns.

'Mr Coggins,' I said. 'You helped move the body, as I recall.'

'Yes, I did,' growled Coggins. 'I didn't know her, the corpse. Mr Harrington, the Justice, he knew her. The old fellow who looks after the church, he knew her too, and got himself into a fair old state about it. But I didn't know who she was.'

At this point he fell silent and seemed still to be brooding on the shabby treatment dealt to him and his potting shed.

'Come along, Coggins, there's a good chap,' urged his employer. 'Tell the inspector what you told me.' He looked apologetically at me. 'Coggins is a little nervous, but he is anxious to do his duty as a citizen.'

'I didn't know her,' repeated Coggins obstinately, adding unwillingly, 'but I'd seen her.'

'Where? When?' I asked, expecting to be told he had seen Rachel in the past shopping in the High Street. But he confounded me.

'Earlier on that morning, really early, *and she was alive then.*'

'Why did you say nothing of this to us?' I gasped.

'What for?' returned Coggins. 'I didn't know *who* she was. I told you that. I just *saw* her. When I got a look at the body, I thought to meself, that's her, the same woman. But I didn't know her name and, as Mr Harrington and the other gentleman *did* know her name, there wasn't any point in my saying anything. So I didn't. Besides, nobody asked me.'

I felt like burying my head in my hands. Coggins's attitude was not unusual. It was all too familiar. He didn't want to be involved in something that was none of his business, and would cause him further inconvenience. His only concern was for his employer's garden, because if there were any damage there, he would be called to account. But, with the arrest of Lamont, a doubt had entered his head. It was natural that he took his concern to his employer first, and not to the police.

Mr Williams urged again, 'Please, Coggins, tell Mr Ross exactly what you told me earlier. I am sure he will understand that you did not at first realise the importance.'

'That's it,' said Coggins. 'That's what I saw – I saw *her* early on, alive and arguing with Dandy Jack, down near the river.'

'Dandy Jack?' I cried. Surely a hitherto unknown suspect was not about to enter the case?

Coggins had the grace to look discomfited. He glanced at his employer and mumbled, 'Sorry, sir.' He turned back to me. 'I should have said Mr Lamont, as lives at Fox House. Some of the local fellows call him Dandy Jack, because he strolls round the place with that walking stick, and the moustache, and always turned out like a toff. It's a sort of local joke, sir.'

Revenge is sweet and I felt an ignoble moment of pure delight at the thought of that fine fellow, Charles Lamont, going by the name of Dandy Jack in the public houses of Putney, and being the object of mirth and derision.

'Coggins became concerned when he heard of Mr Lamont's arrest,' Williams explained. 'He was shocked as indeed we all are. He came to me and I told him he must lay his information before the police immediately. But he didn't want to come alone, so I have come with him,' finished Williams tactfully. He did not add that unless he'd come with the gardener, he couldn't be sure the man would come at all.

'Biddle!' I called.

Biddle appeared promptly.

'Fetch pen and paper! This witness is about to make a statement. Sit there and take it down. Please begin at the beginning, Mr Coggins. Don't leave anything out, however trivial.'

Coggins stared at Biddle and at Biddle's pen and paper and then at me. 'All right, I'll do me best. Mr and Mrs Williams had been away. I wanted the garden to look all neat and trim when they got back the next day. So I went in to work early and was there at six of the morning. It's a good time to be working in a garden. The birds are singing; the dew is on the grass and all's right with the world. Well, all's right in my world, at any rate.'

'I'm sure it is,' I urged him. 'Don't go too fast, or the constable will not be able to keep up.'

'All right,' growled Coggins. 'Keep your hair on! After a while I heard the church clock strike seven. I carried on working, but don't ask me to be exact for how long, because I can't be sure. But the clock hadn't struck eight. My back was requiring a rest and I took a fancy for a cup of hot coffee. There's a fellow sets up a coffee stall by the bridge of a morning. He does good business with people going across to work on the Fulham side. The quickest way for me to get there is out of the back gate and along the path by the river. I stepped out of the gate and just before I turned to the left – towards the coffee stall – I chanced to look to my right. There I saw two people and one of them was Dandy – was Mr Lamont. He was talking to a woman. I took a look at her and thought that she wasn't the sort I'd have expected to see him bothering with. She was as plain as a pikestaff and not a young'un. They seemed to be having a bit of an argument. I thought it probably about the price. I know it was early for that sort of thing. But the drabs are always on the lookout for a customer at any time of day. Not that she looked like any kind of dollymop, as I was saying. But then, perhaps she was just down on her luck, and trying to stay out of the workhouse. Then they walked off into some trees a bit beyond, so I thought they'd come to an agreement.

'I thought no more of it. I went off to the bridge and drank my coffee. I had a bit of chat with a couple of people I knew who turned up there.' Coggins glanced a little furtively at his employer. 'Again, I can't say how long I was there but it couldn't have been very long. As I was walking back to my work, along the same path, I heard someone hollering. I saw it was Mr Harrington, the magistrate. There was a group of 'em round a body lying on the mud: Mr Harrington, the old chap who looks after the church, and some kids.'

Coggins paused. 'There was no corpse lying on the mud when I went past earlier, I can tell you that! Well, they were beckoning to me to come over there and give them a hand. I helped move her. Mr Harrington had the idea to put her in my potting shed.' Coggins turned to his employer. 'It wasn't my idea!'

'Quite, quite, Coggins,' Mr Williams placated him.

'So that's it, then. I didn't get much of a look at her face when we were carrying her, but when we laid her out flat on my bench – ' Coggins scowled dreadfully – 'and knocked my cuttings on to the floor, I saw her better. I recognised the woman who'd been talking to Dandy Jack – Mr Lamont. I still didn't think I needed to say anything. Mr Harrington and the other gentleman, they knew her by name, so they knew more than me. I didn't think Mr Lamont could have anything to do with it. Why should he? I thought perhaps she'd approached another fellow and he'd cut up rough. Then the police came, local bluebottles first off, and then you.' Coggins fixed me with an accusing eye. 'All trampling over the lawn and knocking the shrubs about. I thought you'd never be finished. I don't know how long it was before they moved her out. It was evening before I even got started in the garden. I had to come in early the next day, too, to finish it off. Talk about having my time wasted!'

'What of police time? This was a murder and you could have helped with important information! You were able to fix the time of death, man. Didn't you realise that?' I demanded.

'Of course, not!' argued Coggins. 'Police work isn't my business. Gardening is. It wasn't until I heard you'd arrested Dandy – Mr Lamont, as I thought I'd better mention it to Mr Williams.'

There was little point in venting my exasperation at the gardener's late decision to come forward. We all have our priorities; and for Coggins, that meant his disrupted working day and destroyed cuttings. Nor, at first, must it have appeared possible to Coggins that a local resident for many years, a gentleman and employer of other staff, could have anything to do with the death of a woman

Coggins had assumed an amateur prostitute. 'Is there anything else, Coggins? No? Then please read the account as the constable has written it down and, if you agree with it, sign it.'

Coggins, still frowning, read through it, and wrote his name in a surprisingly clear hand.

'I lost some of my best cuttings,' he said, 'through you lot fooling around with dead bodies in my potting shed.'

Even then Fate had another surprise to spring on us. Late in the afternoon Sergeant Morris reappeared, having searched Fox House. He had a mysterious parcel, wrapped in newspaper, under his arm.

'What have you there?' I asked him.

'Not quite sure, Mr Ross, so I thought I had better bring it in. I gave that butler a receipt for it.' Morris set the parcel on the desk and unwrapped it. I was reminded of one of those parlour games that people play at Christmas.

Unwrapped, the object proved to be a small wooden box with highly decorated panels on both top and bottom, and all four sides. The designs were made up of flowers, birds and foliage for the most part; but on the top was a scene of a harbour with some odd-looking boats floating in it. It was brightly painted in greens, blues and pinks.

'I can't open it, sir,' explained Morris. 'There is a narrow strip along this end that moves to the side, just so far and no further, but then that's it. You're no more forward with opening it. Being as it's a fancy piece, I didn't like just to break into it. It might be a jewel casket, but it don't rattle, if you shake it. It don't weigh much, either. I reckon it's foreign.'

Constable Biddle, ever curious by nature, had sidled into the room to find out what Morris had discovered. Neither the sergeant nor I had noticed him, so we were both startled when he announced loudly, 'It's a Chinese puzzle box!'

'What are you doing there, my lad?' demanded Morris. 'Who asked you to come into Mr Ross's office?'

Too fascinated by the box to heed the reproof, Biddle went on in awed tones, 'It's just like the one in *The Treasure of Kublai Khan.*'

'You mean them rubbishy novels you read, I suppose?' Morris snapped. 'I told you they'll end with turning your brain. Seems to me, they already have!'

'No, no, Morris, wait.' I put out a hand to stem Morris's ire. 'Biddle, do you know anything about these boxes, learned from your reading?'

'You put secret things in them,' Biddle assured us breathlessly. 'In *The Treasure of Kublai Khan*, a box like that contains a map showing where the treasure is hidden. It's in a pagoda.'

'Do you know how to open it?' Morris and I both shouted at him.

Biddle picked it up. 'If you give me a minute or two, I might.' He studied it, frowning.

'That bit moves,' said Morris impatiently, indicating the narrow strip. 'But that's all.'

Biddle moved the strip and then tried all the other sides, with the strip still out of position. The top of the box, with the harbour scene, moved about a quarter of an inch, as if it would slide open, but didn't.

'Sit down, Biddle,' I invited.

Biddle seated himself, put the box on the desk, and began anew to try all the sides. He managed to find another narrow strip that slid aside. After that the top of the box moved a little more. After much fiddling around, Biddle gave a cry of triumph, and the lid with the harbour scene slid out altogether to reveal the interior. Morris and I leaned forward. The box was empty.

'So much for that,' grumbled Morris.

'No, there will be another compartment, Sergeant,' Biddle promised. 'Look, the hole isn't deep enough. There must be a drawer somewhere, underneath it.' He pushed and pressed at the sides; and the opposite end of the box to that with the sliding strips could be raised about an inch and a half. Beneath it could be seen a small knob. Biddle pulled it and a drawer slid out with an unexpected tinkle of a tune. In it was a folded paper.

'Well done, boy!' said Morris and Biddle blushed furiously at the rare praise.

They both watched me as I took out the paper and unfolded it.

'We have him, Morris,' I said. 'We have Dandy Jack!'

'Who is he?' asked the bewildered Morris.

'Biddle will explain to you. I must take this to Superintendent Dunn at once.'

Chapter Nineteen

DUNN SPREAD the letter out flat on his desk and together we bent over it and read.

My dearest wife,

By the time you read this, I shall be far away. This is not how I would have wished our married life together to end, but it is inevitable. Clearly, the police feel they are now in a position to make an arrest and they will come to apprehend me at any moment. It is only left for me to leave the country. Once I have gone, my hope is that they will cease to pay attention to you, as you are clearly guiltless in the matter of Sawyer's death.

I have no regret for removing Sawyer from our lives, other than that it has resulted in the present regrettable situation. She was a dreadful woman, and brought about her own demise. If she had but taken the money she must have saved over the years with us, and left, as I hoped to persuade her to do, all this could have been avoided. But I had overlooked how much she enjoyed having us in her power . . . and her greed.

She assented without any hesitation to a meeting near the river that morning. I had told her I wished to discuss the new situation without fear of being overheard by other staff. But from the first our discussion went badly. She began to demand even more money. She gloated at the hold she had on us. Had she been in any way reasonable, I swear to you I would not have killed her. But she left me no alternative. I believe you will understand because your uncle left you with no alternative, all those years ago. I know that what you did that day, you did for us both. So did I.

I know how much this letter will distress you. But I beg you to believe I have acted at all times in the way I believe best for us both. Please be sure to destroy this letter immediately after you have read it. It must not fall into other hands. My love and regard for you remain undiminished, dear Amelia, and I beg you will not think of me with anger. I have not abandoned you, for you remain always in my heart.

Your loving husband,
Charles Lamont

Dunn and I straightened up and looked at one another.

'But she didn't destroy the letter,' I said. 'Lizzie was right. These are Lamont's last words to her. In reading them, she heard his voice. It was just as though he breathed them in his death agony.'

'He did,' said Dunn grimly. 'Because in keeping this letter, she has sent him to the gallows.'

Faced with the letter, Lamont had no choice but to admit his guilt.

'I still deny that I went to meet her with the intention of killing her. But it was clear she had no intention of being reasonable. She became objectionable, taunting me. I lost my temper. I seized her neck, meaning only to shake her. But she just dropped down dead at my feet.'

Lamont paused. 'It was remarkable. I was quite horrified for a moment or two. But I had to dispose of the body and any evidence; and very little time to do it in. I needed to return home quickly. The girl, Harriet, would have left hot water outside my bedroom door. She would be returning soon to fetch the empty jug and washbasin of water. If she found the jug standing still full but now cold outside my door, it would upset her routine and I couldn't be sure what she'd do. She might knock at the door, even venture to look into the room, or go down and tell Johnson, who would come up and knock. My absence would be discovered.' Lamont sighed. 'But you had worked that out, hadn't you, Ross? That is why you were so anxious to quiz Harriet.'

'Every household has its morning routine,' I said. 'Oddly, it is the part of the day the most fixed in its procedure. If it varies, it is generally because of some necessity.'

Lamont nodded. 'I don't suppose I ever faced a more

difficult necessity than I did then. To get rid of a corpse! How on earth does one do such a thing? I dragged Sawyer towards the river, but she was a strongly built woman, as you saw for yourself. Her weight and that of her clothing, and the treacherous nature of the ground under my feet, all slowed me. I could hardly move her at all. I must have lost the cufflink then. When I realised, on returning home, that it had been torn from my shirt, there was no time to return and look for it. It was such a tiny thing. I thought there was a good chance it would be overlooked.'

'It took three men to carry her from the river bank to a nearby garden,' I told him. 'I am not surprised you found it difficult to move her. A dead weight is rightly called so.'

'There you are, then,' said Lamont resentfully. 'I had no choice but to leave her on the mud. I hoped that the rising river would take her. It would have done, but for pure chance. It those wretched brats had not come digging in the mud . . .' He gave a twisted smile. 'It is like a game of cards. You have to play the hand you're given. Sometimes fortune favours you, and other times it doesn't.' He leaned forward, suddenly anxious and urgent. 'But my wife had no part in it, no part in the murder of Rachel Sawyer at all. My letter makes that clear.'

'He is anxious to point out to us that the letter makes clear his wife had no part in the murder of Rachel Sawyer. We have no evidence to the contrary and she will not be charged with that,' I told Lizzie that evening.

'And the murder of her uncle?' Lizzie asked.

'Pelham won't want to lose two clients to the hangman at once. It would damage his reputation! He will fight to save her from the gallows and he may succeed. Lamont wrote of what Amelia "did that day" but he does not specify in his letter exactly what it was she did. When questioned on that sentence, he said it referred to the guilt she had always felt for having panicked when she found her uncle dead before the parlour fire. Instead of calling the doctor immediately and leaving the body where it was, she ordered that Isaiah Sheldon be taken upstairs. Instead of laying him out decently, she quite lost her head and ordered the application of mustard plasters. She has always felt since, claims Lamont, that she treated the corpse with disrespect.

'Well, I don't think that explanation will wash! But it still leaves it unclear to what he referred in the letter.

'At any rate, neither Rachel nor Mills can be called to the witness stand. Pelham will seek to get the charges against her reduced, if not dismissed. If convicted of anything, I fancy she will face prison, but not the rope.'

Lizzie shuddered. 'She would not survive long in prison,' she said simply.

'She is a strong and resourceful woman,' I countered.

'She will have nothing, no future, to survive a term of imprisonment for,' Lizzie replied.

I was not sure I agreed, but Lizzie's mind was made up on that point so we fell silent, sitting in our tiny parlour with the tea table between us. A muffled clang in the distance told us Bessie washed up with her usual vigour.

Suddenly, Lizzie asked, 'Did Canning come to the Yard today with his solicitor?'

'Oh, yes, he did, I forgot to tell you,' I admitted. 'I didn't see him myself. I understand Dunn delivered a stern lecture to him about wasting police time, and sent him on his way.'

'I wonder how that will end,' said Lizzie.

Elizabeth Martin Ross

We were soon to find out. The following evening Ben returned home with a letter, delivered to him at the Yard. It was from Miss Alice Stephens and requested that, if convenient, both he and his wife would take tea with her and her niece at their hotel, the coming Sunday. They were to return to Southampton on the following Monday.

Jane Canning and her desperate situation had been a great deal on my mind. From everything Ben had told me, I found it difficult to imagine that the odious Hubert Canning would agree to anything that would please his wife. The discussions that had been taking place in the few days since her return with their daughter from Southampton could only have been acrimonious. Miss Stephens appeared to have great confidence in a certain Mr Quartermain. But I have come across the Cannings of this world in the past. Their self-esteem coats them like armour. They can seldom be brought to concede the smallest thing or admit any point of view but their own.

Certainly, from Ben's account, Canning had never done so. The only time he'd agreed to anything Jane wanted was in hiring the nursemaid, Ellen Brady.

My one hope was that Canning might have been so alarmed by being obliged to go to Scotland Yard, with his solicitor, and receive what amounted to a dressing-down by Superintendent Dunn, that he might be persuaded to offer something to bring about a speedy settlement. Dunn's stern warning might sway him where his wife's feelings would not.

There was something else. It was clear he wanted his child returned under his roof. But he didn't care twopence where Jane went. My personal opinion was that Jane had not turned out the domestic mouse he'd anticipated when he married her, and he had become anxious to be rid of her. But not through divorce, which would make it a public matter. Instead he'd planned to pack her off privately to the notorious clinic. As for the child, that was a different matter. She would one day be his heiress. He would want to keep her close, to exercise the control over her, in fact, that Isaiah Sheldon had once wanted to exert over Amelia. Poor little Charlotte, she would discover, as she grew older, just what a dictator her papa was.

The hotel was small but neatly appointed, very quiet, and clearly much in use by elderly ladies. The air bore the odours of lavender water and cough drops. Miss Stephens explained to us that she had arranged with the management to have private use of the hotel's library that afternoon. I decided, when we entered the cramped room, that the management had not made any particularly generous gesture. I couldn't think anyone else would want to use it. The title 'library' was exaggerated. The reading matter on offer consisted of an assortment of magazines, some improving literature donated by various religious organisations, and the complete set, in several bound volumes, of a biography of Albert, the late Prince Consort. The chairs were hard. The carpet was worn and did not fit the floor space, suggesting it had come from elsewhere, demoted to this seldom-visited nook. The motley collection of dried flowers and foliage in an ugly urn, filling the hearth, needed to be taken out and dusted, or preferably thrown away.

We all squeezed in, the ladies' crinolines taking up so much of the available space that Ben found himself pinned against the wall. Tea was brought by a maid nearly as old as most of the residents must be.

'Jane and I are most obliged to you both for coming,' Miss Stephens said. 'We are delighted to make your acquaintance, Mrs Ross.'

I returned the compliment. The truth was, when Ben had told me of the invitation, nothing would have prevented my coming along. I was anxious to meet both women. Miss Stephens was much as I would have expected: a prim maiden lady of high principles but who would have little understanding of the wretchedness in a bad marriage. She had been shocked into offering her niece sanctuary. If Jane had simply written from St John's Wood and requested that she be allowed to return to Southampton, leaving her husband, Miss Stephens would have refused outright. Jane would probably have received a letter reminding her of her 'duty'. But the exhausted, emaciated and barefoot wretch who had appeared on her doorstep could not be refused.

Miss Stephens had once accepted that Canning would make a suitable husband for Jane. Now, perhaps predictably, she had made a complete about-face and Hubert Canning had become the enemy. Canning had let Miss Stephens down. He had presented her with an unwished dilemma. Canning had not kept his part of the bargain. He had called Miss Stephens's powers of judgement into question. Canning had failed in his Duty.

My real interest lay in observing Jane Canning. She must look much healthier now than when she'd arrived on her aunt's doorstep. But she was still very thin and obviously deeply unhappy. Her misery could be read in the early lines that aged her features, and in the continual twisting of her hands in her lap. I wished I had Hubert Canning before me so that I could tell him to his face what I thought of him. It surprised me, and I think Ben also, when Jane now spoke up.

'I understand, Inspector Ross, that my husband does not wish to press any charges against me with regard to my having taken our child when I left home.'

'It is largely a domestic matter, Mrs Canning, that is the Yard's view,' Ben replied. 'We found the child reported missing by her father. You have returned your daughter. Charges would be difficult to frame, involve more public expenditure and frankly we have other fish to fry, as the saying goes. What happens now, that is between you and Mr Canning. He agrees. I think he is anxious to have the police out of his life. Perhaps you've reached some decision?'

Miss Stephens spoke abruptly. 'The wretched man wants the whole business expunged, rubbed out as if written on a slate.'

Having spoken, Miss Stephens clamped her lips together lest harsher words escape them.

Jane, after a glance at her aunt, took up the conversation again. 'My aunt has been more than kind and supportive. She engaged a lawyer to act for me, as you know, Mr Quartermain. She felt it would be better than we two women trying to deal with Hubert. Mr Quartermain explained to me that, in the eyes of the law, my husband is the aggrieved party. I have no grounds on which to divorce him.'

Miss Stephens twitched at the sound of the dreaded word 'divorce', but managed to keep silent.

'He certainly has grounds to divorce me, on the other hand.' Jane gave a rueful smile. She sounded remarkably calm and practical. I wondered how long the effort of maintaining this could last.

'I deserted him,' Jane continued. 'I took his daughter without his permission and lived with Charlotte as a vagrant on the streets of London and on the open road. We begged food and drank from streams and horse troughs. Twice kind farmers allowed us to sleep in a barn. Otherwise, we crawled into the hedgerows for shelter.' Her calm façade cracked a little and she looked down at her hands, now tightly clasped as if to stop that relentless twisting by force. 'I cannot tell you how horrified I am now to think of my own actions, and the harm that might have befallen Charlotte. I can only say that rational judgement had deserted me, arising from my fears of being incarcerated in some asylum, or those spas to which they send women who are – difficult.'

'I am a police officer and not any kind of judge,' Ben told her gently.

'But you are a kind man, kind to me and to Charlotte from the first time we met you near Waterloo that night. I am grateful.'

I could see that Ben was at a loss to reply. He gestured feebly at her to go on.

Jane continued more briskly. 'Hubert does not wish to divorce me for fear of public scandal.'

And for fear of the details of his treatment of his wife becoming common knowledge! I thought.

At this point Miss Stephens made a stifled sound as if she would clear her throat, but intended to announce she wished to make a statement. Her niece threw her a nervous glance.

'I cannot find words to condone Mr Canning's behaviour,' Miss Stephens began, 'but that is the one point on which he and I are agreed. There is no question of a public divorce hearing in an open court! It is quite unacceptable to have anyone and everyone know the details of one's domestic existence. To have reporters sitting there and listening, scribbling it all down to print in their newspapers? No, no, it cannot be entertained.

There is an inelegant but apt saying: one does not wash one's dirty linen in public.'

Miss Stephens shook her head. 'No such thing will happen in this case. If Jane is to return to live with me in Southampton, there will be unavoidable gossip. We accept that, but we must hope to ride it out. However, for her to return as a *divorced woman* is unthinkable. I am involved with several charitable committees and the ladies who are engaged in such good work must be above scandal. I would be asked to resign by the committees. Mr Quartermain understands that.'

So did I. Miss Stephens felt obliged to offer Jane a home, if needed. But the offer would be withdrawn if Jane were a divorced woman. So much for the charitable ladies and their good works! I thought furiously. I caught Ben's eye on me and fought back the words on my tongue.

Jane intervened hastily to take up the explanation. 'After much negotiation conducted by Mr Quartermain, to whom I am extremely grateful, Hubert has consented to a separation without a divorce. The details have been agreed. I am to return to Southampton and live with Aunt Alice. In the first instance, Hubert will explain my absence by telling everyone here that I have returned to care for my aunt who is ill. After a while, people will forget to ask where I am or accept that I will not reappear. That is Hubert's hope. People may assume that I am indeed locked up in some institution and delicacy will prevent them asking for details.

'Hubert will make me a monthly allowance so that I shall not be a financial burden on my aunt. I am not to discuss our private affairs with anyone. I am to conduct myself with what Hubert calls "decorum". I am above all to avoid any contact with the wine shippers with whom he does business.'

Jane's voice faltered. 'Our daughter is to remain in London with him. It is the hardest condition but I must accept it. No court would grant me custody.' Jane looked at Ben and essayed a faint smile. 'Officers, when they arrest pickpockets and such people, often invite them to "come quietly", or so I've heard.'

Ben smiled back at her. 'They do sometimes say that. I've never said it, even as a young constable, or don't recollect doing so.'

Jane's smile had already faded. 'Well, then, I am to "go quietly". In return for my cooperation in all ways, I am to be permitted three visits a year to Charlotte. One will be at Christmas, one at Easter and one on her birthday, which falls in July. I am to make no other attempts to see her or communicate with her, or the visits will cease and not be restored. I have managed to persuade Hubert that Ellen Brady shall remain as nursemaid for the time being. That is so that Charlotte will be in the day-to-day care of someone she knows and trusts.'

'The nursemaid expressed great fondness for your daughter when I spoke to her,' Ben said.

Jane nodded. 'Ellen is a good, kind girl and Charlotte loves her. I was quite surprised that Hubert agreed to her remaining as nursemaid. I do fear that Mrs Bell, who has never liked Ellen because she did not engage her, will prevail upon him to dismiss her eventually.'

Miss Stephens spoke up. 'Canning will not dismiss the girl too soon because he will fear she will go to another household and gossip. It is the best solution to this sorry situation that we could hope for. It is all due to the efforts of Mr Quartermain.'

Jane turned to me. 'I don't know what you think of us, Mrs Ross, and of all this. But I want you to know that I do believe Hubert loves his daughter. He wishes to be free of me, but Charlotte's welfare is another concern altogether. He will look after her. I would not have you think I am leaving my child in the care of someone who has no interest in her wellbeing. I know she will be excellently cared for.'

There is a world of difference between 'excellently cared for' and 'loved'. But I told Jane I understood. It all confirmed what I'd been thinking earlier. I added that I was glad everything had been settled so quickly and that she was not to be cut off from her daughter completely.

'Yes,' she said. 'It is more than I expected. Hubert can be vindictive. But Mr Quartermain persuaded him how important it would be to Charlotte.'

There was no more to be said. We drank our tea. The maid popped her head through the door and offered to 'refresh the pot', but we refused and rose to take our leave. Miss Stephens thanked us again for coming and told us that she had arranged with the cabman who had brought them to the hotel to return on Monday and take them to Waterloo.

'He is a man of most alarming appearance,' she said

thoughtfully, 'but he selected this hotel for us so his judgement is sound.'

'His name is Wally Slater,' I told her. 'You may rely on him completely.'

Ben and I walked slowly together down the road in silence. I slipped my hand into his and he squeezed my fingers. An omnibus came rumbling by, the hooves of the sweating horses clattering on the road. Ben hailed it and we climbed aboard and made our way homeward.

I do not think either of us was ever more pleased to approach our little house within earshot of the great railway at work at Waterloo. The great engines groaned and clanked behind us as we crossed the bridge. Great clouds of steam billowed into the air. There were pleasure craft on the river. Folk wore their best. Bessie opened the door to us with a broad grin and a 'Here you are, then!' which is not the way any well-trained maid should greet her returning employers. Constable Biddle, off duty, was sitting in the kitchen with his latest delivery of lurid reading. An empty plate scattered with cake crumbs was before him. His Sunday suit was near to bursting at the seams and his collar had lost a stud and was askew. Home had never appeared such a warm and welcoming place.

Chapter Twenty

IT WAS almost two weeks since I had visited Miss Stephens and Jane Canning with Ben. They had returned to Southampton. Ben had new cases to investigate and I was back in Aunt Parry's over-furnished drawing room, drinking tea and listening to her litany of complaints. She now moved on effortlessly to the next of these. Frank had left London to visit his prospective new constituency. But he had written to her with a description of the place and community he would in future represent (providing he was elected).

'It does not sound the kind of place I would have wished for him,' she lamented. 'I had hoped for some peaceful rural constituency where he might follow the pursuits of a country gentleman. Instead it is a place where they make all manner of pottery, the whole population engaged in it. The air glows red all night, Frank writes, from the furnaces that never go out. Great clouds of smoke hang constantly above, and can be seen from miles away.'

'I think Frank would find a rural constituency a trifle dull. He has always liked to be where things are happening and to face a challenge. He adapted to life in Russia and, after that, to life in China,' I went on to assure her. 'He will have no problem adapting to his new situation.'

'I dare say,' said Aunt Parry, clearly unconvinced. 'He also writes he is considering becoming engaged to be married.'

Goodness! I thought. Frank has wasted no time.

Aunt Parry paused to take solace in a buttered scone. 'I do hope he has chosen wisely. Her name is Patience Wellings. I have looked in several books of reference, but I cannot find her family. I understand her father is in commerce. My late husband, Josiah, was in commerce and so I have no objection to that. It is just that I had hoped for a more elevated connection for Frank.'

I was relieved to hear that Frank appeared to have been guided by common sense. I said I looked forward to meeting Miss Wellings.

'So do I,' said Aunt Parry gloomily.

It was best to change the subject. 'Have you had any luck finding a new companion, Aunt Parry?'

She brightened. 'Yes, Miss Rosa Featherstone will arrive in a week's time, from Birmingham. She is a schoolmaster's daughter and so I hope she will be able to read aloud clearly, without stumbling over long words, as Laetitia Bunn used to do. I hope for the best, Elizabeth, as you know I always do. But I have had so many disappointments concerning companions. All the ones I have liked best have left to be married . . . as you did. You abandoned me with no thought, Elizabeth, and to marry a policeman. Do not think I have anything but a high opinion of Inspector Ross – but really, murder!' She shuddered.

'He does not always have to investigate murders,' I protested.

'It seems to me he is always engaged in that way,' Aunt Parry retorted. 'Every time you come to visit me, the inspector is busy with yet another gruesome crime. Such a disagreeable business and I do wonder that Inspector Ross has chosen to make a career of dealing with it.'

'Well, someone must do it,' I offered.

'I dare say,' returned Aunt Parry fretfully. 'But you did not need to marry him, all the same. What on earth do you talk about over dinner?'

I could not resist replying, 'Sometimes about the current murder investigation, Aunt Parry, though of course not always.'

She sat back and stared at me. 'Really, Elizabeth, life is unpleasant enough. Do ring for Simms. All the scones are gone and those crumpets are quite cold. We need more and hotter ones.'